Take a Bow

Sawyer's Cove: The Reboot

Libby Waterford

Also by Libby Waterford

Sawyer's Cove: The Reboot

Take Two

Take a Bow

Take It All

Take a Chance

Take Me Over

Hot Take in Steamy Shorts: A Kissed by Romance Anthology

Take Another Look in A Kiss at Midnight: A Kissed by Romance Collaboration

Never a Bride

Can't Help Falling in Love

Can't Make You Love Me

Can't Fight This Feeling

Can't Hurry Love

Weston Reunion

Flirting with Her Professor

Her Reunion Fling

Falling for Her Ex

Also by Libby Waterford

Sawyer's Cove: The Reboot

Take Two

Take a Bow

Take It All

Take a Chance

Take Me Over

Hot Take in Steamy Shorts: A Kissed by Romance Anthology

Take Another Look in A Kiss at Midnight: A Kissed by Romance Collaboration

Never a Bride

Can't Help Falling in Love

Can't Make You Love Me

Can't Fight This Feeling

Can't Hurry Love

Weston Reunion

Flirting with Her Professor

Her Reunion Fling

Falling for Her Ex

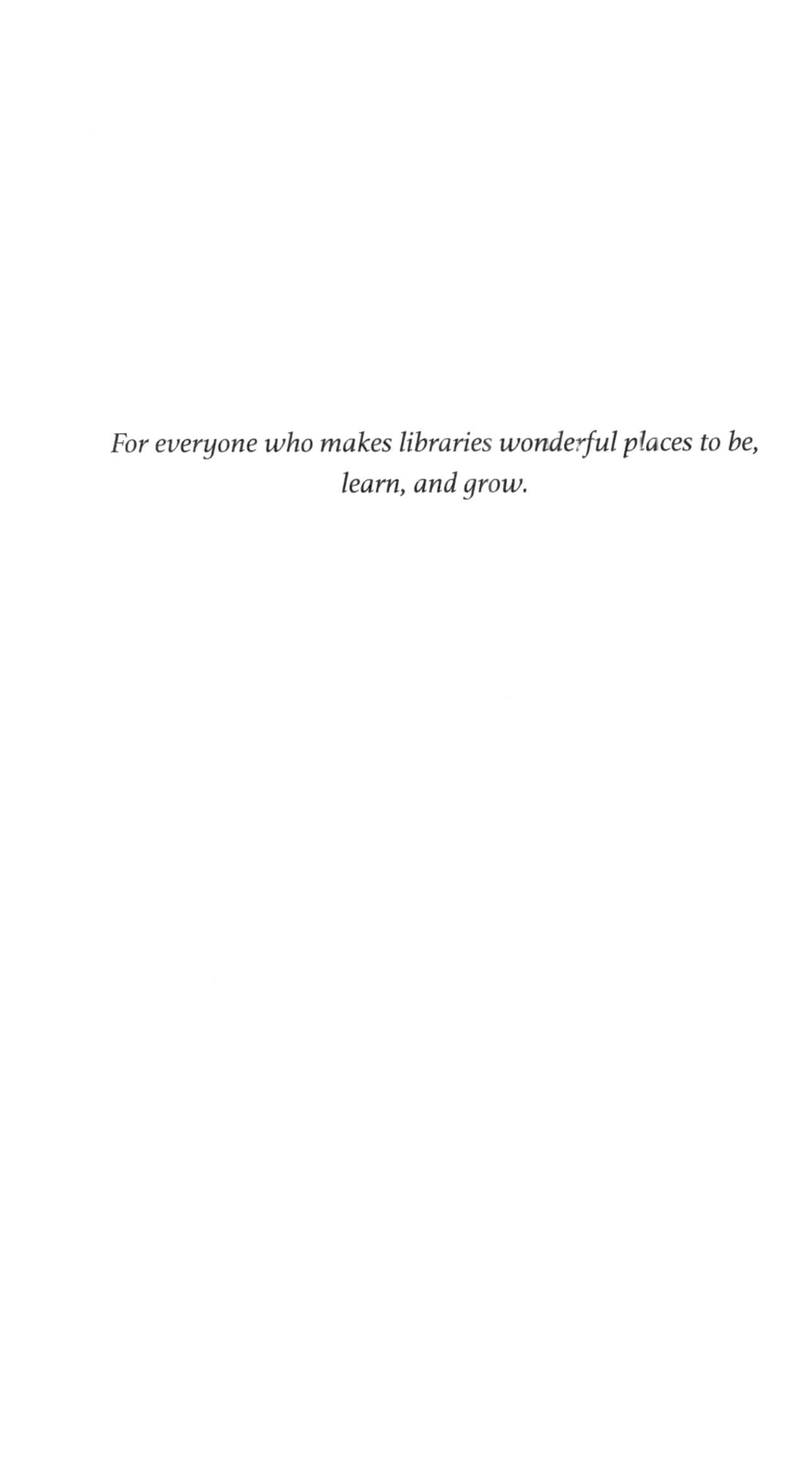

For everyone who makes libraries wonderful places to be, learn, and grow.

"What in the world would we do without our libraries?"

— Katharine Hepburn

Chapter One

Sometimes being the stranger in
town is the only way to be
seen.
Honey, I'm a stranger in my own
limousine.

— "Stranger," The Nash
Speedwell Experience

"In five hundred feet, turn left on Dandelion Road."

Nash peered out the window of his pickup, looking for anything in the dense trees that could possibly be considered a road.

"Turn left on Dandelion Road."

"There is no road," Nash told the insistent mechanical voice of his maps app. "Just a bunch of trees. Wait—"

A break in the green showed a dirt road and rusty

signpost almost hidden by the glossy leaves of a maple sapling. Nash made the sharp turn and nosed the truck onto the road—more of a track, really. He winced as the truck hit a deep depression and the entire vehicle jolted. He patted the dash reassuringly. It might have been a rental, but he'd bonded with the silver beast on the drive to Misty Harbor from the Boston airport.

"Almost there."

Warner, the owner of the rental house, had said the place was at the top of a rise, and the track was indeed quickly rising in elevation. Nash shifted the truck into low gear and pushed the gas pedal down. The truck had no trouble with the climb, and suddenly the hill hit its apex. The road became a paved driveway for a two-story wood frame house, light gray with white trim, save for the cheerful bright blue front door.

Nash parked right in front and climbed out. He dug the keys Warner had given him out of his jeans' pocket, but instead of heading for the door, he walked around the side, passing tidy beds full of shrubs and flowers just beginning to fade as summer got ready to melt into fall.

The back flagstone patio was populated with generic weatherproof outdoor furniture. But the furniture didn't matter. The view was what had drawn Nash to this property when he was looking for somewhere to hang his hat while shooting the new episodes of *Sawyer's Cove*, the television show that had launched his career, and it didn't disappoint.

From this vantage point, the Atlantic Ocean spread out to the horizon like a dark gray blanket someone had spilled glitter all over. The late August sun lit everything up in Technicolor, from the green of the trees surrounding the house to the vivid blue sky. The house not only had a spectacular view, it also boasted access to the coastline. He spotted the entrance to a rocky trail that led from the patio down to a private stretch of beach.

Misty Harbor's public beach and harbor were a little way north, hidden from Nash's eyeline behind a jutting spit of land. This spot was still technically Misty Harbor, but the beach belonged to the owners of the dozen or so houses on this side of town.

Nash itched to explore, but the groceries sweating in the bed of the truck forced him to do the responsible thing. He reluctantly turned away from the ocean and dutifully unloaded the food into the kitchen—open floor plan, gray granite, and stainless steel everything— then grabbed his suitcase. He surveyed the rest of the ground-floor rooms—bathroom, living room-slash-dining room with French doors onto the patio. Upstairs were two bedrooms and another bath. He stashed his bag in the bedroom with the best view, washed his hands, then went back to the truck for the final item he'd brought with him—his guitar.

He set the case with his beloved Gibson on the dining room table and literally scratched his head. His brown hair was getting a little floppy, but he'd wait to cut it until he'd met with the *Sawyer's Cove* producers and discussed his character's look for the show.

Now what?

He'd planned his trip to Misty Harbor weeks ago, thinking it would be smart to get settled before heading into what was going to be weeks of back-to-back shoots. They were filming all ten episodes of the limited series revival roughly in order, but, due to scheduling, there would be some overlap. As a principal on the show, he was going to be needed for most of the ten-week shoot.

He could work on his lines for the scripts he'd already been given, though the first table read with the entire cast wasn't for another ten days. He'd had some idea he'd hang out with Jay, the friend he never got to spend enough time with, but Jay and his girlfriend-slash-co-star Cami had flown to Paris to celebrate their birthdays and recharge before the show started production. Cami was also producing the series, and Nash knew she'd been working herself to the bone all summer. Selena Echeveria, the showrunner, was coming to town in a few days, but she was currently still in Los Angeles, working on things from there. The last he'd heard from Ariel and Crosby, the other members of the core *Sawyer's Cove* cast, they were going to be arriving shortly before the table read.

Nash glanced at the guitar guiltily. He knew what he should be spending his afternoon doing, but he figured another few hours of procrastination wouldn't matter. He turned his back on the guitar case, grabbed the truck keys, and locked the door behind him. He'd looked forward to the peace and quiet of Misty Harbor, the privacy and beauty of this out-of-the-way beach house. But now all he wanted was company. And he had some idea where to find the best company he knew.

Mimi dropped a piece of paper on Pauline's desk.

Her co-worker and friend looked up, elegant eyebrows drawn together. "Are you going to tell me why you're interrupting me, or do I have to guess?"

"Can you proofread this press release? I've read it ten times, and I'm going cross-eyed." Mimi paced back and forth in the small office on the second floor of the Misty Harbor Library, while Pauline bent her head over the printed sheet she'd been given. Her friend kept her dark hair short, and she looked more like a model with her swan's neck and perfectly smooth dark brown skin than a small-town librarian who specialized in 19th century town history.

But Mimi knew people weren't always what they appeared to be. She paused at the window and looked down at the park next door to the library, recognizing a few of the locals enjoying the warm afternoon weather. Her gaze shifted, and she took in her reflection in the glass, her own curly hair coming out of the hasty bun she'd tied it up in earlier, the expression on her peach-tinted face unusually pinched. She turned away from the window and resumed pacing, feeling itchy in her skin. She pulled her red cardigan around her middle, buttoning and unbuttoning it compulsively.

"You don't need this comma," Pauline said, circling

the offending punctuation with her pencil. "And I think you used the British spelling of 'traveling.'"

"Thanks. You are a gem," Mimi said, scooping up the sheet.

"I know," Pauline said lightly. "But you didn't come to bother me over a comma. What's going on?"

"That's unusually perceptive of you. I must be a mess." She resisted the urge to unbutton her cardigan yet again.

Pauline laughed. "I do have some social skills, you know."

"You know what I mean."

"Lucky for you, I do know what you mean," Pauline said wryly.

Mimi chewed on her bottom lip. "It's just the fundraiser—I need to knock it out of the park. We're starting Mr. Russell's scholarship fund, and I'm worried no one will donate. And the *Sawyer's Cove* production is starting soon, and it's going to disrupt things in town for weeks. Months, even."

"I thought you were all about that show? You've been the one rolling out the red carpet for them since it was announced."

"True," Mimi admitted. She'd been an early cheerleader of the reboot and convinced the library board to let the producers use it as a location for some scenes. Her own brother was one of the stars—she wanted it to be a success, and she knew it would do great things for the town. "I guess I'm just nervous."

She wasn't only nervous about the success of the

annual library fundraiser. Every day that brought them closer to the start of the *Sawyer's Cove* production brought her one day closer to seeing a certain member of the cast. She had no business being nervous about that, but she was. The rub was, she couldn't tell anyone to get reassurance everything was going to be okay. Not her mom, who she could talk to about anything and everything, with the very big exception of her love life. Not Pauline, who wasn't particularly interested in the nuances of interpersonal relationships. And definitely not her brother Jay, who, even if he hadn't been out of town with his girlfriend taking a well-deserved vacation, was the last person she could talk to about this particular quandary.

"The fundraiser is going to be an unqualified success," Pauline declared. "And it's not for over a month. You're going to burn out if you don't calm down about it. And everyone keeps saying the benefits of the *Sawyer's Cove* production outweigh the drawbacks. So, we'll just have to put up with it when it gets started."

Mimi allowed herself to take a deep breath as Pauline's reasonable tone washed over her.

"Okay. You're right. I need to chill."

"Precisely," Pauline said, waving toward the door. "And you need to let me get back to work. The deadline for this grant application looms."

"I won't bug you anymore. Today, at least." Mimi paused in the doorway. "We on for the show this weekend?"

"I think so." Pauline had become her frequent

companion to the weekend music shows at Jay's bar, The Cove. Mimi made a hobby of booking acts for the bar, but she hadn't booked this one, a folk-rock group that had approached The Cove directly. Even so, she was looking forward to checking them out. She loved live music, and Pauline was fun to go with and never cared if Mimi left with someone else. "Is it okay if Colin comes?"

"Colin Bailey?" The librarian assistant who worked part-time at the front desk checking out books and helping patrons, and part-time for his dad's landscaping business was the only "Colin" she knew. She'd known him since he was born, in fact, and even babysat him for a few years back in the day.

"Yeah. He told me he's always wanted to check out the music at The Cove but his friends aren't interested, so I said he could come with us. If that's okay."

"Sure." Mimi examined Pauline's pretty face for any clue this was something besides a friendly co-worker get-together, but she gave nothing away. Mimi was aware Pauline was asexual and hetero-romantic, but that didn't mean Colin knew. "Like as friends?"

"Of course," Pauline said. "Now go back to work so I can go back to work. Please."

"Right, okay, off to my office." She closed the door firmly, feeling mildly guilty about taking up her friend's time when she was the one who needed to get her shit together.

There was no reason to be so stressed over the return of *Sawyer's Cove*. So what if Nash Speedwell was going to be among the group of actors and crew descending on the town? So what if he'd specifically texted her several times over the past six weeks to remind her he was coming and he was looking forward to seeing her? So what if the last time he'd contacted her, he'd said he might arrive in town as early as today? Those texts were simply glorified booty calls with one of the most desirable men in America. And since that's all Mimi had ever wanted or expected out of their acquaintance, there was seriously nothing to be nervous about.

She walked briskly back to her closet-sized office located off the employee break room. She didn't have time for a personal emotional crisis. She had work to do.

To show exactly how not bothered she was about Nash's imminent appearance, she decided to put on his album. She clicked the play button on the music app on her computer and started streaming The Nash Speedwell Experience's self-titled debut.

If she had a vinyl copy, she probably would have worn it out from the number of times she'd listened to the album since it came out last year. She'd fallen in love with the poppy alternative sound, with its heavy country influences. Well, "fallen in love" was a strong phrase. She *really liked* the entire album, from the radio-friendly tracks to the couple of slow burns tacked on to the end. Nash sang each song in his mellow, soulful baritone, with an occasional twang that always made her insides clench.

He was as expressive a singer as he was an actor, and Mimi always felt as if he was singing directly to her. Of course, every fangirl and fanboy who'd been smitten with Nash since he played skinny-armed Will O'Connell on *Sawyer's Cove*, or more recently been exposed to him as a brawny-armed hero on the historical epic *Hawk and Bone* probably felt the same way.

She hadn't seen him since the album came out; he'd just finished recording it the last time he swung through Misty Harbor to spend a couple of days hanging with Jay before he went to Europe for a multi-month shoot. At the time, he'd been hesitant about putting the thing out in the world. He shouldn't have been. The album rocked, and it had gotten good reviews in the trades. Strangely, he hadn't done much promotion for it. In fact, unless you were a diehard Nash Speedwell groupie, you probably wouldn't have heard about The Nash Speedwell Experience at all.

No matter how much she liked the album, Mimi firmly declined to be labeled a Nash Speedwell groupie. She supposed when viewed from a certain angle, their interactions could be interpreted as those between a famous actor and devoted fan.

But no—actors didn't text groupies. They didn't make a point to see them whenever they were in town.

On the other hand, whatever had happened between her and Nash in the past didn't comfortably fit into any relationship box. They'd never dated. They didn't talk on the phone. They weren't pen pals.

They didn't fuck in silence and then ignore each other the rest of the time. No, they talked. But the talking was always a prelude to something physical happening, and the post-coital conversation was usually abbreviated, since Nash was always going somewhere, heading to a shoot, or back to his home base in L.A.

He occasionally mentioned wanting to spend more time in Misty Harbor, but he never did, and Mimi was glad. He was a vivid part of her fantasy life, and a much smaller part of her real life. She didn't need him to spend more time in Misty Harbor—she had enough of him those handfuls of times he'd ended up in her bed. In between, she could always watch his shows, or listen to the album if she needed a Nash Speedwell fix.

She corrected the two errors Pauline had pointed out, then sent the press release to her contact at the local newspaper. They'd already sold about half the fundraiser tickets, and she hoped a little more publicity would help sell the rest.

Her favorite of Nash's songs, "Stranger," started playing, and she kicked up the volume, singing along under her breath as she rooted around the bottom file drawer in her desk, looking for last year's fundraiser program. She needed to update it for this year and get it to the printer soon. Nash was singing about tumbleweeds and limousines, and she was so lost in the music and her task, she jumped when the door to her office cracked open.

Mimi's mouth was already parted to ask what the intruder wanted, but it dropped further when she saw who was standing in her office doorway: Nash Speedwell himself.

Chapter Two

Tumbleweeds roll down Hollywood Boulevard.
Neon lights lie so pretty.
This desert town will let you down
hard.

— "Stranger," The Nash
Speedwell Experience

"Hiya, Mimi."

Mimi Orlando stared at him, pert mouth ajar. He registered the soft blush on her high cheekbones, the general air of messiness in her office, and the fact that his music was playing over her laptop's speakers, a little tinny, but clear.

He grinned. "Hey, I know this song."

She closed her mouth, fumbled with her computer keyboard. The music abruptly cut off. "Nash."

"Hey." He couldn't help the warmth that infused his voice. Being around Mimi always grounded him. He hadn't known how anxious he was to see her until he found himself tracking her down at work. Now that he thought about it, he probably shouldn't have just shown up with no warning.

She didn't look particularly happy at the interruption. He cursed himself for forgetting just because he was on no particular schedule at the moment, it didn't mean everyone had the same freedom.

"I should have texted first, sorry."

"It's okay." She pushed some of her curly hair behind her ears. It was longer than the last time he'd seen her, and a different color. Today it was mostly her natural brown, with a thick shock of electric blue. "You just get into town?"

"Yeah, this morning. Got settled into my place, but I thought maybe you'd want to get together later. You free for dinner?"

"I might have to work," she said quickly.

"Oh." He was surprised at the disappointment flooding his gut. "How late is the library open?"

"Six. I have a lot of work to do on our upcoming fundraiser. Sorry."

"It's okay." Again, he reminded himself the world didn't revolve around him. "Maybe tomorrow?"

He didn't mistake the hesitation on her part this time. "Um..."

Was it something he'd said or done? Something he *hadn't* said or done? He and Mimi had always been straight with each other, and he didn't think that had changed in the months since he'd last seen her.

"Let's catch up before things get busy with the show."

Her eyes flicked to her computer screen and back. "Yeah, okay. Tomorrow night. You want to meet at The Cove?"

He dug the laid-back vibe at Jay's bar, but the food was nothing special. "How about the seafood place at the harbor? I've been craving oysters."

"Harborview?" She seemed surprised at the suggestion.

"Yeah, that place. Seven?"

"All right."

"Great." He couldn't help smiling again. It really was good to see her. "I didn't mean to bother you at work. I'll let you get back to it."

"It's okay." She smiled back, but it didn't quite reach her eyes.

"See you tomorrow, Mimi."

"Bye, Nash."

He'd been dismissed. He backed out of her office, wondering if he should feel insulted at the lukewarm welcome, crossed through the break room he'd been directed to by the guy working at the circulation desk, and headed into the quiet, inviting lobby of the library. If Mimi wasn't free to hang out, he'd have to find something else to fill the rest of the day. He passed a bookshelf marked "New Releases," spotted a recent biography of a favorite musician. On impulse, he grabbed it and went to the desk.

"Hey, how do I check something out?"

"You need a library card." The guy was young, probably early twenties, and looking at him with wide eyes. His name tag read "Colin." Nash pegged him for a *Hawk and Bone* fan.

"And how do I go about getting one of those, Colin?"

The kid started at the use of his name, cheeks coloring a little. "You need some proof of residency. We only issue them to town residents." Colin's voice was apologetic.

Nash considered. "Well, I'm a temporary resident. I'm renting a house for a while, but my ID has a California address. Is there anything you can do? I'm good for returning the book. Mimi Orlando can vouch for me," he said, with his winningest smile.

"Uh, just a second."

Colin got up and went to the other end of the desk, where a middle-aged woman was checking in a stack of books. They conferred under their breath for a minute, while Nash tried to appear as trustworthy as possible.

Colin came back. "We can issue you a temporary card. You won't be able to request items, just check out ones we already have. If you bring something like your rental agreement, I can give you a permanent card. We're a no-fine library, so we're not worried about that, but we do need an address to bill you in case you lose an item."

"Sounds like a deal. What's a no-fine library?"

"We don't charge fines for overdue books, but you can't check out anything new if you have books overdue. It cuts down on labor not to have to keep track of fines, plus fines can be a deterrent to some people using the library."

"Makes sense."

"It was Mimi's idea."

"Of course it was." Mimi was brilliant and cared about Misty Harbor just as much as her brother, who had a hand in everything going on in town, on top of owning the popular bar at the end of Main Street. She was beautiful, too, no matter how many times she insisted she was merely handsome.

He supposed he saw what she meant—she wasn't conventionally pretty like Cami or glamorous like Ariel Tulip, his other *Sawyer's Cove* co-star. She didn't look much like Jay, her brother. They had the same mom but different dads, and she took after their Italian mother, except for being about a foot taller than her, with lighter skin. She wasn't polished—she was real. Her oval face was constantly delivering expressions, with high cheekbones, a sassy mouth, and intense hazel eyes framed by thick brown lashes all getting in on the action. Sure, she was handsome.

She was also beautiful.

He was looking forward to dinner tomorrow night very much.

He handed over his ID to Colin, along with the address of his rental house. He glanced around the space, while Colin tapped at his keyboard.

The main floor of the library was larger than it seemed from the outside. There were stacks of books, of course, but now he noticed a staircase leading down to a below-ground level, with a list of everything that could be found down there, from fiction to DVDs, a Maker lab, and a seed library. The rest of the first floor was filled with reading tables, computer stations, and an entire wall of windows that looked out onto the small park next door. Comfy-looking gray armchairs lined up facing the windows, inviting you to sit and read by the natural light.

Colin checked out the book and handed over Nash's ID and new library card, which had a bright red "temporary" sticker attached.

Temporary. It fit—he was always temporary, no matter where he was. He was always traveling somewhere new for work. Each season of *Hawk and Bone* had been shot in a different location. By now, he felt like he knew eastern Europe better than he did Los Angeles, or the town in Tennessee where he'd grown up.

Misty Harbor had been home for three years while they'd shot the original *Sawyer's Cove*, and he'd been back several times over the intervening twelve years, but he was still just temporary.

He thanked Colin, put everything in his wallet, and stuck the book under his arm. If the library closed at six, he could sit and read for a while before he went in search of a meal. He picked out an armchair in the corner and sat down.

Half a chapter in, something on the page spurred the glimmer of an idea for a song. He'd learned long ago he needed to capture ideas right away or he'd lose them, and they'd never return in quite the same way. He dug out his phone and opened the notes app, where he tossed down everything he wanted to remember. He typed out a few phrases, hoping they'd make sense whenever he got around to looking at them again.

He had an entire folder of half-written songs on his phone. He'd been having trouble finishing anything since he'd recorded the album. It had been meant to be a one-time thing, but he'd be lying if he said he didn't still have the bug.

With his phone open, he succumbed to the temptation to check his email and feeds. He liked a few of his *Hawk and Bone* co-stars' recent posts, commented on a couple. He responded to a text from his sister-in-law to let her know he'd arrived safely in Misty Harbor, knowing she'd pass the news on to the rest of his family. He and his parents had a good relationship, but they weren't super attached to their phones and didn't text much. He'd just spent a few days with them in Tennessee before heading northeast; he'd call his mom in a day or two to check in.

His email had the usual spam, and a reminder from Lacey, his contact at Rainbow Canyon, the L.A.-based LGBTQ+ community center he'd been a supporter of for over a decade, about his deadline. He was cutting it close. They were putting together a benefit album, and he'd promised them a song—a song he hadn't written yet.

He sent a brief email assuring Lacey he'd get them the recording soon, then scrolled through his ideas file. He had the first half of about sixteen songs. What if he just combined two of them, Frankenstein-style? He shook his head. He'd never pretend to be much of a songwriter. It was a hobby. The Nash Speedwell Experience was basically a vanity project, and he knew it. But this was serious—he cared a great deal about the cause the group was raising money for, and they deserved his best work. He had no business lounging around, reading for pleasure, when he owed them a song.

He pushed up out of the chair, tempted to punish himself by returning the book altogether, but took it with him. He'd pick up some takeout, return to the silence of his lonely rented house, and force himself to work on the song until he had something usable.

His phone rang as he reached the truck. The rental vehicle was temporary, too. He longed for something permanent, something that was his. He glanced back at the library. The stout stone structure was a hundred and fifty years old and still thriving. It buzzed with life, just like Mimi.

He answered the phone on autopilot.

"Nash, you picked up." Mary-Anne's distinctive high-pitched voice had him holding the phone a few inches away from his ear.

"Sure did," he said unnecessarily. "How are you, Mary-Anne?"

"I'm the best agent in the biz, is how I am. Guess who wants to test you for the spinoff of the biggest superhero franchise of the decade?"

"What?" There had been rumors of a slate of new

superhero films being put together by one of the biggest studios. "They want me to audition?"

"They want to skip right to the chemistry reads, Nash. They want you for Moonshot—you know, that radioactive astronaut? Five-movie deal, with options for more."

"Seriously?" Nash had appeared in a few movies, but the bulk of his resume was TV. Where *Sawyer's Cove* had made him well-known for a certain niche audience, the mainstream success of *Hawk and Bone* had pushed him into a different level of fame entirely. The fact that his character was going to be killed off in spectacular fashion in the soon-to-air fourth season meant he was looking for a new gig. The *Sawyer's Cove* reboot was just a blip—Mary-Anne had been looking for something big for his *Hawk and Bone* follow-up. He'd assumed he'd be able to land another action-oriented series, but taking the mantle of Moonshot, a superhero in a multi-film franchise, was a whole new ball game.

"I'll let you know when they want you to fly down to North Carolina. It may not be for a while, so don't get your hopes up too high." Mary-Anne was the master of dropping tantalizing possibilities, then stifling expectations.

He laughed. "I've been doing this long enough not to get my hopes up about anything."

"I knew you'd become fully jaded eventually," she said. "I told you when you first walked into my office with your farm-boy optimism, it wouldn't last."

His laugh turned brittle. "Hollywood ultimately grinds us all down to dust, I guess."

"Hang in there, superstar."

"I'm not going anywhere," Nash assured her. "Keep in touch."

"Will do."

Nash took a second to digest the news. If this panned out, it would mean an entirely new chapter of his life. As much as he felt at loose ends, he hadn't exactly expected to jump into something so major. He had the strongest urge to ask Mimi what she thought. But she was working. He was just the guy in between jobs with nowhere to go except the pizza place to pick up dinner for one.

Chapter Three

You turn my head around, then
put it back on straight.
You make my knees weak, and
you're never late.

— "Cranberry Girl," The
Nash Speedwell Experience

If Mimi thought she'd been on edge before, she was even worse by the end of Friday. She'd impulsively accepted Nash's dinner invitation, and now she found herself tearing through her closet, trying to figure out what to wear to Misty Harbor's second-fanciest restaurant on date night. Even though this wasn't a date.

Right?

True, they were going out to dinner, just the two of them, in public. He'd texted her earlier to say he'd pick her up at 6:45, so far traditional date-behavior. And he'd said yesterday he wanted oysters. Weren't oysters code for getting laid?

The getting laid part she was comfortable with. It was the main purpose of every one of their previous encounters, after all. She'd already changed the sheets on her bed, tidied her bedroom, and checked her condom supply. Her minuscule apartment was visitor-ready.

Now to make her body visitor-ready. She put on a relatively new matching bra and panties set. The smooth cream-colored wireless bra fit her small breasts snugly and comfortably. She didn't believe in being uncomfortable, not even for someone as hot as Nash Speedwell. At work she usually wore pants, but she did have a few skirts and dresses she loved, so she chose a white short-sleeved sundress with multi-colored flowers embroidered all over it that showed off her upper arm tattoo of a rose growing out of a book. She pinned her hair back from her temples, threw on some lip gloss and the pair of baroque pearl earrings Jay had given her for her thirtieth birthday.

To complete the look, she slipped into flat espadrilles she'd bought on a whim and rarely wore because they weren't particularly practical. But this evening wasn't about being practical. It was about sharing a meal with someone she sincerely liked.

And then sex.

The knock on the door gave her pause. She'd

assumed Nash would text when he got there and she'd head outside, but there he was, standing at the door to her apartment. He wasn't dressed fancy, but he looked put-together in dark wash jeans, a button-down shirt in a flattering shade of green, and polished brown cowboy boots. The brown of the boots was repeated in his leather belt, which was studded with an ornate dark silver buckle. He could have looked silly, but he was Nash Speedwell. He looked edible, and she was about to suggest they stay home and skip the meal in favor of the main course, but he spoke first.

"You look great. All set? Our reservation's at seven."

"Sure thing." She grabbed her shoulder bag and brushed past him, catching his scent, clean with a hint of leather. He led her to a big silver pickup truck. "Yours?"

"Rental," he said. "It's the newer model of the one I had when I was filming *Sawyer's Cove* the first time around."

"What happened to that one?" she asked as he started the engine and headed for the harbor.

"I think it went to a charity auction," he said after a brief pause. "I wanted to drive it back to L.A. after the show wrapped, but I didn't have time."

"Sounds like you miss it."

"It was a great little truck."

"You're such a cowboy cliché tonight," she said with a laugh. "All you need is a Stetson and a drawl."

"Oh, you mean a hat like this?" He waggled his eyebrows as he reached behind the seat and drew out a buff-colored cowboy hat. He ducked down to put it on.

He was too tall to sit up straight and not crush it against the roof of the cab. "Howdy, ma'am."

She giggled. "Of course. I don't know why I'm surprised."

"Hold this for me?" He passed her the hat, and she took it, surprised at the weight in her hands. She brought it to her face and took a whiff. It smelled like the leather band on the inside, and a little of Nash.

She put it on her own head, sliding down almost as far as he had, since she was nearly as tall as him. "What do you think?"

He took his eyes off the road for a quick glance at her. His brown eyes seemed to darken, then he looked at the road again. "Suits you," he said, a smile playing at the edges of his mouth.

"Really?" She folded the sun visor down and looked in the vanity mirror. The hat was too big for her, certainly, but it did add something to her overall aesthetic. She'd never had a problem with her looks—she had always been a tall girl, long arms and legs, but not waifish. She was sturdy, small tits, solid hips and thighs, with a face that was appealing if not beautiful. She appreciated her strong body and that it enabled her to do everything she wanted to do—whether it was race around the library, get down on the floor with the toddler reading group, or go dancing for hours. She never had trouble finding a guy to take home at the end of the night either. Confidence made up for whatever she lacked in the feminine wiles department.

"You look good in hats," he said.

"Well, that's true," she said, because she always tried to be honest. She did look good in hats.

A few minutes later, they'd parked and were greeted at the hostess stand by a young woman who took one look at Nash and promptly turned scarlet. She managed to do her job, however, grabbing two menus and leading them to a table on the deck with an impeccable view of the sun setting behind the town, tangerine clouds scudding lazily in the sky over the metal-gray ocean.

Once they'd taken their seats, Mimi had to tease him. "I always thought eyes bugging out was just an expression, but now I've seen it for myself. I thought that girl's eyes were going to fall right out of her head."

"That's a vivid image," he said lightly. "And it would have ruined my plans to order oysters."

"Still on the oyster kick. You know, I'm a sure thing. You don't have to lure me with aphrodisiacs."

"What do you mean?" His brow furrowed, and Mimi felt a little foolish. Was he seriously not expecting this night to end the way every single one of their encounters had ended so far?

"You know what I mean. You don't have to order oysters just to get me in bed."

He was silent for a long, uncomfortable moment. Finally, he smiled, but it wasn't his easygoing, expansive, patented Nash Speedwell smile. This smile was small, and it made him look disconcertingly regular.

"Mimi, I want to order oysters because I like them. And this date doesn't necessarily have to end in bed."

It was Mimi's turn to be silent. She took a sip of water, cleared her throat. She decided she better set something straight before this night got any weirder. "I don't date. And we don't date each other. Therefore, this is not a date."

He seemed entertained by her assertion. "So what is it if it's not a date?"

"Two people eating a meal together at a prearranged time."

"Okay. Fine. But 'date' is a lot more efficient."

"Stop saying 'date,'" she said, a bit desperately.

Their server came by to rescue her and take Mimi's order for the beet salad appetizer and glass of Prosecco and Nash's order for a New England pale ale and oyster sampler platter—two of every variety of local oyster they had, with all the trimmings.

"That's a lot of oysters," she said. "What if I don't like them?"

"Do you like oysters?" he asked.

"Love them. But that's not the point."

"You seem to have a lot of preconceived notions about this whole night," Nash said.

"So do you."

"Well, let's get on the same page. Why did you say you were a sure thing?"

"Nash, be serious. Every time we've hung out over the past eight years, sex has been involved."

He looked genuinely surprised. "It has?"

The server returned with their drinks. Mimi met

Nash's pint glass with the rim of her champagne flute and smiled instinctively at the merry clink.

"Cheers. Maybe you have a girl in every New England town with a population of eight thousand, but I remember."

"I'm that memorable?" He raised an eyebrow.

She stuck her tongue out at him. "I'm just saying, don't blame me for thinking this is the prelude to the main attraction."

He sipped his beer and looked at her appraisingly. She had the unnerving thought he was looking at her with fresh eyes, closer than he'd ever looked at her before. She shifted under the scrutiny.

"Why don't you date?"

That wasn't what she thought he'd say.

"What?"

"You said you don't date. Why not?"

"I'm not looking for companionship."

"So you like being alone?"

She didn't exactly approve of the word he'd chosen. "I like living alone," she said truthfully. "I like my own company. But I'm not alone that much. I have work. I spend time with friends, at the bar, at shows. I have company whenever I want it."

"I'm sure you do." There was no trace of judgment in his voice. "So why don't we date? What would you call all the other times we've gotten together?"

"That was hooking up."

"Friends with benefits?" he offered.

"Are we friends?"

"Yes," he said, as if it wasn't up for debate.

"Then I suppose. Friends who fuck."

He cringed. "Mimi."

"Sorry, did I shock you?" She glanced around. The restaurant was full, but the tables were far enough apart that no one could have overheard. No one seemed to be paying much attention to them anyway. It was mostly tourists this time of year. Mimi didn't see anyone she knew. A youngish couple at a table across the way kept throwing them glances. Probably wondering if they could come over and ask for a picture with Nash.

She leaned forward and lowered her voice anyway. "We don't date because there's no point in dating someone who's the definition of a casual hookup."

"Should I be offended by that characterization?"

"It's just the truth," Mimi said. "And it's nothing to be ashamed of. Casual sex is a perfectly acceptable basis for a relationship."

"So that's what you want?"

"Yes," she said automatically. Then she frowned. Wasn't it? She'd never imagined any other option, so she'd never given it much thought. "Isn't that what you want?"

The server returned, bearing a giant silver platter. She set it down on the table with a flourish. A dozen oysters nestled in the crushed ice, little white ramekins filled with different savory accompaniments alongside. Her beet salad was placed like an afterthought at her elbow.

Nash didn't answer her question. "We should eat these, and I'll think about it and get back to you."

Mimi nodded wordlessly. What did that mean? What was there to think about? Either he wanted to keep fucking her or he didn't. There was no real in-between for them, was there?

But she really did enjoy oysters, so she accepted his invitation to partake with gusto. The first one went down easily. Cold and briny, it woke up her entire system. She squirted some lemon juice on the second, and that one tasted even better.

Nash matched her oyster for oyster, laughing a little when one of the little guys slithered off the shell into the ice before he could get it into his mouth. Mimi's concerns faded as they drank and ate and talked about books they'd been reading. He told her about a biography he'd picked up at the library yesterday afternoon, and she told him about the mystery series she'd been bingeing.

After a while, they ordered their main courses—steak for Nash, fish for Mimi. The sun was well set by the time they finished their meals and the couple that had been eying them before stopped by their table.

"Hey, sorry to bother you, but we love *Hawk and Bone*. Could we get a picture? We're on our honeymoon."

"Sure thing," Nash answered kindly, his drawl returning. "Crowd on in here."

It looked like the newly married guy was going to try to take an awkward selfie, and Mimi took pity. She'd been out with Jay enough times when he'd been approached for a picture that she knew it was easier to offer to take the photo so everyone could be on their way sooner.

"Let me," she said, extending her hand.

Nash gave her a grateful smile and then slipped on a more practiced one for the photo. The young couple thanked him, and they even thanked her for taking the photo, which was nice. Usually, she felt invisible in these situations. Which was understandable since she wasn't famous.

"Thanks," Nash said when the couple had gone and they were alone again. "You didn't have to do that."

"No problem," she said. "It must happen all the time."

"A bit," he admitted.

"Do you ever say no?"

"I have once or twice when I didn't get a good vibe from the person asking. But I don't mind. They're usually legit fans, and if I really don't want to interact with anyone, I'll stay out of sight. Easy solution."

"But what if you want to go out and be anonymous?"

"The ship has kind of sailed on that one." He shrugged. "But I'm really lucky, Mimi. I'm grateful every day for my career. Taking pictures with fans is not the worst part of my job."

"What's the worst part?" she asked.

He hesitated, then shook his head. "Nah, no one wants to hear the famous guy complain. You ready to take off?"

She let it go. They'd been having a good time since

their somewhat awkward conversation about dating and expectations—she was honestly surprised at how good a time they'd had. Nash was excellent company, and an attentive listener.

"Yeah, I'm ready."

He turned his whiskey brown eyes on her. "So, your place or mine?"

Chapter Four

Your hair slips through my fingers
like time slips in a stream.
Why can't I remember the color of
your eyes, but I know your
sheets are cream?

— "Cranberry Girl," The
Nash Speedwell Experience

"Excuse me?" Mimi blinked at him with her expressive hazel eyes. He'd been mesmerized by them all night—she couldn't keep her emotions out of them. When she was having fun, they sparkled with joy and laughter. When she was uncomfortable, they went matte and dark. Now they were round with surprise, and he had to laugh.

"I'm sorry, honey. I couldn't resist." All evening, in the back of his mind, he'd been mulling over the way she'd characterized their relationship. She was right. Every time they hung out, they always ended up in bed, sometimes literally, sometimes figuratively—quickies in one vehicle or another, and one time in the storeroom at The Cove, which they both had sworn never to tell Jay about.

She relaxed and scrunched up her nose. "I was going to say yours, but—"

"I'll have you over soon, I promise," he said. "There's a grill. We can have a summer cookout."

"Sounds fun."

"Come on. I'll take you home."

She unhooked her bag from the chair and pulled out her wallet. "We need the bill."

He smiled again. She was adorable. "I took care of it."

"When?" She looked more put out that he'd snuck one by her than that he'd paid.

"Before."

"Oh. Well. Thank you."

"You're welcome."

She stood up, and he admired the way her body just kept on going, long lines with the hint of curves under the pretty, frilly dress she was wearing. He was attracted to her, and it would have been simple to keep things status quo. He'd have happily taken her to bed that night, or any night.

But it bothered him that she thought that was the only thing they were capable of. And since he was going to be in Misty Harbor for a while, he no longer wanted to be a hookup.

He meant it when he said they were friends. He liked her. He respected her. And he remembered how damn good it felt to bury himself deep inside her, how enthusiastic and uninhibited she was in the bedroom. But those encounters had always been rushed, and a little secretive, as neither of them had wanted the complication of Jay knowing about that aspect of their relationship.

They had more time now. He wanted to take his time with her, to get to know her, to deepen their friendship. And they couldn't do that if they were constantly fucking.

He escorted her back to the truck. It was completely dark, and a cool breeze had kicked up from the water. He wished he had a jacket to wrap around her shoulders. Mimi wasn't a delicate flower, but she deserved to be taken care of with as much consideration as if she were a violet that could be easily crushed instead of the sturdy sunflower she was.

"Do you have any plans this weekend?" he asked as they drove to her place.

"I'm going to a show at The Cove tomorrow night with some friends."

Mimi no doubt had tons of friends. "Sounds fun. Who's playing?"

"A folk-rock group, the Lazy Susans or something like that."

Nash waited for the invitation to join her, but Mimi

said nothing. By taking sex off the table, had he taken away her incentive to spend time with him?

He was about to ask her straight-up when she said, with a hint of shyness, "You could stop by and check them out if you want." She told him the start time; she'd be there a little early to snag a good table.

"I'll be there."

He parked across the street from her apartment, shut off the engine, and walked her to her door, without giving her the option of declining. She hesitated at the doorstep, and he felt a little awkward, too. They'd spent the entire evening together without touching once, yet he felt closer to her than ever before. He'd have leaned down and kissed her cheek if he wasn't sure she would make fun of him for it. Still, he was surprised and pleased when she leaned in and wrapped one arm around his shoulder to give him a half-hug.

"Goodnight, Nash. Thanks for dinner."

"My pleasure, Mimi."

She didn't invite him in, and he was glad. It would've been a lot harder to stick to his plan of deepening their friendship and keep his hands off her in the confined space of her shoebox apartment, with the memory of the various times they'd had sex on her couch, on her bed, and one awesome time on the kitchen floor.

He shook his head as he climbed into his truck. She was right. They *did* have sex every time they saw each other. But she was also wrong—he didn't have that kind of relationship with anyone else. For one thing, the girls he dated were usually younger than him and more interested in their careers than anything else. He had gotten a bit of a reputation on the gossip blogs for being a player, but while he enjoyed the company of women, he'd never met one he'd seriously connected with.

The fact that he'd been seeing Mimi on and off for... he counted back...*eight years* was eye-opening. Had it really been that long since the first time? Jay had just opened the bar, and Nash, proud of his friend's second act, had come out for the grand opening, but he remembered he'd spent most of the night talking to Mimi.

He'd met her in passing when they were still doing the show, but during those years she was mostly away at college. Plus, she was two years older than Jay, who was two years older than Nash. The age difference had seemed greater when he was twenty-two and she was twenty-six, but now that he was thirty and she was thirty-four, it barely even crossed his mind.

Mimi had always been attractive, but tonight she'd been rather luminous.

He had the odd sensation he was trapped in some generic cable rom-com. Was he seriously considering dating his best friend's sister?

He'd left the porch light burning before he left to pick up Mimi, and as he gained the hill on Dandelion Road, the warm glow welcomed him back. His house was starting to feel homier. The bed was comfortable, and he could just hear the lap of waves on the shore if he left his window cranked open and didn't have a fan going. The sea breeze was nicer than any artificial one.

He gazed at his closed guitar case, then took off his

boots and took out his phone. He grabbed some scrap paper from a stack on the kitchen island and a pen. He'd been thinking about the wisp of a song that had come to him the day before. Staring at Mimi all night had loosened another fragment of an idea.

He scribbled a few words on the paper, opened his guitar case. The familiar scent of wood and glue hit him, taking him back to the first time he'd held a guitar, thirteen and so excited he almost dropped it. He strummed a few chords and warmed up his fingers, then fumbled through a few half-baked melodies before one caught his ear. He immediately repeated the order of the notes, again and again until he had the fingering memorized.

He sang softly under his breath as he worked, fitting the snatches of lyrics to the melody. Then he'd reach a wall and start all over again from the beginning. He was shocked when he looked up and saw two hours had passed since he'd first sat down with the Gibson. He had the bones of a song, maybe a pretty good song, and he had to capture it before it left his hands and head. He set his phone down on the coffee table, set it to record, and played the whole thing through twice.

His last thought before falling asleep later that night was wondering what Mimi would think of the song.

Chapter Five

You taste tart like cherry, sweet
like rain.
Dark like morning, deep like pain.

— "Cranberry Girl," The
Nash Speedwell Experience

Mimi worked a half-day on Saturday, wanting to get the fundraiser program finished so the committee could sign off on it on Monday.

She worked in silence rather than to her usual weekend playlist. It wasn't so much that she didn't want to listen to music, it was that she was having enough trouble focusing on work while her mind seemed unable to stop reviewing last night. Every word she and Nash had exchanged was burned into her brain, and she couldn't stop thinking about it. The entire evening had been bizarre. He'd said they were friends as if it was a given. Then he hadn't wanted to hook up. But he was coming to the show tonight, and he wanted to have her over to his place to grill.

What in the ever-loving hell was going on?

The most surprising thing about the entire situation was that she could have felt rejected by him not wanting to sleep with her, but she felt—relieved? And puzzled. He'd flipped their script, and now she was even more off-balance than before.

She was probably overthinking this. Maybe Nash really did just want to be her friend. She had lots of friends—she could always use one more. The fact that she'd seen him naked in multiple different positions over the years wasn't relevant. Of course, she'd never been friends with an ex before. Not that he was an ex. They'd never been together, so they couldn't be exes. And they weren't over anyway. Were they?

So yeah, she was confused. And she still found him sexually attractive—who wouldn't? The guy was six feet of pure muscle, with a handsome face, thick brown hair, pretty light brown eyes, even white teeth, and gentlemanly manners. He looked good in a cowboy hat, for fuck's sake. Of course she was attracted to him. But that didn't mean she couldn't be his friend.

For real.

She liked him as a person, after all, not just as a sex object. After their extended conversation last night, it was nice to know she hadn't been hooking up with a vapid jerk all these years. Nash Speedwell was an interesting person, a good guy, and easy on the eyes. Her brother was all those things, too. She could start thinking of Nash as another little brother.

She considered the idea for ten seconds, then rejected it. No, she'd never think of Nash as a brother. He was too good in bed.

When the program draft had been sent, she went home, surveyed her mostly empty fridge before opening the freezer. Jackpot—a burrito was hidden behind an ancient bag of baby peas and container of chicken stock. She threw the burrito in the microwave, then called her mom.

"Whatcha doing?" she asked when Deb picked up.

"Working. Whatcha doing?"

"Just got home. Eating lunch."

"Lunch sounds good. I should do that." Deb sounded distracted.

"Mom, you've been working even more than usual lately. Is everything okay?" Her mother was the assistant manager at the Misty Harbor Inn, a local landmark and where much of the cast and crew of the *Sawyer's Cove* reboot would be staying during production.

"Oh, it's fine. The inn's just busy. The beginning of the season was so slow, now we're finishing out the summer with a bang, and soon all the TV people will be arriving. I'm extending some of our seasonal workers' contracts through the fall."

"It sounds like you should take a break. Want to grab some dinner with me later?"

"Aren't you going to The Cove for the show?"

Deb, though she seemed to live at the inn most days, always heard everyone's news first.

"I am, but the band doesn't start until nine. We could go to the Bakeshop or get Thai."

"You know what, sweetie, I don't think I can. I have a stack of timesheets to go through."

"Brunch tomorrow?"

"Yeah, that sounds good. You want to go out or stay in?"

Deb wasn't much of a cook, but she made an out-of-this-world French toast. Still, Mimi was anticipating the weather turning cold as the summer faded away; opportunities for sunny Sunday morning brunches would soon be a distant memory.

"Let's go out. I was just at Harborview and noticed they do a weekend brunch. My treat."

"Fancy. It's not Mother's Day and I forgot, is it?"

"No. Just...I miss you." They'd both been working too hard to find much time to hang out this summer.

"Okay, sweetie. I'll meet you there. Ten?"

"Better make it eleven," Mimi said. She was not a morning person as a rule, but the night after a show, she was even slower to roll out of bed.

"Love you."

"Love you, too," Deb said.

That left her the entire afternoon to kill before meeting up with Pauline and Colin and...Nash Speedwell. She should probably warn Pauline Nash was coming. Not that she'd know who he was. Pauline had limited interest in current pop culture.

Head's up, I invited Nash Speedwell to
join us tonight.

The second male lead of Sawyer's
Cove?

You know who he is?

I looked everyone up on IMDb when
they announced the reboot. I do have
research skills, you know. Hello?
Librarian?

Oh good, so yeah, he's coming.

As your date?

NO

She'd capitalized the "O" by accident, sort of, so she
followed up with a softer:

No. We're friends. He's one of Jay's
best friends, too.

I'll let Colin know. He mentioned he saw
him at the library the other day. He
might appreciate the warning.

Thanks. See you later.

Pauline gave her last text a thumbs up. Great. Now all
Mimi had to do was last until 9 p.m. without obsessing
over seeing Nash again. Easier said than done. Her
apartment was already clean from yesterday's non-date
experience. She didn't have any errands to run. She

thought about vegging in front of the TV or reading, but then she remembered one crucial piece of the fundraiser she'd been putting off. Her outfit.

Shopping was her least favorite activity, and there was nowhere to buy fancy clothes in Misty Harbor. She would have just worn her go-to simple black sheath dress like last year—except someone had commented on the photos of the event afterward that it made her look like she was at a funeral. She couldn't disagree. She grabbed her laptop and prepared to sacrifice her Saturday afternoon for fashion.

Three hours later, she'd done the impossible— ordered an attractive non-black dress in a size she thought would work after reading the online reviews of said dress in minute detail. It was in her budget, besides. She felt so good about her efforts, she ordered a pair of shoes to match while she was at it. She could figure out jewelry and hair later.

But when she looked at the clock, she realized she needed to eat—she'd made the mistake of going to a show at The Cove on an empty stomach before.

She changed out of her T-shirt and into a tank top, threw on some deodorant and lip gloss, and headed for the Bakeshop. She could get there just before they closed, then eat on the beach.

Trevor was working. The kid was a favorite of hers. He'd moved to Misty Harbor with his parents as a high schooler and had a hard time fitting in at first. She'd noticed him coming into the library most days after school, had gotten him a volunteer position shelving books, and then a reference when he'd applied to work with Zelda at the Bakeshop once he graduated. That was a few years ago now, but he seemed content to fill the same orders for croissants and lattes day in and day out. It probably didn't hurt that the Bakeshop was a hub of Misty Harbor gossip.

"Mimi, what's up, girl?"

"Not much," she said, which was true if she didn't include her back-to-back non-dates with Nash. Her life was usually work, books, friends, music, throw in a few hours of TV, repeat. "Is it too late to order food? I need fuel for the show tonight."

"Zelda's catering a wedding tomorrow, so the kitchen is very much up and running."

"Whose wedding?" Mimi wondered idly as she debated getting something besides her usual.

"Some out-of-towners are getting married at the inn, I guess." Trevor shrugged, pursed his bright red lips.

Mimi remembered when he'd first started wearing makeup, showing up to the library in lipstick and blush. He hadn't said anything about it, and she hadn't either, but once they got to know each other a little better, he'd told her he simply liked wearing makeup because it made him feel good. She'd said that's why she liked dyeing her hair. It was fun and made her feel colorful and happy.

"Exactly," he'd agreed and smiled, and they'd been friends ever since.

"I'll have a mozzarella panini," she said, "if that's okay."

"Anything for you, Mimi, you know that." Trevor keyed in the order. "You want an iced tea?"

"Perfect. And I better get a cookie, too."

"Yes, you'd better," Trevor agreed, with an indulgent smile. "So, when are Jay and Cami coming home? Isn't filming starting soon?"

"So I gather, and the lovebirds should be back this week."

"Isn't it wild that the rest of the *Sawyer's Cove* cast is going to be here, like walking around Misty Harbor?" Trevor was a fan of the show and kept his finger on the pulse of all the reboot news.

"Pretty wild."

"Someone told me Nash Speedwell's in town already. I'm, like, kvelling. I mean, I'm used to Jay, and even Queen Cami, but I think if I ever met the person who played Will O'Connell, I would basically melt into a puddle on the spot. Like, I'm cool with famous people usually—remember when Justin Long came in that one time? I was so, like, blasé about it or whatever. But *Will O'Connell.* He's, like—iconic. I'm not going to be able to handle it, Mimi—seriously."

Mimi laughed nervously and worried a little for Trevor's oxygen intake. "Breathe, sweetie. He's just an actor, like all the rest of them."

"No, he's not—Nash Speedwell was the reason I figured out I was queer. He's like the reason half the guys who came of age in the last fifteen years knew they were queer. Either you watched him on *Sawyer's Cove* all twinky and sensitive with his guitar playing and sucking face with Noah, or on *Hawk and Bone* with all that leather and fur and homoerotic subtext. Nash Speedwell is basically in the bi-curious starter kit."

She choked on her iced tea. "Really? He was that formative for you?"

Trevor held up a slim, pale finger. "Super cute." He held up a second finger. "Super nice." He held up a third finger. "Plays an instrument. How do you not fall in love with that?"

Mimi swallowed uncomfortably. "You know he's straight in real life, though?"

"That's what they all say." Trevor waved his hand airily. "Though it doesn't matter. He's just a fantasy. Except! He's coming here. So he's no longer in the fantasy realm. He's a real person, apparently."

"Yes, that's the problem," Mimi agreed.

When Nash had just been part of her fantasy life, a dream who popped in and out with no consequences, everything was so much simpler. Now she was getting to know him as a real person, and she didn't know what she was supposed to want out of this scenario. Even if they got to know each other and became real friends, he'd still be leaving at the end of the shoot, off to his next project. He'd never be a permanent part of her life. So why were they even bothering to engage in this performative "let's be friends" thing?

"I heard he gives tons of money to LGBTQ charities," Trevor said. "I mean, hot *and* generous? Even if he's straight, a boy can dream."

"Well, maybe he's just a good ally." Mimi supposed

she didn't know with a hundred percent certainty Nash was straight. He'd never mentioned he wasn't, but that didn't mean anything.

"That just makes him dreamier," Trevor said. "Oops, let me get your panini from the back."

Trevor flitted off, and Mimi wondered how to tell him not only was Nash Speedwell in town, he was a friend of hers. A very intimate friend. Not that she'd tell him that part—she trusted Trevor, but things like that had a way of circulating around Misty Harbor despite anyone's best intentions. And the last thing she needed was Jay getting wind of it.

Trevor returned, carrying her sandwich wrapped in brown waxed paper. "Here you go, sorry about word vomiting on you before. I'm just so stoked we're not only getting new *Sawyer's Cove* episodes, but it's all happening right here."

"Don't say 'vomit' to customers, please," Zelda said, emerging from the back laden with two enormous trays of cookies covered in plastic wrap.

"Sorry, Zelda," Trevor said cheerfully. "But it's just Mimi."

"Hi, Zelda. Looks like you're busy."

"I swear, the season started off slow, but we've gotten busier every week. I'm going to be a wreck by Labor Day."

"Is that a good thing?" Mimi asked doubtfully.

"Anything that means we don't have to worry about making rent is a good thing."

"You won't be too busy to do the desserts for the library fundraiser, right?"

"When is it?"

"End of September."

"That's fine. But you better get your order in soon."

"This week, for sure. Thanks, guys, I'll get out of your hair."

She escaped the Bakeshop before she could be drawn into further conversation about Nash or the fundraiser. She needed to unwind, and her favorite way to do that was going to see a band play live. Even if Nash was going to be there, she'd simply ignore him and get lost in the music.

Chapter Six

Cranberry lips, cranberry tongue.
Come on, honey, let's have
some fun.

— "Cranberry Girl," The
Nash Speedwell Experience

Nash had been to The Cove lots of times, but always when Jay was with him, either working the bar or working the crowd. He'd been proud of his friend for pulling himself together after things fell apart in the wake of *Sawyer's Cove* getting canceled. It had taken a while, but the bar had turned out to be the best thing for Jay—an outlet for his energy and love for his hometown.

Misty Harbor wasn't that different from the Tennessee town Nash grew up in, small, incestuous, and steeped in history. Misty Harbor differed in that it welcomed tourists and industry, and even though its location made it unsuitable for commuting to any of the nearby big cities, it still managed to foster culture and a passable nightlife. And where the only reason he went back to his hometown was for the obligatory holiday visits with his family, more and more he found himself looking forward to visits to Misty Harbor.

At first it was about visiting Jay, who'd tried to cut off contact with everyone from the *Sawyer's Cove* days once he decided acting wasn't in his future. Nash had grown too fond of his friend to allow himself to be ghosted. Since Jay never left Misty Harbor, that meant Nash had to go to him. Eventually, visiting the seaside town was both about seeing Jay and being able to relax and be himself. He didn't flaunt himself, but if he ran into fans, they were cool.

Of course, there was another reason he looked forward to visiting Misty Harbor.

Mimi.

She was a breath of fresh air after being around Hollywood types. Nash loved acting, he loved his job, and he liked the people for the most part. Most of his best friends were in the business, Cami and Ariel included.

But Mimi was grounded. She was real, and she didn't bullshit him. She didn't apologize for being herself, and she didn't pretend to be anything but what she was. He liked being around her. She made him feel normal, like someone whose life wasn't flying to obscure locations to wear makeup and dress up for months at a time, then spending his weeks at press junkets and weekends at fan conventions.

His downtime had been severely limited since he signed on to *Hawk and Bone*—if he wasn't in production, he was doing press, and when he wasn't doing press, his schedule was booked with fundraisers for the charities he supported, and sometimes industry events, like awards shows and parties, that were part of the job. He'd spent his last birthday appearing in a promo video for Rainbow Canyon for free.

Honestly, he'd been relieved when the producers of *Hawk and Bone* broke the news they were killing off his character. His initial thought was maybe he could finally take a vacation.

Of course, it wasn't long before Selena and Cami had approached him with the *Sawyer's Cove* reboot, and he'd told himself shooting the show back in Misty Harbor might be as close to a vacation as he was going to get.

The superhero franchise he was going to test for would be like that, but on steroids. Which was another issue. He'd had to bulk up for *Hawk and Bone,* and he'd already begun to lose the extra muscle now that he wasn't under the watchful eyes of the trainer and dietician. That fit for his *Sawyer's Cove* character Will O'Connell, who'd never been a big guy, though he supposed good old Will could have developed muscles after high school graduation. Nash could only imagine more protein powder and extreme workouts in his future if he was offered the part.

He should be excited about it. And he was. It was

incredibly validating to even be considered for a role like Moonshot. Being in a franchise like this was the logical next step for his career.

But it wasn't a step to take lightly.

There was also the matter of his music.

He'd spent a lot of the day working on his song for the charity album. It wasn't the best thing he'd ever written, but it wasn't the worst. He needed to find a recording studio to lay down a track to send to the organizers. Maybe Mimi would have a recommendation for him. She knew the local music scene better than anyone else he knew.

There was the woman herself, near the stage, easy to pick out in the half-full bar, with her height and blue hair. She was dressed much more casually than she had been for their dinner date, in slim jeans, flat sneakers, and a tight black tank top that showed off her long, toned arms, complete with the tattoo he remembered her getting a couple of years back.

We're not going to have sex tonight. When he reached her table, gave her a quick hug, and breathed in her subtle, clean scent, he had to remind himself why that was again.

Because any time spent with Mimi was time well-spent, and he needed to make her understand it wasn't all booty calls between them.

"Hey, you made it," she said, with an overly bright smile.

"Sure did." He studied her face. She seemed...edgy. He couldn't remember her being nervous around him before. She usually treated him with polite dismissiveness, as if she could take or leave him, which was both amusing and provoking. But since he'd changed the rules on her, she seemed to be overcompensating for something.

"Here comes Pauline," she said, waving over an attractive young woman wearing a similar outfit to Mimi, except where Mimi's tank was black, Pauline's was white.

He gave the newcomer a smile.

"Where's Colin?" Mimi asked.

"He'll be along," Pauline said. "Are you Nash Speedwell?"

"That's me."

"Pauline isn't super up on pop culture. But ask her about what was going on in Misty Harbor in eighteen fifty, and she's got you covered." Mimi didn't sound like she was joking, and Pauline didn't correct her.

"Okay." He'd have to ask more about that later. "What can I get you to drink? First round's on me."

"Vodka tonic, please," Mimi said.

Pauline wrinkled her nose. "How you can drink that vile stuff is beyond me. I'll have a Stella."

"You got it." Nash bellied up to the bar and was greeted by Danica. He'd met the bar manager a few times on previous visits to The Cove.

"Hey, Nash. You know Jay isn't here, right?"

"Yeah, I'm here with Mimi."

Her eyebrows rose. "Mimi?"

What was so strange about that? He gave her their

order, and she happily opened a tab for him and told him she'd bring the drinks by in a minute. When he got back to the table, another familiar figure had joined their little group.

"Colin, right?" he asked the rangy young guy. "From the library?"

He got a chin lift in return. "Hey."

"You have the unparalleled good fortune of spending your evening with three of Misty Harbor Library's finest," Mimi said before dragging Pauline out of her seat. "Let's go powder our noses before the show starts."

As soon as they were gone, Colin asked, "Are you here as Pauline's date?" Before Nash could react, he went on, "Because I sort of have a thing for her, and I guess I need to know what I'm up against."

"I just met her, man," he said, trying to tamp down a laugh by biting the inside of his cheek. "But she seems awesome."

"She is," Colin said on a sigh. "Sorry. It's just—she's been really consumed writing this grant for the Captain Zachariah Bragg exhibit and she's finally done and—wait—are you here as *Mimi's* date?" He said the last part as if it was truly unbelievable.

"Um..." Nash didn't know how to answer the question. "Would it surprise you if I said I was?"

"Pretty much. Mimi doesn't date, as far as I know. I've heard some people say she's gay and in the closet and that's why she's never in a relationship, but she told me herself she's straight, so that's not it."

"Is this an appropriate conversation to have about your boss?" Nash asked.

"Oh, Mimi used to babysit me. She basically gave me 'the talk' before my parents got around to it. Small town, you know? Besides, she's, like, the coolest boss ever."

This was why it had been a good idea to come out tonight. Maybe Mimi's co-workers were a little odd, but at least he was getting to know more about her.

The band started warming up, and Danica delivered their drinks. She eyed Colin when he asked for a Red Stripe. "Do you have ID?"

The kid handed over his license. "I have a baby face, but I'm twenty-five. Pauline's twenty-eight, but I don't think that matters if you really like someone. Do you?"

It certainly never had bothered Nash that Mimi was four years older than him, so he shook his head. "Definitely not."

The women returned from the bathroom, and while the conversation with Colin had been enlightening, if unexpected, he was glad for Mimi's return. They sat boy-girl-boy-girl and clinked their various drinks together as the band launched into their first song of the night.

It was too loud to talk, but Nash didn't mind just listening to the music, which was more than decent folk. The singer was a pretty woman with long blonde hair and a throaty alto voice. She was accompanied by a male guitarist and drummer and another blonde on tambourine. It could have been annoyingly retro, but their sound was vibrant and modern, and Nash enjoyed himself. He also enjoyed Mimi, who was watching, rapt, her bright eyes wide open, her hand keeping time by tapping her thigh. Pauline was into the music, too, and Colin looked like he was making an effort to get into it, even if his gaze kept sliding to Pauline. It was cute, because she would occasionally catch him and give him a look that was hard to interpret, but it seemed like she was into him, too.

Nash turned back to the band, which was when he realized the guitar player was making definite eyes at Mimi. What the hell? Yes, he was throwing glances in Mimi's direction and—was that a wink? Nash snapped his gaze to Mimi, looking for her reaction. She looked happy and not particularly concerned by the attention. Maybe even liked it.

He experienced an unfamiliar rumbling sensation in his chest, and his fist tightened around his bottle of beer. He stared hard at the guitar player, wondering what she'd see in the guy. He had hair so long it swept the top of his collar, and a sort of melancholy hangdog look. He supposed some chicks would dig that. But not Mimi— Mimi should be with someone who challenged her, who supported her. Someone who'd offer her more than a tepid one-night stand.

Wait, was this strange, hot feeling jealousy?

Huh.

Maybe he needed to make this an official date between them after all.

Chapter Seven

Jules: We've been wanting to do this episode for a while, and, with one thing and another, it's only happening now, but no judgment.

Erika: This is a judgment-free zone. Except when we review things. And critique things. And judge the hell out of things. Wait.

Jules: Look, we're not judgey, we have opinions.

Erika: Yes, we have lots of opinions. Nonjudgmentally.

Jules: So what is your opinion of The Nash Speedwell Experience?

Erika: I was honestly pleasantly surprised.

Jules: Same! The album was super listenable.

Erika: I listened to it to prepare for this episode, but I actually found myself playing it just because I wanted to hear a few of the songs again this week. It might go into permanent rotation. Way to go, Nash.

The Lazy Susans finished their set, and Mimi clapped and whistled along with the rest of the appreciative crowd. She glanced over her shoulder at Nash, and he was clapping, too, though his expression was a little pinched. Maybe the music hadn't been his cup of tea, though she would have thought he'd like the tunes, since his album had a definite folk influence.

"What did you think?" she asked, leaning over into his space to be heard over the hubbub of the crowd.

"Not bad," Nash said. "You liked it?"

"Yeah, they were great," Mimi said, unafraid to admit to liking something, even if it made her look foolish. She owned her likes and dislikes, and to hell with anyone who judged her, even Nash Speedwell.

"You want to get a refill?" Colin asked Pauline. She nodded, and he jumped to help her scoot out her chair.

Mimi grimaced as they left. "Poor guy," she said. "I don't know if he knows what he's doing."

Nash looked after them appraisingly. "He told me he has a thing for her. Is it not reciprocated? She seems to like him, too."

"I didn't think so, but what do I know?" She laughed. "I'm no expert."

"Colin also interrogated me about you. His eyes went about as round as beer cans, thinking I might be your date."

"Oh, yeah? And what did you say?"

"I don't think I was definitive either way, but I'm certainly glad to be here with you, date or not," he said, turning those melting brown eyes on her. She suddenly felt in danger of becoming a Nash Speedwell groupie.

"Lots of drama at The Cove tonight," Mimi said, laughing a little to clear the air between them. "Almost like an episode of *Sawyer's Cove*. Who likes who, and who's dating who."

"And who's eye-fucking who," Nash said, nodding in the direction of the stage.

"Excuse me?"

"The guitarist. He was staring at you the entire set."

Mimi had noticed the guy giving her a look, and she'd returned it—he was cute, and talented. Her friends were always supportive of her flirtations, and she and Nash were apparently friends.

Then again, it wasn't a very friendly tone of voice he was using.

"He wouldn't be the first musician I've picked up at The Cove," she said, with saccharine sweetness. "And he probably wouldn't be the last."

Nash's jaw muscle twitched for a second, but then his expression dissolved into a sheepish smile. "None of my business, I know. But you could do a lot better, Mimi. He's a folkie," he scoffed.

"I usually go for bass players anyway." He was taking this better than he could have.

"Bass players? Seriously?" Nash flicked his eyes to

the stage, as if looking for any errant bass players. "I don't play bass, you know."

"I do know," she said. "That's why it could never work between us." She said it lightly, as a joke, but it seemed to fall flat, because he didn't laugh. "Anyway." She stood up from the table. "Want a refill?"

"Sure, I'll go with you," he said.

Craving a moment alone to clear her head, she said, "Someone has to hold down the fort."

As if some sadistic screenwriter had written it, Pauline and Colin appeared at that moment.

"We're back," Pauline said brightly, holding up her fresh drink and looking between Mimi and Nash.

"Always so helpful, Pauline," Mimi murmured.

Nash trailed her to the bar like a confused duckling imprinting on a dog. "So, what is it about bass players? Their inability to carry a melody?"

She waited her turn for Danica's attention behind a couple of bearded guys in flannel. "They're uncomplicated," she said. "Singers are narcissists, drummers are too energetic."

"What about lead guitarists?"

"They're fine." She shrugged, knowing he was fishing and happy to stymie his efforts. "There's something about bass guitarists—they just curdle me." She winked at him.

"Huh?"

"Sorry, it's a line from *Some Like It Hot*. Marilyn Monroe joins an all-girls band because she has a thing for saxophone players—tenor sax in particular—and she can't afford to sing with male bands anymore."

"I saw that movie a long time ago, I think."

"One of my favorites."

"We should watch it sometime," Nash said.

Mimi was saved from answering when Danica asked if they wanted the same again. "Yes, please," she said. Nash nodded in agreement, then moved a little way down the bar to snag a menu.

"How are you getting along with Jay out of town?" Mimi asked Danica.

The pretty bartender grinned as she cracked the cap on a new bottle of vodka. "Oh my gosh, it's so relaxing. Jay's an awesome boss, but he can be a little micro-managing. I'm looking forward to the start of filming so he'll be out of my hair again."

Mimi laughed. "He thinks he's so laid-back, and yet he's so controlling."

"Tell me about it." She tipped her head toward Nash. "I didn't know you and Nash were a thing."

"What? Who says we are?" Mimi really did feel like this was high school all over again. Why did everyone care so much about her and Nash and their relationship status?

"Oh, sorry, never mind. I just thought—he said—" Danica looked flustered. "Don't mind me."

"It's okay—not your fault." Mimi wasn't exactly upset, but she glanced over at Nash, who was concen-trating on the single-page menu so hard, he might have been memorizing a Shakespearean soliloquy. "Add this to his tab."

"You got it."

Nash sidled back up and asked for an order of sliders and sweet potato fries. "You want something to eat, Mimi?"

"No, I got food from the Bakeshop earlier. Which reminds me, I've got a friend I want you to meet sometime," she said, thinking of Trevor.

"Any friend of yours," he said easily.

They went back to the table with their drinks. The band was gearing up for another set. Mimi considered positioning herself in such a way that Nash couldn't miss it if she kept flirting with the guitar player, but in the end she didn't want to lead the guy on. The musician, that is.

She was probably not going to score with Nash Speedwell tonight, and that was fine, but she couldn't muster the enthusiasm to get with someone else. It was a pickle. He didn't seem to want her like that anymore, but it was a big drop from Nash Speedwell to second place. She shifted her chair so her back was partially to the band and she could see her table mates much better. Colin and Pauline were talking about who had the best pizza in town.

"Antonio's gets my vote," Mimi put in.

"But that's not a pizza place, it's an Italian restaurant. Doesn't count," Colin said.

"I think Harbor Pizza wins because they have gluten-free options," Pauline said.

"But you aren't gluten-free," Mimi argued.

"I can take my dad there when he visits. He doesn't eat gluten."

"Seriously? I think gluten is the only thing my dad puts in his mouth," Colin said, making Pauline smile.

"Harbor Pizza is pretty good," Nash said, surprising Mimi by having an opinion on the subject. "I like their Hawaiian pizza."

Pauline wrinkled her nose. "I thought people who liked Hawaiian pizza were a myth?"

"You're looking at one," Nash returned. "I like the sweet and savory combination." He glanced at Mimi after that comment. "And they deliver late, which is a plus."

"I remember reading on your Wikipedia page that you released an album. What do you think of the music tonight?" Pauline asked in her precise way.

"Uh...they're good," Nash said.

"Even the guitar player?" Mimi couldn't resist asking.

Nash shot her a look, then asked Pauline, "What kind of music do you like?"

"I'm agnostic when it comes to music," Pauline said. "I like everything. Which is good, because Mimi drags me to every show, without regard to genre."

"I've been getting more into jazz," Colin said. Three pairs of eyes gave him disbelieving looks. "What? I can't be into jazz?"

"You should both listen to Nash's album. If you like this band, you'll like his stuff. It's better," Mimi said, pretending not to see Nash's satisfied smile.

"Do you have a band?" Pauline asked him.

"Nah, just a couple of friends who pitched in and recorded the album with me."

"You should play at The Cove," Mimi said, suddenly wondering why he'd never done it before. "They have local musicians on Sunday nights."

"First of all, I'm not local," Nash said. "Second of all, I don't play live."

"Third of all, you're living in Misty Harbor while the show shoots, so close enough," Mimi rebutted, "and fourth of all, why the hell not?"

Nash shifted uncomfortably in his chair. "I just don't. The album was a fluke. I'm not a real musician."

"That's bullshit," Mimi said calmly. "Besides, you can't have stage fright. You're an actor."

"Are you kidding? Actors have the worst stage fright. And it's not about that anyway."

"Didn't you play guitar on a few episodes of *Sawyer's Cove*?" Mimi had watched the talent show episode about sixty times and distinctly remembered Nash, as Will, doing an acoustic cover of "Wonderwall," by Oasis. "Doesn't that count as performing live?"

"The magic of television," Nash declared. "All done in a studio; I just lip-synced on the day."

"Yeah, but you sang it in the studio. I don't get it." He was so talented. It had never occurred to her that any of this was *hard* for him.

Nash cleared his throat and changed the subject. "Anyway, I'm glad you like the album. Really. It means a lot that you like it."

"I love it," Mimi said softly, unable to prevaricate.

"Thanks." His eyes filled with something like gratitude, and Mimi wondered again how someone as put-together and successful could need even more validation than your average bear.

A minute later, Nash was busy eating the sliders that had been delivered, while Mimi picked at the sweet potato fries he pushed in her direction. When the band started up again, Colin and Pauline got up to dance. Mimi thought they looked good together, Colin towering a full foot over her friend, with eyes only for her. She shook her head and hoped they knew what they were getting into.

"You don't approve?" Nash asked, bellowing to be heard over the band.

"It's not that." She wondered if Pauline would mind being outed to Nash. "Don't worry about it. Hey, so why did Danica think we're dating?"

Nash choked on his fry. "I don't know. I just told her I was here with you."

"You did what?" Mimi frowned. "Okay, we need to get our story straight right now. What is going on between us? Are we dating? Are we friends? Because Jay is coming home soon, and I don't think either of us wants him to hear you and I are an item."

Nash laughed disbelievingly. "Why not?"

"Why not? Why do you think we've never told him about us before?"

"Um. Because...it was a casual thing he didn't need to know about?"

Mimi was surprised by the accuracy of that statement. "Exactly. Now we're all chummy, and it looks suspicious."

"It's suspicious that you and I are friends? Everyone knows Jay and I are close. Makes sense you and I would be, too."

"Okay, so we're going with that. You and me and Jay—all good friends."

"Aren't we?" He seemed confused.

"Yeah." Mimi smiled slyly. "Then you need to watch the catty remarks about my predilection for bass players. My friends are all supportive of my flings."

"Your flings?"

"Yes, my flings. Of which you, until recently, were one." Was that too far? Even a super chill person might not like being reminded they were one of a long line of guys in her bedroom.

But Nash just gritted his teeth and said, "Fine. I'll be supportive of your flings. Speaking of which, they'll be finishing their set soon." He nodded toward the stage.

Mimi followed his gaze all the way to the guitarist. The guy was decent-looking, and a good musician.

And she had no desire to so much as chat with him, let alone sleep with him.

Telling herself it had nothing to do with Nash, she shook her head. "You're right. I can do better. And I have a brunch date tomorrow, so I better not stay up too late tonight."

Nash's satisfied smirk at the front half of her statement faded in the wake of the second half. "A brunch date?"

"With my mom," she said, laughing at the comical way his expression changed to one of relief. She was in big trouble if this was how their friendship was going to go—him cock-blocking her by being himself, her teasing him, a little turned on by his jealousy. She had lots of friends, and this was not how she behaved with any of them.

Chapter Eight

Friends and lovers, lovers and
friends.
What's the difference when we're
all playing games?

— "Puzzle Piece," The Nash
Speedwell Experience

"Glad I got a reservation," Mimi commented the next morning when she and Deb slid into their seats on the Harborview deck. They were shaded by a big sun umbrella, but that didn't help with the humidity, which made the late summer air feel as thick as the Bloody Mary she ordered from their server.

Her mother ordered the same and studied the menu. "I haven't been here in years. What made you think of it?"

Mimi avoided answering the question while she

debated quiche versus omelet. She'd inherited so many things from her mom—from her hazel eyes to her no-nonsense attitude and work ethic. They'd always been close, even during Mimi's adolescent years. Deb had been seventeen when she was born, finished high school while her mother took care of newborn Mimi during the day.

The relatively small gap in their ages had always been a plus as far as Mimi was concerned. Her mom remembered all too well what it had been like to be a hormonal teenager. And as tough as it was sometimes growing up with a single mom and bratty little brother, Deb had never taken out her stress or worry on Mimi and Jay. She'd always made them feel wanted, loved, taken care of.

With the perspective of adulthood, Mimi knew Deb had no doubt sacrificed her own well-being and sanity to give them as secure a childhood as she could. And now that they were grown and independent, Deb was still as hardworking as ever. She never asked for anything for herself, so Mimi and Jay liked to spoil her when they could.

Deb fanned herself with the menu. "It is hot today, right? I'm not just having hot flashes?"

"I don't know about the hot flashes, but it's definitely hot," Mimi agreed. "Maybe we should ask if they have a table inside."

"No, the view is so pretty," Deb said, looking across the choppy ocean. "This is great. Thanks, sweetie."

"You're welcome. And to answer your earlier question, I came here for dinner the other night."

"Oh? With the girls from the library?"

"No. Um..."

Even though they shared everything else, Mimi had never felt overly comfortable talking about men with her mother. Mostly because Deb had never been in a relationship the entire time Mimi had known her. And while Deb seemed perfectly content, Mimi felt like there was some soreness there. On the other hand, there were precious few people she could talk to about Nash. Deb had known him for fifteen years, after all.

"I had dinner with Nash."

"Nash? Is he in town already?" Deb looked surprised, then ordered the omelet Mimi had been thinking about from the server when she came around again. Mimi decided on the quiche for a change of pace.

"He got in Thursday. Wanted to get settled before the shoot."

"Well, that's nice. I can't believe all the kids will be back in town. Just like the old days."

"Those kids are all thirty-plus, remember?" Mimi said.

Deb groaned. "Don't remind me. Makes me feel old."

"You're fifty-two and look like my older sister," Mimi said dryly. "But I know what you mean."

"Well, tell Nash I'd like to see him. Maybe we should all have dinner when Jay and Cami get back."

"He said something about hosting a barbecue," she said. "He's renting a house down on the south side."

"Oh, it's lovely down there."

Mimi took a fortifying sip of her drink, the acid of the tomato juice bright on her tongue. "Are you surprised Nash and I had dinner?"

"Should I be? He's your brother's best friend."

Mimi said nothing, waiting for it to sink in. Deb's face grew thoughtful. "You and Nash?"

"No, not exactly," Mimi said. "Well, it's complicated. He says we're friends, but he's wooing me, I think."

"And do you want to be wooed?"

That was the question, wasn't it?

"I don't know. I've never wanted to be wooed before. Or to woo anyone, for that matter."

"But this is different." It wasn't a question.

Mimi sighed. "I don't know. I like him, as a person. The problem is, we've already slept together. Quite a few times. I've never had a relationship with someone I've slept with. It's usually a one-and-done kind of thing."

Deb made a face.

"Sorry. TMI? I know we don't usually talk about this stuff."

"It's okay. I get it. You know, I've been a bit selfish over the years, quietly relieved you never seemed to want a long-term relationship. I wouldn't have been much help to you if you had. But it's okay to change your mind. It's okay to try something new. And Nash is a good person. He's been a good friend to your brother."

"You never wanted a relationship either," Mimi said. "Did you?"

Deb's smile held a hint of sadness. "It wasn't part of the equation for me."

"I know you had me and Jay to take care of, and that made things complicated, but when we grew up, you could have pursued something. You still could, for that matter."

Deb hummed and gazed out over the water again, but Mimi didn't know what she was thinking.

Despite her tendency to get pregnant at the drop of a hat, her mother was the least promiscuous person Mimi had ever met. In fact, Mimi had sometimes thought she was so enthusiastic about her own sexual freedom to make up for her mother's abstinence, which was kind of twisted. Or maybe she was simply the cliché of the fatherless girl acting out by having lots of casual sex.

That idea was repulsive to her. She prided herself on never being a cliché. She was no meek, tidy, buttoned-up librarian. She was bold and a little wild. She dyed her hair and had a tattoo. Yes, it was a book tattoo, but a tattoo nonetheless. She lived alone, but she didn't own a single cat. She didn't sleep with strangers because she was self-loathing, with abandonment issues. She was just patently uninterested in couplehood.

Which was why her arrangement with Nash had been perfect, up until a few days ago.

Stupid, beautiful man making her question thirty-four years of singledom.

Deb broke into her ruminations. "Have you thought about what Jay's going to think of all this?"

Mimi winced. "I've tried not to."

"Well, you might want to tell him yourself before the town gossip circuit relays it first."

"I know." Her brother wasn't toxically overbearing, but he did take his role as the third leg of their little family stool very seriously. He wasn't happy if he didn't know Deb and Mimi were thriving, and she imagined it would take an adjustment period for him to picture his sister with his oldest friend.

But that was if she and Nash were even a thing. So far they'd had one confusing dinner, a group outing, and nary a kiss between them.

So why was she more on edge than ever? She'd been jittery with anticipation before he arrived in Misty Harbor, not sure how their intermittent fling would be affected by his long-term stay. But instead of having more sex due to his proximity, they were having none because he was trying to prove a point.

She didn't have to take this relationship solely on his terms. Why shouldn't she march over to his place and tell him this was ridiculous? They should fuck and get it over with. She had a pretty good track record of getting men into bed when she set her mind to it.

She and Deb finished brunch by sharing ice cold lemon basil sorbet and made plans for lunch later in the week.

"And when Jay comes home, we'll do dinner. You know, I'm impressed Cami got him to leave the county, let alone the country."

"She's a very persuasive woman," Mimi remarked.

"That she is. Now, you have a nice day off."

"You, too. Don't work all day," Mimi instructed.

"Same goes for you, sweetie." Deb hugged her good-bye, and they got into their separate cars.

Mimi blasted the AC and took stock. She'd showered that morning, and yes, the humidity had dampened her a little bit, but she didn't think Nash would mind a little sweat. Instead of heading back to her apartment, she navigated to the long cross-town boulevard that led away from downtown Misty Harbor to the big beach houses on the south side of town. She'd once been to a friend's bachelorette party at the house Nash had rented. It was hard to find, but Mimi remembered the turn-off. She nosed her small car down the track and gunned it up the hill. She was glad it hadn't rained in a few days, or she would have had a harder time scaling the steep dirt road in her front-wheel-drive compact.

Her stomach had been jumpy since conceiving her little plan, but calmed when she pulled in behind Nash's silver truck parked in front of the attractive beach house. He was home. She'd been low-key horny since he'd walked into her office Thursday afternoon. Clearly, sex was the best course of action here.

Nash answered thirty seconds after her confident knock. He smiled at her lazily, his eyes creasing at the corners. "Hiya, Mimi."

"We should have sex."

Chapter Nine

They can try to shut us out, but
    we'll never stop knocking
    down walls.
Every one we knock down, we'll
    make a garden in the rubble.
We'll fill it with love.

— "Untitled" for Rainbow
Canyon, The Nash Speedwell
Experience

"You better come in," Nash said, opening the door wide enough for Mimi to slip inside. She looked dewy and delectable in linen trousers and a white T-shirt.

"Thank God for your air conditioning. I was melting out there," she said, which explained the dewiness.

"I know, I went for a run on the beach this morning, and it was even bad down there."

"New England humidity," Mimi said as she positioned herself under the ceiling fan in his living room.

"Would you like something cold to drink?" he asked.

"I think we should have sex," she said.

"You said that."

"And you didn't say anything back. This is silly, Nash. We're grown-ups. We don't need to justify anything. And whatever imaginary relationship you think is growing between us is just that—imaginary. Why not just do what we know we're good at?"

"Haven't you ever heard of romance?" Nash said.

"I've read plenty of romance novels," Mimi assured him. "But that's fiction."

"Look, I know we have great sex. Remember that time in the stockroom at the bar?"

She smirked. "I remember."

He chose his words carefully. He didn't want to scare her off, and he didn't want to make any promises he couldn't keep. "I don't think I can just see you around town and have sex with you once in a while. I think I need more."

"More?" She acted like he'd suddenly started speaking Swedish.

"You don't have to want that, too. But maybe you could try it out? See how it feels?"

"How would I do that?"

"Well, let's say we're two people who like each other but haven't slept together yet. We might...talk. Kiss, even.

Without having sex. I think they call it making out." His gaze snagged on Mimi's lips, an unpainted, pale pink. The last time he'd made out with someone had been on camera for *Hawk and Bone*, a couple months ago now. He very much wanted to end his make-out dry spell with Mimi Orlando.

"I've heard of it," she said wryly. "But isn't that a bit juvenile?"

"Don't knock it 'til you've tried it."

"We've made out before," she argued. "The first time it happened."

"That was eight years ago," he reminded her.

"Which is why this is silly."

"If you don't want to, that's totally fine. We can still just be friends. I'll always be your friend, Mimi. You don't have to worry about losing that." He got a little anxious thinking about a world in which they weren't in contact at all. He really wanted to keep her in his life. But not as an on-demand booty call. He was old enough to know that was no longer what he wanted from her.

But what did she want?

She looked around the room, her gaze landing on his guitar. "Okay, so let's pretend we're...that we like each other." She made a face like a grossed-out middle schooler. "What would we do?"

"We could talk. How about that drink?"

She composed her features, probably reminding herself she was, technically, a mature adult. "Sure. Sparkling water?"

"You got it."

He took his time in the kitchen. He wondered, not for the first time, if the stakes in the game they were playing were too rich for him to be bluffing like this. Of course, it didn't help that she came into his home looking soft and oozing pheromones. He stuck his head in the fridge to cool himself off. The air conditioning helped, but it was still hot as hell outside. Mimi had brought the heat inside, and now he had no escape.

He filled two glasses with ice from the freezer, then to the brim with sparkling water. He vaguely wanted to add a slice of lemon or sprig of mint, but his home-making skills were limited after years of living in rentals and hotels. A couple of years after *Sawyer's Cove,* he'd played a chef in a TV pilot that didn't get picked up, and the research he'd done for the role was the extent of his cooking experience. Not that Mimi cared if her water had a garnish. He just wanted to put his best foot forward. He'd never spent this much energy to make sure a girl stuck around before. It was a new and not entirely comfortable sensation.

He returned to the living room, where Mimi was paging through the biography he'd checked out of her library. He pressed the glass into her hand, let their fingers brush intentionally. She eyed him suspiciously but didn't say anything.

"How's the book?" she asked instead, nodding toward it as she settled onto the oversized couch.

He took the armchair kitty corner to her, both so he

could see her face more easily as they talked, and to avoid any temptation to touch her prematurely.

"Good so far. I got a little distracted and haven't read much."

"Distracted with what? Prep for the show?"

"No, I haven't really started prepping yet, but there's time. I was writing a song."

"A new song?" She leaned forward eagerly. "Are you working on a new album?"

He couldn't help noticing the way her tits strained against the thin fabric of her shirt. He knew what they felt like in his mouth. He forced his gaze to her clear, expressive eyes.

"Not exactly. I have a bunch of partial songs but haven't been able to finish anything lately. This song, though. It's almost done. I think."

"How long does it take you to write? What's your process? Do you compose on the guitar? Can I hear the song?"

Nash laughed at her animation. She really dug everything about music. "I don't have any set process. Every song comes to me differently. Sometimes I write the melody first on the guitar—but for this one I wrote the lyrics, then worked on the melody after."

"God, I wish I could play an instrument." Mimi sighed. "I'm like the world's most un-musical music lover."

"Have you ever tried?"

"I made it through exactly one piano lesson before my teacher told my mother her money would be put to better use literally any other way than trying to get me to make sense of reading music and notes. I think I have a blind spot in that area."

"Lots of musicians only play by ear," he said. "I started by imitating Jack White."

"You must have a good ear. And a good memory."

"Two things that make acting a job I can actually do," Nash agreed. "But it's never too late if you want to learn."

She leaned forward again. "Why? You want to give me guitar lessons, Mr. Speedwell?"

He shifted in his seat, ignoring the way her sultry voice made his shorts feel tight. "That's a possibility," he said lightly. "Though you could probably learn more from YouTube."

"So let's hear it," Mimi said, sitting back. "Your new song. I want to hear an unreleased Nash Speedwell track. You already know I'm a fan—the ship has sailed on any plausible deniability on that score."

He looked at the messy stack of handwritten notes he'd piled on the coffee table. He didn't need them. He'd worked on the song until he could play it by heart. But though he had no particular songwriting routine, what definitely wasn't part of the process was playing the song for another human being until it was polished and shiny and impervious to criticism.

This song was done, maybe, but it was raw.

"Um...it's not ready for primetime."

"I'm not asking you to perform at the Grammys," she said. "It's just me."

Mimi may not have been musical, but she had

discerning taste. She listened to everything from Neil Young to Kendrick Lamar. And she had opinions on all of it. What if she didn't like this song?

Some of his thoughts must have been playing on his face, because she said, "What if you play it and I don't say anything? I'll just listen. Pretend I'm not even here. Close your eyes if you want. Can you play the guitar with your eyes closed?"

She looked uncertain, and he laughed again. This was why he liked being around her. She was so unapologetically real. She didn't tailor her words or actions to conform to any particular way she thought she was supposed to be. She just was. And he liked who she was. Very much.

More than he'd ever admitted to himself before.

He found himself picking up his Gibson. He wasted a minute needlessly tuning it.

Mimi, true to her word, tucked her legs beneath her, folded her hands in her lap, then relaxed her face into a neutral expression.

Why was he so nervous? She was right—there were literally no stakes to him playing this song for her. He'd played for Jay more than once; he'd jammed with friends in private all over the world. Just because he made it a rule not to perform live, didn't mean he was incapable of it. He had a healthy ego. He knew he could play the guitar proficiently, and he knew how to imbue his playing style with soul, thanks to his acting ability, if nothing else. But he couldn't eradicate the fear that anyone who ever clapped at one of his songs was only doing it because he was Nash Speedwell. Forget *Almost Famous*, he was already famous.

He'd never felt like he'd earned any of the accolades that came through his music. How would he know if anyone only gave it a listen because of his name? He wished he could have put his album out with his name nowhere near it, but instead he'd put it right there on the cover, because he wasn't stupid. He wanted to sell copies because that meant more money for Rainbow Canyon. Every time he was able to send a healthy chunk of change their way, he felt like he'd done something worth doing.

Closing his eyes as she'd suggested, he felt out the fingering and started to strum. When he began to sing, his voice came out almost too soft to hear over the chords. He stopped, started over, forcing strength into his voice.

After the first verse, Nash cracked his eyes open and kept them on the French doors to the patio instead of looking to Mimi for her reaction—or non-reaction, as it might be. He stumbled slightly over the chorus—the last line wasn't quite right, but he kept on until the end. The last notes faded away in the bright, sunny living room.

When the room was silent but for the faint whir of the ceiling fan, he made himself turn to Mimi.

She was looking at his guitar. Her face was blank, but her eyes gave her away every time. She couldn't keep her emotions out of them. They were shiny, almost as if they were glazed with tears, but that couldn't be right, could it?

He hadn't meant for the song to be sad.

"The chorus needs a little work—" he began just as she said, "Nash. That was gorgeous."

Chapter Ten

Our flowers will grow stronger
    than bricks.
Every arm open, every heart free.
Every song for you, every song
    for me.

        — "Untitled" for Rainbow
Canyon, The Nash Speedwell
            Experience

"Oh." Nash's shoulders dropped about a foot.

Mimi found herself leaning toward him, wanting to ride the line between encouraging and gushing. "I mean, yeah, maybe that one line, about finding a place whether there's rain or sun, sounded a little rough? But the whole thing was just...lovely. You captured how I feel about the library."

His forehead wrinkled. "The library?"

"Well, yeah. For me, the library has always been about making a place for people who need one. When I was a kid, I'd go there and feel instantly better. Why do you think we offer so many programs? It's not just a place to get books. It's about community."

"I never thought about it like that before. But I got that feeling when I was there the other day. It's so inviting, I felt like staying a while, in a cocoon of books."

Her chest went warm and fuzzy. She worked so hard to cultivate a welcoming environment at the library, and he'd expressed his experience perfectly. "Exactly. Sometimes I think I'd be happy living in a room made entirely of books. But it's probably good I don't, or I'd never leave."

His smile was fond. "No, you shouldn't be sequestered away. You make the world better by being out in it."

"Oh. Thanks." She touched her mouth self-consciously. No one had ever said anything like that to her before.

"I'm glad you connected with the song. I must confess, I wasn't thinking about the library when I wrote it."

"I'd be surprised if you had been. What's the inspiration, then? Or do you not want to say?"

He shrugged. "It's for a charity album, so I guess I was thinking about the kids who grow up feeling out of place, and I just want them to know there is a place for them, if they can hang on long enough to find it."

"Are you talking about queer kids?"

"Mostly. You wouldn't believe how many messages I get from people—young people—like twelve, thirteen sometimes, who watch *Sawyer's Cove* and say they didn't know a gay person could be so well-adjusted in high school."

"Well, that was the beauty of Will O'Connell. He was the least fucked up of all the Cove kids and dealt with his problems in the healthiest way."

"Yeah, sometimes I thought he was too good to be true, but then I remembered I was on a TV show and none of it was real." He laughed self-deprecatingly, then bent over his guitar, plucking at the strings idly.

She leaned toward the music like a plant being played Mozart. "I know, it was almost like they were just making it up as they went along," she teased. "But it's cool you have so many people who look up to you."

He frowned, glancing at her through his long golden-brown lashes. "It's a big responsibility."

"You wear it well."

"Thanks." He kept playing as if he wasn't aware he was doing it. "It never feels like enough."

"Is that why you're doing the charity album?"

"The least I can do is financially support folks who are much more qualified to give those kids real help than I am."

"Give yourself credit, Nash. You do a lot more than most people."

He didn't answer, but abruptly stopped playing and set the guitar aside.

Apparently, the private show was over. She fought a pout. She could have stayed there for hours watching him noodle on the instrument. For all their banter about bass players, obviously she found his guitar playing more than passably attractive.

Oh, who was she kidding? She'd lived thirty-four very full years and never seen anything as hot as Nash Speedwell playing guitar in a preppy blue polo, his flat-front khaki shorts showing off muscled legs dusted with light brown hair and ending in enviably perfect bare feet. His hair was rather long and swept back in a faux pompadour. She wondered if they were going to make him cut it for the show. His guitar looked well-used—the plain blond wood looked good with the neutral beach-friendly decor of the living room.

But Nash could have been wearing a ratty bathrobe in the middle of a garbage dump, and he'd still be gorgeous strumming that guitar with his agile, clever fingers.

Her panties were damp from more than the over-whelming humidity. God, she was just as stupid around Nash as Marilyn Monroe was around saxophone players.

Speaking of which. "So this 'let's talk' thing...you aren't punishing me for being easy, are you?"

He grinned at her. "Honey, nothing about you is easy."

"Thank you." That was the type of compliment she could understand—one couched in criticism.

"You're welcome," he answered gravely.

"Well." She stood up quickly. Her legs were rubbery after having been folded underneath her for so long. "I guess I should go."

He nodded and stood as well, but his smile seemed forced. "Sure."

"I mean, I probably interrupted you doing something important. Some important rock-star-actor business."

"It's Sunday," he reminded her. "Even rock star actors need a day off."

"Thunderstorm tonight," she plowed on. "I bet you'll have a great view of the storm over the ocean from upstairs."

There was a pause. If this had been six months ago, he would have asked her to come see for herself, and they would have spent the afternoon fucking and forgetting all about the view.

But this wasn't six months ago.

"I heard tomorrow's supposed to be cooler." He crossed his arms, causing the sleeves of his polo to strain over twin swells of muscle.

"That's good. I like the warmth, but not the humidity. My hair doesn't need any more inducement to frizz."

He glanced at her hair. "I like the color. It matches the sky."

They both turned to look out the French doors. The sky beyond was indeed a bright light blue. But Mimi saw gray clouds gathering on the edge of the horizon. There would be rain before long.

"What night would be good for you to have that barbecue?"

She shifted from romantic notions of riding out the storm curled up in bed with a book and Nash to mentally consulting her calendar. "Technically, I'm done at six every day, and I take a half-day on Friday." She could take a night off to be social.

"Then I'll see when Jay's back in town."

"Great. Do you think we could invite my mom?" Wait, that sounded as if they were hosting this thing together. "I mean, you. Could you invite my mom?"

"Of course."

"She says hi."

He waved at no one. "Hi, Deb."

"Okay, well, then. I guess we'll be in touch." This was weird. Why was she still there? Why wasn't he kicking her out?

It was almost as if neither one of them wanted to say goodbye.

"Okay."

"Okay." She took one step toward the front door, then another. He didn't stop her, so she kept going. "Thanks for the drink. And the song."

"Mimi?"

She stopped.

"You really liked the song? It was all right?"

"Geez, between you and my brother and Cami—are all actors really attractive bags of insecurity?"

He let out a sharp, short laugh. "Pathetic, isn't it?"

"Not pathetic." She walked back to him, leaned in, and kissed his cheek. "Your song was beautiful. Thanks for playing it for me."

She walked out of the house and got in her car before she could throw herself at him yet again.

Chapter Eleven

Hours later, Nash had recorded a decent enough demo of the now completed song and emailed it to Lacey at Rainbow Canyon. He'd have to book time at a recording studio to make the final version. Maybe when he was in North Carolina for his chemistry read, he could find somewhere suitable. Then there was always Boston, which was about two hours' drive from here.

He wished, not for the first time, for his own

recording studio. He'd always planned, once he hit some phantom career milestone, to take time off and find a house with a soundproofed studio and big patio with a fire pit. Come to think, a more permanent version of this house.

He was surprised when he looked out the French doors again and it was dark. He grabbed some leftovers out of the fridge and ate them standing up over the sink, thinking about Mimi.

She'd been clear earlier—she wanted to sleep with him again. It had taken a heroic effort, but he'd pivoted, bought himself some more time. Somehow, she'd gotten him to play her the song, and he hadn't disintegrated into nothingness afterward. How about that?

Whatever they were building between them was good. He hadn't fucked it up yet, and she was still interested.

The only problem with the situation was, now he was heading up to his big bed alone.

The window over the sink that faced the back yard suddenly lit up with a flash of white. He counted to twenty before he heard the far-off rumble of thunder.

He'd like to make love to Mimi during a thunderstorm. The electric crackle in the air would only underscore the electricity they built between them. The noise would barely compete with the moans he knew he could pull out of her. Mimi was noisy. That time in the storeroom of The Cove, he'd had to shove three fingers into her mouth for her to suck on to help her stay quiet enough to keep their hookup on the down-low.

God, she was hot.

Now he was hot. For her. And she was all the way across town, and he had only himself to blame.

He was contemplating how foolish it would be to get in his truck and drive through a thunderstorm to her place when his phone rang.

His hopes that it might be Mimi asking for him to do exactly that, or at least have some phone sex, were dashed when he saw the name on his screen. It was the wrong Orlando.

"Jay, what's up, man?"

"It's not too late, right? I have no idea what time it is," Jay said, his deep voice made even more gravelly with what sounded like exhaustion.

"No, it's good timing. You saved me from doing something unwise."

"How many times do I have to tell you frosted tips are not your look?"

Nash chuckled. "Luckily, hair dye is not involved. Hey, where are you?"

Jay yawned before answering, "We're at JFK, waiting for our connection."

"Back stateside already?"

"Cami was getting too stressed about the show to enjoy Paris, so we decided to come home a couple of days early." Jay yawned again, and Nash found himself echoing his friend with a sympathy yawn of his own. "Honestly, I'm getting a little stressed, too. I was thinking maybe we could get together and run lines this week if you have time. I need the practice."

"Sure, of course. I was going to suggest the same thing." It had been years since Jay had professionally acted, and being Parker Wild would come back to him, but that didn't mean rehearsal wasn't a good idea. Nash could use the refresher of what it was like to inhabit Will, too. "I'm open. Hey, what night's good for you and Cami to come grill at my place? Mimi's free, so it's up to you."

"You've seen Mimi already? When did you get there?"

"Thursday." Nash wished he and Mimi had discussed how they were going to ease Jay into their... whatever it was. It had never seemed like a big deal to omit how intimately he was acquainted with Jay's sister, because their encounters were so infrequent, it didn't seem to matter. But if things with Mimi kept escalating... well, he didn't think Jay was going to be upset, but there were bad ways and good ways to go about letting your best friend know you'd slept with his sister, repeatedly, and were now trying to get her to date you.

Another flash of lightning. The rumble came after twelve beats this time.

"I can ask Cami, but I think the only night that's bad is Wednesday. It's trivia night at The Cove. Let's do it tomorrow."

"You won't be jet-lagged?"

"Nah. I'll be okay. It's been too long, bro."

Nash smiled. He'd missed his friend, too.

"Safe travels."

"You, too. I mean, yeah, whatever."

"And maybe sleep on the plane?"

"It's, like, a forty-five-minute flight, but yeah."

"Bye, bro."

Jay hung up without saying goodbye, and Nash was glad his friend had Cami there to make sure he boarded the plane. Jay wasn't the most experienced traveler, but Cami was a pro. Nash was certain she was taking care of their boy.

He turned off the downstairs lights and paused in the darkened living room by the French doors. The lightning flash was completely visible this time, a jagged line of light illuminating the ocean, the churning mass of clouds behind it like something out of a special effects house.

It was a real, live, old-fashioned thunderstorm at sea.

It was beautiful.

He wished Mimi was there to watch it with him.

Chapter Twelve

Cold beer and apple pie.
American picnic, American style.
Light up the grill and light up my
    bliss.
American woman, give me a kiss.

— "Fourth," The Nash
Speedwell Experience

Yes, we're jet-lagged, but we have to
get back on Connecticut time. No food
allergies. What can we bring?

> Booze is always appreciated.

JAY

I'm on it.

> Are we in a group chat now?

CAMI

Sorry. I thought it would be more
efficient.

> It's cool.

> Might as well treat me like the third
> wheel I am.

CAMI

Oh stop.

JAY

Who else should we invite?

> Is anyone else in town?

CAMI

Not yet.

JAY

You mentioned Mimi? Should I call her?

> Go for it.

> And your mom.

> And um, Pauline?

From the library?

And Colin.

JAY

Already making friends in Misty Harbor.
I love it. We're going to make you an
official resident soon.

6PM

Alcohol.

JAY

You got it, buddy

Nash spent a small fortune at the high-end food market in the strip mall near the freeway and fought a little rush-hour traffic to get home in time to get the grill warmed up. He'd realized while on his daily beach run he should invite his landlord, who he knew was a friend of Jay's, so he'd texted Warner to let him know about the get-together.

It dawned on him that while his ostensible purpose in Misty Harbor was to work, he was socializing with true townies. Cami counted, since she'd officially moved in with Jay earlier that summer.

It felt good to be somewhere he could put down roots if he wanted to.

And he was looking forward to seeing Mimi again. He'd almost texted her six times during the day, but reminded himself she was working. Jay wouldn't forget to invite his sister.

It was only after Jay arrived and was helping him

unload a case of beer, a few bottles of wine, and an excellent bottle of Scotch from the back of his Land Rover Defender that Nash realized why he should have put aside his hesitance and reached out to Mimi. They still had no game plan when it came to telling Jay.

"Good to see you, man." Jay gave him a rib-crushing hug once the alcohol was brought in and set up on the patio.

"You, too, Jay." His friend looked rested despite his jet lag. He had a few new laugh lines around his mouth, but they looked good on him. His brown skin was clear, and his dark eyes bright. "Seems like Paris agreed with you."

"It was surprisingly fun," Jay said.

"I'm assuming you guys actually saw some of the sights and didn't stay in the hotel room the entire time?"

Jay coughed and threw Nash a dirty look. "We went out," he insisted. "Um. Museums. Restaurants. It was great. It was Paris."

"Paris has great museums and restaurants," Nash agreed, laughing. "But seriously, it's amazing you and Cami reconnected. I always thought the two of you made the best couple."

"I haven't screwed it up yet," Jay said. "And happily, I don't think she's going to let me."

"That's great." There was a beat of silence as Nash tried to come up with a segue from Jay's love life to his own. He was saved from his own indecision by the sound of a car pulling up to the front. He heard the horn blare once and lifted his eyebrows at Jay.

"It might be Cami. She's still getting used to driving."

They walked the path around the house to find a mud-spattered sky blue Fiat 500 parked at an angle behind the Land Rover. Cami slammed the driver's door noisily. The petite blonde had fire in her eyes when she rounded the hood, her arms waving.

"What kind of a road is that? My baby barely made it!"

Nash winced. "Sorry. It rained last night, and it's a little muddy."

"The owner should think about paving it," Jay put in.

"It's perfectly passable in my truck," Nash said.

"My Land Rover didn't have issues," Jay added.

"Well, good for your boy vehicles." Cami glowered. She then sighed and broke into a wide smile. "Let me start over. Nash. Hi. How the hell are you?"

Nash grinned and wrapped his arms around his friend. He hadn't kept in as close touch with Cami as he had with Jay over the years since *Sawyer's Cove* ended, but they saw each other from time to time when they were both in L.A. He lifted her off her feet and planted a smacking kiss on her cheek, grinning even harder at Jay when he gave them an unamused look.

"Camille, you look fantastic. All those museums and restaurants really did you good, huh?" He winked at her.

Her lightly tanned skin was already flushed from the summer sun, but her cheeks grew even pinker. "Paris is always restorative," she said, a little primly.

"I'll bet," he said. "Well, you're the early birds, so you can help me finish setting up." He put his famous friends to work setting out plates and cutlery and chips and dips and all sorts of party goodies while he adjusted the temperature of the grill. The first chicken thighs were hitting the heat when the next guest arrived.

Warner trudged around the house carrying a bottle filled with dark amber liquid. He was dressed in baggy, faded jeans and a wrinkled blue and white striped button-down shirt. With his messy sandy blond hair going gray at the temples, he looked rumpled, to say the least.

Jay greeted him with surprise. "Hey, Warner."

"Orlando." Warner nodded stiffly. "Hello, Speedwell." He handed Nash the bottle of booze. "I'd love a snort if you've got a glass."

Jay blinked at the man. "I think I've only seen you outside The Cove, like, three times. How did you possibly hook up with Nash?"

Nash glanced between them as he cracked the seal of the top-shelf bourbon. "He's the one Cami should petition for the road paving."

"Why?" Jay's expression remained blank.

"He owns this place," Nash said, waving at the house. "He's the landlord."

"Guilty as charged," Warner said. Nash had cottoned onto the fact that Warner liked to talk as if he were a character in a 1940s noir. "And I'm not paving anything. The dirt road keeps people away."

"It does make the place feel nice and secluded," Nash said. "I haven't seen a single soul up here, not even on the beach. Except—" He was about to say when Mimi stopped by.

Speaking of which, where was she? It was well after six.

Nash poured Warner a couple of fingers into a lowball glass from the bottle he'd brought, then allowed Jay to lead him to the side of the patio for conversation while he checked on the chicken. Pauline and Colin showed up next—together, Nash noted with a smile. Deb arrived a minute after them, and he lifted her up in a big hug, much the same way he'd greeted Cami.

"You look wonderful," she said. "Mimi said you were settling in here. You need anything? I brought some eclairs from the inn's kitchen."

Nash thought he saw Jay shoot them a look at the mention of Mimi's name.

"Here, let's put those in the fridge. They'll melt out here." He led her into the house through the French doors.

"At least the storm drove out the humidity," Deb said. "I can't wait for fall. I like the crisper air."

"Oh, I don't mind the heat," Nash said. He opened the fridge door, and Deb found a spot for the eclairs. "How's everything at the inn?"

"Busy. The television show will keep us busy until the holidays. I had to extend all my summer hires. It's good."

"Excellent." Deb had worked at the inn so long, she felt responsible for the entire place. "When are they going to put you in charge already?"

She smiled. "My boss is never going to retire. And if he did, the company that owns the inn would probably bring in some young transplant from one of their New York hotels."

"Seriously? But you're the heart and soul of the place."

"Sweet of you to say. I can see why Mimi likes you."

"Does she?" He smelled gossip. And who better to mine for clues to Mimi's heart than her own mother? He wasn't above it.

"Well, we all do," Deb said, backtracking. "You're an honorary Orlando, you know that, right?"

If he was an honorary Orlando, did that make pursuing Mimi less awkward, or more?

"I'm grateful, Deb," he said simply. "What can I get you to drink?"

"Something fizzy and cold."

They went outside, and as he showed her the soft drink cooler he smelled charred barbecue sauce.

"Shit!" He ran to the grill, turned the thighs just before they started burning.

Meat back under control, he checked his watch. Where was Mimi? He was about to grab his phone when a tall, curly-haired figure came stomping around the side of the house. His relief at seeing her mixed with perplexity—why was she covered in mud?

Her jeans were splattered with brown sludge from thigh to ankle, and the Dr. Seuss characters printed on her T-shirt were obscured by the muck. There was even a streak down the side of her face. Her mouth was set in a grim line.

Her mother was closest. "What on Earth happened to you?" Deb asked.

Cami and Jay crowded around her, followed by Pauline and Colin. Nash hovered on the outskirts of the group, not truly family, not co-worker.

What was he to Mimi, again? Simply a friend.

"The road was so soft after the rain. I was trying to get up the hill, skidded and overcorrected, and got my car stuck in some mud on the side of the road. Which wouldn't have been terrible, except I slipped as soon as I got out of the car to start walking. So here I am! The party can start!" Mimi said, with false brightness.

"You poor thing." Deb clucked—or was she chuckling at her daughter's bedraggled state? The Orlandos had a healthy habit of making fun of each other out of love.

"I'll call Ravi to give it a tow. Unless you think we could push it out ourselves?" Jay asked.

"You probably could," Mimi said doubtfully. "But your clothes wouldn't survive. Better let Ravi deal with it. Thanks, Jay."

"You're a mess," Cami said, grimacing.

"I'll stay outside," Mimi volunteered.

"No."

All eyes turned to Nash. He hadn't meant to sound quite so forceful. "I mean, you can clean up inside. I'll show you. Deb, can you watch the chicken?"

He waited to make sure Mimi was following him, then went back through the patio doors and directly upstairs. He heard her pause to remove her muddy sneakers, then continue behind him. He waited at the door to his room.

"You can borrow something of mine to wear," he said. "And you can wash up in my bathroom. None of the others have soap."

She looked at him, her eyes dancing. "You want me to wear your clothes?"

Yes. "Better than getting dirt everywhere."

She shrugged. "Not sure anything will fit, but thanks."

He opened the dresser drawer and pulled out a muscle tee that wouldn't be much baggier on her than her own. He frowned. The pants would be a problem. He grabbed a pair of sweatpants with a drawstring waist.

"These might be okay." He handed her the items and nodded at the door in the corner of the room. "Shower's in there."

She let her fingers brush his as she took the bundle of clothes. "You sure you don't want to join me?"

She was utterly unkempt and completely kissable. He couldn't spend any more time in private with her without giving in. He was close to losing this game.

"I have to turn the chicken." His voice was hoarse.

She took the rejection in stride. "Of course. You do that."

With effort, he backed out of the room without touching her.

How much longer could this go on?

Chapter Thirteen

Mimi couldn't help smiling as she washed the sweat and mud off in Nash's shower. She opened the cap of his body wash and sniffed experimentally. She couldn't identify the different spicy notes, but it smelled expensive. She poured a small amount on her palm and lathered up, the tingling on her skin having more to do with feeling like she was being surrounded by Nash's masculine warmth than the suds themselves.

She felt her hair and decided washing it would be more trouble than it was worth. She didn't think she'd gotten too much mud in it anyway. She rinsed the fragrant suds off regretfully, but she couldn't stand in his shower indefinitely while he hosted her entire family and some of her friends.

She toweled off and opened the door to the bedroom, shivering when the air-conditioned air hit her damp skin. Now for the problem of clothes. She eyed her underwear dubiously. She hated the sensation of putting on dirty underwear after a shower, but the alternative was wearing Nash's clothes commando. She shivered at the implied intimacy and wondered if he'd imagined her slipping into his clothes, naked in his bedroom.

At first glance, the space seemed as impersonal as a hotel room, but she noticed an old-fashioned iPod sitting on the table next to the king-sized bed. A pair of running shorts was slung over a straight-backed chair, and a silver laptop peeked out of a utilitarian gray backpack. He'd chosen a room with a stellar view of the ocean.

She was learning things about him this summer. For one, Nash Speedwell didn't do excess. He liked things well-made and simple, and she admired how straightforward he was about everything—even his failings.

But he was too hard on himself. He stretched himself too thin. She knew it was dangerous to do things only because you thought you should.

Was that partly what this whole restraint thing was about? Not giving in to something that had no purpose other than pleasure? Wasn't he allowed simply to enjoy her, for enjoyment's sake? Wasn't she?

She made it her mission then and there to make sure Nash enjoyed this party, if nothing else. And if she had her way, she'd see he enjoyed the afterparty as well.

She slipped into the sweats sans underwear. They fit pretty well once she cinched the waist tight. Her bra was fine, a simple wireless bralette in light blue. She put that back on, then the shirt, which looked like a normal white cotton tee but was soft as cashmere and probably cost as much as the dress Mimi had ordered for the fundraiser.

Barefoot, she went back downstairs, her dirty clothes balled up in her hand. She hunted around the deserted kitchen until she found a paper bag. She stuffed her clothes inside, stashed the bag by the door, then detoured to the fridge to grab a beer before heading out to the patio. The food was being served, the partygoers sitting down at the large round table.

Nash was at the grill. The air smelled of charred meat and spices and salt air from the beach just over the hill. She smiled at him and felt his eyes on her as she went to get a plate.

"You find everything you need?" he asked as he selected a juicy thigh for her. His voice was low and sweet.

"Just about, thanks."

She winked and sauntered over to sit next to her mother and fill the rest of her plate with green salad. She opened her beer, pleased with herself, and life, and the beautiful late summer evening in good company. All that would make it perfect was if Nash was sitting next to her instead of across the table.

Deb, Warner, Pauline, and Colin were gossiping about the latest rumor about the old movie theater on Spring Street, just off Main. It had been vacant for years, and there had been rumblings that some out-of-town developer was going to turn it into condos.

Jay was usually the first one to obsess over the possibility of development in Misty Harbor, but instead he asked, "How are ticket sales coming on the fundraiser?"

"Getting there. Over half sold," Mimi said. She was still nervous about pulling it off, even though every year since she'd taken over as head librarian, the event had raised more money than the last. She'd been up early going over their rental order, hemming and hawing about numbers.

"Awesome. I got my tickets," her brother said.

"Tickets for what?" Cami asked from her seat next to him. "You taking me on a hot date?"

"Hottest ticket in town—the annual library fundraiser," Jay said. "It's at the inn, of course. But it's always really fun. There's a silent auction and music. Who's playing this year?"

"Alabaster Poppy," Mimi said. "They're doing it practically for free, which is great for the budget. I hope they aren't too much for the older crowd."

"What should I donate to the auction?" Jay asked. "Is a *Sawyer's Cove* script too boring?"

"That would be great," Mimi said. "Or how about a gift card to The Cove?"

"I want to donate something," Cami said around a bite of salad. "What about a day as an extra on the set?"

"Seriously?"

Cami nodded. "Yeah, it's no problem. Just put me as the contact person, and I'll set it up for whoever wins the item."

"That would be incredible, thank you so much, Cami. I'll give the auction coordinator a heads-up." Mimi shouldn't have been surprised by Cami's generosity, but she was still getting to know her future sister-in-law. Not that Cami and Jay were officially engaged, having just gotten back together after twelve years apart, but Mimi could see the writing on the wall. Her brother was more than smitten—he was head over heels for the love of his life, and Mimi was beyond happy for him.

"I'm feeling left out here," Nash said. "Fundraisers are my specialty. Let me donate something, too."

She gave him a gracious nod. "The Arthur Russell Scholarship Fund thanks you in advance."

"Who's Arthur Russell?" Nash asked.

"He was the head librarian when I was growing up," Mimi said. "He's the reason I wanted to become a librarian."

Nash leaned forward on crossed arms. The position made his muscles flex and strain the sleeves of his T-shirt, but Mimi valiantly kept her gaze on Nash's butterscotch eyes. "Tell me about him."

"He was wonderful. The epitome of an old New

England geezer—wild white hair, big fan of cable-knit sweaters. Everyone called him Art, but I called him Mr. Russell. He really believed in the library as a community resource. He made it a safe space for people who didn't have anywhere else to go. I learned a lot from him."

Nash gave her a funny look, as if he was figuring something out. "I see."

"He died about three years ago. I wanted to set up the scholarship fund right away, but his daughter didn't sign off on it until recently. She's had a hard time. I think she didn't want to consider his legacy until she'd come to terms with his death. I get it. I cried for a month."

"You were close."

"Yeah." She still missed him, his reassuring presence, the way he got excited over little things, but also saw the big picture and knew things generally worked out in the long run.

"So, this fundraiser is a big deal," Nash said.

"I'm trying to set up the scholarship right. Shooting for fifty thousand to start. Then we can afford to award it to more than one kid per year. It's for Misty Harbor residents who want to study library science or education."

"That's amazing," Nash said. "And you're doing a hell of a job, Mimi."

"Thanks." His frank praise meant a lot. Sometimes she worked so hard and felt like only a handful of people noticed. But then she'd see the folks who used the library for all kinds of things and knew even if they didn't have a clue who she was, she'd helped make their experience possible with her leadership, and that felt good.

"What do you think your crowd would like?" he asked. "Show swag? Signed photos?"

"You know what people would really love is for you to sing some songs from your album."

Mimi twisted her head sharply to look at her brother, who she'd kind of forgotten was there. The rest of the table had occupied itself with other subjects while she was telling Nash about Mr. Russell.

"Jay." She said his name like a warning.

Nash frowned. "You know I don't perform live."

"But it's for a good cause," Jay said. "I bet she'd sell the rest of the tickets in about five minutes if you were added to the bill."

"No," Nash said shortly. "Sorry, Mimi."

"It's okay." She glared at her brother. What was he up to?

He put up his hands innocently. "Just thought it might be a good fit. Isn't this year a western theme?"

"There's no theme," Mimi said. "We're celebrating the library, and by extension Arthur Russell, that's all. I just want it to be a great night, one that honors his legacy. His daughter's been so keyed up, it can't be a flop. But we have the music covered, thanks, Jay."

"How about some *Hawk and Bone* memorabilia?" Nash suggested. "I can get a few of my co-stars to autograph something."

"Better leave yours off," Jay said, grumbling. "It'll be worth more."

"What's gotten into you?" Mimi asked. "You're being rude."

"He's just jealous," Nash said, seemingly unbothered. "But put me down for that, okay, Mimi? I want to help."

She smiled her thanks, and he smiled back. Her gut gave a small, not unpleasant lurch.

"I better get the eclairs out of the fridge. It's starting to get dark." Nash pushed back from the table.

Mimi found herself hissing at her brother. "What is your problem?"

"No problem. I just think Nash needs to leave his comfort zone once in a while," Jay said.

"Are you serious right now? The man who'd never been out of the country until a week ago thinks Nash needs to get out of his comfort zone?"

"Why are you defending him?" Jay asked. His eyes narrowed. "And why are you wearing his clothes?"

"I got mud on mine, remember?" Mimi said. She hoped she wasn't blushing. She didn't need her brother in her business, not when she wasn't doing anything worth him bothering her over—at the moment anyway.

"You guys are weird," Jay grumped. "I'm getting another beer."

Chapter Fourteen

By sunset's light, your glow's so
   bright.
But by morning's sun, you've got
   me undone.

— "Sleep With Me," The
Nash Speedwell Experience

Nash managed to unload most of the leftover food on his guests as they left. He waved goodbye to Warner, Pauline, and Colin, hugged Deb so hard she squeaked then dissolved into giggles, and made plans with Jay to meet up at his place to run lines later that week. Cami reminded him for the tenth time their first all-cast table read was a week from Wednesday at the studio, and he assured her the event was in his calendar in red. He'd silenced a call from Mary-Anne while he was serving his guests eclairs, so he made a mental note to check his voicemail.

One by one, everyone left, until there was only Mimi. She'd been in contact with the tow truck driver, who'd managed to get her car out of the woods, but reported she had a flat tire and bent rim. He'd towed her car to the shop to be worked on the next day.

Nash leaned in the doorway to the kitchen, hip cocked. Mimi was rinsing dinner plates.

"You want a ride home?" he asked. He'd been fighting a near-constant erection since she'd appeared on his patio wearing his clothes. The wave of possessiveness at seeing her dressed in his clothing had his cock paying attention to her every move.

"I guess so. You have an early morning tomorrow?" she asked.

"Not particularly."

"Want to share a nightcap?"

"Don't you have an early morning?"

"I have work, yes. Whisky?"

He went over to a corner counter where he'd put both Jay's gift and what was left of Warner's bourbon and poured them both a shallow glass of the Scotch. He didn't usually drink liquor on casual weeknights at home, but he was technically on vacation. Besides, Mimi was wearing his sweatpants, and he could see her ass very prominently—the Scotch would have to substitute for dragging that ass onto his lap and fondling it.

"Fun party," she said, rinsing the last plate and putting it in the dishwasher. "You're a good host."

"Thanks. It was nice to have people over without it being a work thing."

"Sorry about my brother," she said, drying her hands on a dish towel, which she then carefully threaded through the oven handle. She took the glass from the bar and settled onto one of the white wooden bar stools. He leaned over the bar from the other side, glad they had the entire island between them.

"It's okay. It's kind of his job to needle me," Nash said. He'd been surprised when Jay suggested he play the fundraiser, more by the impulse he had to say yes, if only to put a smile on Mimi's face. He knew Jay didn't mean anything by it.

"Isn't that what he's supposed to do to me?" Mimi said. "I guess you're sort of like a brother to him." She sighed, took a sip. "This is good stuff."

"Yeah. Jay brought it."

"Well, he's good for something anyway." She tipped her glass toward his, and he tipped his back. As they did a silent air clink, Mimi's lips curled into a smile. "Are you scared of me or something?"

Nash choked on his mouthful, and the liquid burned the back of his nose. He coughed. "What do you mean?"

"You haven't come closer than this all night. You think I'll give you cooties?"

He rolled his eyes at her. "I think you're too tempting for your own good."

"If I was too tempting, you'd be on top of me right now."

"Jesus, Mimi. Are you trying to kill me?"

"I know you didn't want to be all physical. Well, fine. But how about partly physical? I promise I won't make you go further than you're comfortable with."

Nash swallowed. More than his throat was burning. He set down his glass. "What did you have in mind?"

"I don't know." Mimi glanced through the big kitchen door into the living room and at the couch. "Cuddling?" She sounded so doubtful about the concept, he barked out a laugh.

"Not really your speed, huh?" he said, with a smile.

"No." She took a swallow. "But I'd give it a shot."

"Okay." He had to admit, while his libido would have been happy for him to throw all his grand notions out the window and get her into bed, cuddling Mimi Orlando sounded like an appealing challenge.

He went around the island and held out his hand. She set down her glass, barely touched, and took it. Hand in hand, they walked to the living room sofa. They were both barefoot already, so he simply sat down, pulling her right down onto him the way he'd been fantasizing about before. But it wasn't overtly sexual. They pulled their legs onto the seat, and she wriggled around until he was framing her body with his, her head on his shoulder, their legs twined together. She might be able to feel his thickening cock behind the fly of his jeans, but maybe not. He let his hands drift over her back, but not lower. Getting them on her ass would have been a bad idea.

"There. How's that?" he asked, surprised by the throatiness in his voice.

"Um." She shifted her weight, her hip pressing into his belly. "Fine."

Neither of them said anything for a minute.

"So this is it?" she asked, sounding unimpressed. "Cuddling?"

"Well, it's supposed to feel good. Be relaxing."

"But I don't want to fall asleep," she said, shifting again.

He chuckled. "Fair enough. Cuddling isn't your thing. Noted." He was about to suggest they sit up, but then she sighed again and buried her nose against his neck.

"You smell good, at least," she said. "I like your shower gel."

"Thank you."

"I used some. I hope that's okay."

He lifted her arm and smelled the soft freckle-dotted skin. She did smell like his own signature body wash. It took everything he had not to nip a toothy kiss into that soft flesh.

"You smell good, too," he said, "and you look really hot in my clothes."

"Narcissist," she whispered.

He grinned into her hair. "No, just an actor."

They fell silent again. He began stroking the arm he'd smelled, cotton to skin and back up to the cotton again. She was soft and warm, and she fit right up against him, like they were made to share this couch. His eyes drooped, then shut, and when he opened them again, there was dove gray light beyond the glass of the French doors.

Mimi was a warm weight on his chest. He felt her breathing against him, deep and regular. He couldn't believe they'd slept together all night and he hadn't tossed and turned. It was a comfortable, extra-wide couch, but still. And Mimi, the self-proclaimed non-cuddler, had apparently slept just as soundly.

He let himself hold her for another minute, wondering what it meant that he felt as content being with her like this as he did when they were talking or having sex. It felt like they were really becoming friends. Which was wonderful—that was what he'd wanted, wasn't it?

He shifted and looked down at her. Her proud nose and slight overbite and the big rings of her curly hair were all so dear to him. Even though her eyes were closed and he didn't have those secret windows into what she was thinking and feeling, he thought she had to trust him a little, like him a little, to sleep plastered against him all night.

He smiled.

She made him feel so good—so normal. His smile dimmed, thinking about his schedule and how straight-forward it was to imagine being with her like this when he wasn't working. But soon the long shooting days would start up again. Granted, they'd be here in Misty Harbor, but the shoot wasn't going to last forever. There was always something taking him on the road, someone who needed his time and attention, whether it was his press obligations or family or the nonprofits he was involved with.

He didn't have room in his life for a personal life. But he was thinking maybe he should start making more space. A Mimi-sized space seemed like a great place to start.

His spine straightened as he remembered he hadn't listened to Mary-Anne's voicemail last night. He'd set his phone down somewhere the night before. He craned his neck to peer around the living room, found it sitting on the coffee table just out of reach. Would Mimi be annoyed if he woke her up before she was ready? They'd never spent a full night together before. He had the impression she was a reluctant morning person. On the other hand, the sun was rising quickly over the horizon, and he knew she had to go home and change before she could get to work. He stroked her head lightly, and she stirred.

"Morning," he whispered.

She let out an unintelligible burble.

He suppressed a laugh. "We fell asleep last night. But I think we need to get up."

She tipped her head up, squinting at him. She had sleep creases on her cheeks from the cotton of his shirt and sand crusting up her eyelids. She looked adorable.

He swiped a thumb over her red cheek. "Sorry to wake you. I'll make some coffee."

"Tea?" she croaked hopefully.

"Tea." He thought about his pantry contents. "I have English Breakfast."

"Perfect." She sat up and swung her legs to the floor, stretched her neck back and forth. He wanted to wrap her up and never let her go. But they both had their days to start. And besides, friends didn't spend all day cuddling on the couch. And that's what they were. Friends.

He got up, cracking his back as he went. Even though he'd slept well, next time they should try to make it to a bed.

He swiped his phone from the coffee table. "You can use my bathroom."

"Thanks."

She went upstairs, and he switched on the tea kettle, then popped a pod into the coffee maker that had come with the rental. He thumbed through to his voicemail and put the phone on speaker. Mary-Anne's high-pitched voice flooded the kitchen in a particularly irritating wake-up call. He winced and turned the volume down slightly. She was telling him negotiations had progressed on the Moonshot role and the producers wanted him as early as this weekend.

He frowned. This all seemed to be happening fast, considering he hadn't even had a face-to-face conversation with any of the people involved. And this weekend was his last free one before *Sawyer's Cove* started in earnest. He'd wanted to relax, maybe take Mimi out on the water one day if the weather held.

But this was a huge opportunity. He had to meet with them at least. He sighed, pushing his own agenda down the list once again.

He had the tea steeped and cream in his coffee by the time Mimi came downstairs, still wearing his borrowed clothes. Her face looked clean and shiny, and her hair was pulled back into a messy bun. She accepted the mug gratefully and stuck her nose in the steam wafting up.

"Thanks. This is great. Could you give me a ride to my apartment?"

"Of course."

"And my clothes are all stiff with mud. I'll return these later."

"You better," he said gruffly. "Those are my favorite sweats."

She took a sip and made a little sound of satisfaction that made him feel as warm as his mug of coffee.

"I can't believe we fell asleep on the couch like that." Her cheeks could have been pink from the steam, but he thought maybe she was the slightest bit embarrassed.

"We must have been really comfortable," he offered.

"I guess."

"You want some breakfast? I usually don't eat until I come back from my run, but I've got eggs." He made for the fridge, but she stopped him.

"No, I'll get something at home. I don't want to put you out."

"You aren't any trouble, Mimi."

"Thanks. But I'd like to go home now if that's okay."

He recognized his own disappointment at their time together ending. He always seemed to want more from her than she was ready to give—except when it came to sex. Why were their priorities so messed up?

"Sure. Give me two minutes." He gulped down a quarter of his coffee before finding his shoes and keys.

"There's another great band playing at The Cove this weekend, if you're interested," Mimi said as they drove down the hill. The road was much drier today, and he spotted the messy area where her car had gone off the road. He gulped when he saw the large tree trunk she could have slid into and was thankful she'd come out of the experience only a little muddy and not injured.

"I might have to fly to North Carolina this weekend," he said apologetically.

"Oh. I thought you were starting work on *Sawyer's Cove* next week?" Mimi said.

"I'll be back in plenty of time." He debated asking for her advice about the role. It was a definite boost for his career, but the fact that he'd be locked in for so many movies, essentially the next several years of his life, was a bit intimidating. But Mary-Anne's chipmunk squeak in his head told him he should probably wait until it was more of a sure thing. "Sorry to miss the band," he added.

"It's not like there won't be other shows," she said lightly, looking out the window. "Travel safe."

"Wait, I'm sure I'll see you before I leave. I don't even have my ticket yet." He turned onto her street, parked the truck in an open space a little way down from her building. "You want to get dinner later?"

She looked back at him and bit her lip. "I don't know, Nash."

"You tired of me already?" He smiled, but he was a little hurt. He knew they were good together. Why wouldn't she let them find out where this was going?

"This is really not my wheelhouse," she admitted.

"Just dinner. Friends having dinner."

"You keep saying we're friends, but friends don't sleep snuggled up on a couch all night together."

"Then more than friends," he said quickly. "Come on a date with me."

"You want to date me?" she asked.

He realized he'd been dancing around it, but the simple truth was, "Yes."

She didn't answer, then her eyes grew wide as she looked out the truck's windshield. "Shit."

"What?" Then he saw. Jay was striding toward the truck. He didn't look happy.

Chapter Fifteen

JULES: I saw someone posted a picture of Nash Speedwell at Jay's bar a few days ago. There's really no way to tell when it was taken, but it seemed recent. He was with a girl and I think it was Jay Orlando's sister.

ERIKA: I saw that picture, too! I can't believe we haven't talked about it yet. Do you think they're dating?

JULES: Nash and Jay Orlando's sister? No. They were probably just both in the same place at the same time.

ERIKA: I know, right? But how adorable would it be if they were together?

JULES: OMG, what if they got married? Then Nash Speedwell and Jay Orlando would be brothers-in-law. I couldn't handle the cute level.

FROM THE SAWYER'S COVE REWATCH PROJECT PODCAST: THE NASH SPEEDWELL EXPERIENCE ALBUM REVIEW

Mimi got out of the truck before Jay could rap on the window like a suspicious cop. She had her purse and the bag of her dirty clothes, and she slammed the passenger door behind her, half-hoping Nash would just drive off and let her deal with this by herself.

No such luck. Nash was out of the truck in a flash, walking around the front and positioning himself between her and her brother.

"What's going on?" Jay asked. His handsome face was tight, and his arms flexed as he crossed them aggressively across his puffed-out chest. Her brother had an overdeveloped sense of familial duty when it came to protecting his sister from perceived threats, even if the threat was his best friend.

"Nash gave me a ride home. You know Ravi has my car."

"But why is he only now bringing you home? And why are you both still dressed in the same clothes from yesterday? And why am I getting a very bad feeling about all this?" Jay's voice got progressively deeper as he went on. It was almost comical how stereotypically protective he was being, except that now Mimi was going to have to explain exactly why Nash was driving her home at eight in the morning, wearing yesterday's clothes. And she couldn't quite get her mind around the fact that they'd actually cuddled so hard, she'd fallen asleep, and no orgasms had been involved whatsoever.

"Jay, relax," Nash said, clapping her brother on the shoulder.

Mimi winced. You didn't tell an Orlando to relax when they were in an agitated state.

Jay turned his glare on Nash. "Fuck you, Speedwell. What's going on?"

"Jay, Jesus, that's a little much." She shook her head at the ridiculousness of the situation. "Nash and I fell asleep on his couch last night. He drove me home. That's all there is to it."

From the corner of her eye, she caught Nash sending her a look. Well, that's what happened, wasn't it? There was nothing else to tell.

"But why did you fall asleep on the couch?" Jay asked.

She looked at Nash, who just gestured back to her. She supposed he was letting her explain to the extent she was comfortable with, but her mind was coming up blank, and the longer they stayed silent, the more incriminating it seemed.

"We fell asleep because we were tired," she said finally. "And the rest of it really isn't any of your business."

Jay closed his eyes, as if in defeat. "You know I'm just going to think the worst, don't you?"

"Nash and me being together would be the worst?" she asked.

Jay's eyes flew open. "Are you together? Is that what this is?"

"Not exactly," she said. She looked again at Nash. He'd been in the middle of asking her out on a date, and she'd choked. She didn't know how to do this, dammit.

But she could learn new things. She wasn't a fossil. And being with Nash, as uncomfortable as it sometimes was not to know exactly what they were doing, made her want to find out what was possible. "We're friends," she said firmly.

Did she imagine the disappointed way Nash's lips curled when she said that? She was tired of dancing around the truth. She and Jay had always been honest with each other. "And we're dating. And if you must know, we've already had sex. Multiple times. But not last night. Last night, we just slept together. Which is weird, but whatever. It happened. So there. Be careful what you ask for, little brother."

Nash was smiling by the end of her little speech, a private little smile that reassured her she'd done the right thing, even if she hadn't exactly run it by him.

Jay's face was burgundy. He turned to Nash. "Is this true?"

"Yep."

"And you guys kept this from me for how long?"

"Sorry," Mimi said. "It never came up."

Jay shook his head. "Wow. Okay." He took a deep breath, then stepped up and got into Nash's face. "You know how I feel about my family, Speedwell. I know you aren't taking this lightly."

Nash straightened his shoulders. He wasn't as tall as Jay, but he was broader, his jaw squarer. He was physically just as imposing, and while Jay didn't back down, Mimi could tell her brother was adjusting his stance to make it slightly less aggressive.

"I do know how you feel. And I'm not taking this lightly. I'm sorry if you felt we were keeping something from you, but we weren't any of your business. Now you know. And I'm glad."

Mimi studied his face. He was glad? God, would she ever feel on balance around this man?

"Okay, well..." Jay cleared his throat and stepped back a foot. "Then I wish you guys well, man."

"Thanks." Nash smiled.

Mimi rolled her eyes. "Well, I'm super happy you two have made peace, but I've got to get to work. Jay—it's all going to be fine, okay?" She wanted to believe it herself.

Jay cocked an eyebrow at her. "All right. I'll get off my brother high horse. You two are adults. And you make sense in a strange way that never occurred to me until now."

"Thanks?" Mimi was confused, but she supposed he meant that in a good way.

"Anyway, I came over to see if you wanted a ride to work."

"Sure, but I've got to change. Give me fifteen minutes?"

"I'll text you about dinner," Nash said, getting back in the truck.

She sighed. It looked like she was going on another date with Nash Speedwell.

❧

Since I picked the place last time, do
you want to pick tonight's spot?

What's your favorite place?

It doesn't even have to be in Misty
Harbor.

LMK and I'll make a reservation.

Mimi laughed the fourth time her phone buzzed in her pocket in less than a minute. Nash always texted in bursts. It could have been annoying, but it was just his thing, and she found it kind of endearing.

She'd spent the morning in a budget meeting and was eating a late lunch from the Bakeshop, standing up in the break room.

Pauline walked in as she was staring at her phone, figuring out how to reply.

"What's up, Mimi?" Pauline asked. "What's got you smiling so hard? A new librarian meme?"

"Nothing," she said, shoving the phone in her pocket. Pauline went to the employee fridge and brought out a bento box of sushi. Sushi, that was an idea. She loved sushi. And her favorite place was up the coast a bit, so they could make an outing of it. "Actually, I'm going out with Nash tonight."

"On a date."

"Officially, yes. A date."

"Good for you." Pauline sat down and took out a pair of chopsticks from a little cloth carrying case. "He really likes you."

"It's just, well, actually dating someone? I'm a little out of my element."

"Aren't you always saying it's good to try new things?" Pauline said. "I have a date, too, by the way."

"What? With who?"

"Colin."

"Oh." Mimi studied her friend. She looked typically calm and collected as she ate her tuna avocado roll in dainty bites. "You don't date either."

"Not in a while. But Colin's interesting. He likes me. And I like spending time with him."

"Does he know you—"

"He knows I'm ace, and he's cool with it. He says." Pauline looked slightly worried. "So I'm trying it."

"Wow, that's great." Mimi knew just because her friend wasn't interested in a sexual relationship, that didn't mean she didn't want companionship, or even romance. And Colin did seem really into her. She smiled at Pauline. "I hope you guys have fun."

"Thanks. We're going to the dollar theater. You and Nash want to come? We all seemed to have fun last weekend."

If she suggested it to him, she knew Nash wouldn't have a problem with it. But she also knew he was envisioning a slightly more intimate evening.

"Thanks for the invite, but I think we're going to do something just the two of us."

"He couldn't keep his eyes off you last night at his place."

"Really?" God, she was so in over her head.

"It's okay, you know."

"What's okay?"

"It's okay to have feelings for someone."

"What? I know that." Mimi clutched her cardigan and pulled it tighter around her middle.

Pauline leveled a look at her. "I've known you for a couple of years now, and you're one of the most fearless people I've ever met. But you—I don't know—it's like you reserve your love for people you know will love you back. Your brother, your mom, even me."

"I do love you, Pauline. I was so lucky the person who was the perfect fit to manage our historical archives also happens to be one of the coolest people I've ever met."

"I love you, too. I didn't know if moving to a small town in Connecticut would be a good fit for me. I was prepared to be lonely, actually. But you were so welcoming. Jay, too. And the whole town, really. I'm glad I ended up in Misty Harbor."

"Me, too." Mimi leaned over and gave her friend a hug.

"But my point still stands."

Pauline was a dear, but she was stubborn as hell.

"I don't hoard my love," Mimi argued.

"You engage in sex so you don't have to risk someone not loving you. It probably has to do with your childhood."

"Pauline!" Jesus, she was used to her friend being straightforward, but this was a lot.

"Sorry. Anyway, I'm just proud of you for trying

something new. And Nash is extremely attractive, financially stable, and professionally successful. He's a catch."

Mimi laughed. Her friend was a trip. "Glad you approve." She had two people in her life who thought dating Nash was a good idea. Now she just had to convince herself.

Chapter Sixteen

Kiss me in the morning, kiss me at
noon.
But by midnight's moon, you're
gone too soon.

— "Sleep With Me," The
Nash Speedwell Experience

"This is your favorite restaurant?" Nash said disbelievingly as they pulled into a strip mall parking lot. He saw a hardware store, package store, and spin studio, but he didn't see anything that looked like a sushi place.

"Just wait. It's in the corner."

Mimi got out and strode across the parking lot without waiting for him. He scrambled out of the truck and followed, admiring the view of Mimi's ass in black capri pants and a tight red tank top. She led him up a set of rickety wooden stairs, and they found themselves on the second floor of the strip mall, with a view of the river and a half-dozen tables full of happy-looking diners.

"Okay, this place is great," he said, taking in the view of the sailboats on the water beyond the mouth of the river.

"And the sushi is melt-in-your-mouth, I swear."

She wasn't exaggerating. Nash had eaten sushi in Tokyo that wasn't this fresh. They ate until they were stuffed, then ordered mochi because they were masochists.

"So, Jay was okay when he dropped you off today?" he asked. He'd thought the encounter with his friend this morning could have been more awkward. Somehow.

"He was fine. He always regrets butting into my personal life," she said. "And since it's you, I think that makes it worse. Or better? I don't know. If you hadn't noticed, I'm not exactly good at this."

"You're doing great. I don't date a lot either," he said.

"So what are all those photos on social media of you with girls about?"

"Okay, so I date. But not the same girls, not for very long." He cringed. "Wait, that sounded worse than it did in my head."

She laughed. "It's okay, I know what you mean."

"I'm good at dinner dates. Movie dates. Lunch dates. But the stuff that comes in between the dates—I kinda want that, I have to be honest, Mimi."

"Okay." He thought she meant it was okay he wanted

that, rather than her agreeing to that with him, and that was okay, too. They were going slow.

"I was thinking tomorrow night we could do trivia at The Cove."

"I'm there."

"And you know I've been with a lot of guys, but I think I've been with you the most times—you know what I mean?"

Nash widened his eyes. "Really?"

"Yeah. And I'm not planning to sleep with anyone else while we're doing this dating experiment. Just so you know."

"Thanks for telling me. And me either."

"Okay. Cool."

Suddenly, Nash needed to kiss her as much as he needed to draw his next breath. "Can we get out of here?"

"Sure. There's a little path by the river if you want a walk."

He paid by leaving a stack of cash on the table and grabbed Mimi's hand as they walked down the rickety staircase together. She let him hold her hand until they got to the path. They passed a couple of teenagers and a man walking a Labrador, then went around a curve and were suddenly alone.

"Can I kiss you, Mimi?"

"Go for it," she said.

He shook his head. She didn't make being romantic particularly easy. But he liked a challenge. He slid his hands around her waist and pulled her to him, the setting sun turning the water lava orange behind them. He leaned forward, brushed her lips with his, barely making contact.

"You are so sexy," he said. He brushed his lips against hers a little harder. "You are a beautiful woman." He brushed once more, more firmly. "You feel so good, Mimi."

He felt her breath coming quick and hot against his mouth and her hands tight on his forearms. Only then did he kiss her full-on, the scent of the water briny around them, the sweet dessert they'd had flavoring their tongues.

Mimi kissed him back, and he was overjoyed to feel her responding to him with as much passion as every other time they'd kissed. She was vital and strong in his arms, and he drank her in, thirsty for her after keeping his distance from her for so long.

She was giggling when they broke apart. "Damn you, Nash. Why are you such a good kisser?"

He smiled, eminently pleased with the compliment. "You're pretty good yourself."

"Just pretty good?"

"Excellent," he amended. "Extraordinary. Enticing. And other 'E' words."

She hooked her fingers in the belt loops of his jeans. "What's happening, Nash?"

"I don't know," he said, only partially honestly. He thought he did know what was happening, but he knew if he said it out loud, it would scare her off. "But I like it."

"Me, too."

. . .

On the drive back to Misty Harbor, Mimi asked, "Where did you get the name 'Nash?' Is it after the car?"

"Nah. My parents met in Nashville. I always assumed I was conceived there."

"Oh, wow." Mimi let out a startled laugh. "I've never been."

"It's a very cool city. We should check it out sometime. You'd love it—the live music is unreal."

She smiled, but said nothing.

"What about you? Where did Deb come up with Mimi?"

"You don't know? Mimi's just a nickname. Baby Jay couldn't conquer my name, and Mimi stuck."

"So what's your real name?"

"Marilyn Margaret. I'm named after my grandmothers. My mom's mom was Margaret, and my dad's mom was Marilyn."

"Perfect grandmother names. I've got a Helen and a Joyce."

"I like Mimi. It's frivolous and girly, and I'm not, so it throws people off. I like subverting people's expectations of me."

"You're great at it," Nash said, with a wink. "Still, I can see you as a 'Marilyn.' Sexy, elegant."

Mimi snorted. "Hardly elegant."

"Classy," he reaffirmed. "Trust me."

"I guess." She turned in the passenger seat, a horrified look on her face. "Please tell me you aren't going to start calling me 'Marilyn.'"

"Why?"

"I don't even know what my mom was thinking. My dad's family didn't want anything to do with me. It's not like they cared what she named me."

There was barely a hint of bitterness in her words, but Nash looked at her, concerned nonetheless.

"What do you mean?"

"The way my mom tells it, I was a complete accident. Obviously. She was a junior, and a hot shit senior, Gregory Ellsworth, asked her to prom. They did the whole nine—corsage, dinner, limo. And a hotel room after. Well, they had slightly too good of a time, because my mom got pregnant with me. His parents were pissed. Mom says he was understanding, but his parents forbade them from seeing each other. Which sounds star-crossed and romantic, but Gregory went along with it, then he went to college and fell off a balcony at a frat party the first week of school and broke his neck."

Nash's stomach hurt for her, for the loss. "Oh my God, that's horrible."

"Really tragic, yeah." Mimi's voice was soft. "His parents basically wanted nothing to do with Deb—or me—and they eventually moved away from Misty Harbor. They never supported Mom, a literal teenager who had their grandchild. So when I don't have warm and fuzzy feelings about those people, you understand."

"I get it." Nash felt a flash of anger toward the people who could have been Mimi's family, but rejected her before she was even born. "You probably don't need to hear this, but you're better off. They sound like complete assholes."

Mimi smiled crookedly. Nash wished he wasn't driving, so he could gather her against his chest and let her feel surrounded by...love, for lack of a better word.

"Total assholes." Mimi sighed. "I have the best family in the world. I couldn't ask for a better mom or a more wonderful brother. But it was hard, you know? Growing up in a small town with that legacy. My mom's kind of famous—and not in a good way—for having two kids so young, no dads in sight. She's got terrible luck with men. No wonder she took herself off the market." She gave a short, unhappy laugh.

"Is that why I'm the first person you've dated?" Nash asked, some of the lines between the dots filling in the more she told him about her past.

"Sadly textbook, isn't it?" Mimi said, and now the bitterness did shine through. "I always strive not to be what people expect, but I guess about some things I'm just as trite as the next person."

"You're allowed to not be perfect," Nash said, needing her to understand just because she wasn't impervious to loss, to pain, she wasn't a failure. "We all have issues, Mimi."

"What are yours?"

He laughed, sharp and loud in the confined space of the truck cab. "You know, the usual. Insecurity. Impostor Syndrome. The perpetual actor's lot of not knowing what your next job is. Feeling like a fraud."

She put her hand on his arm, scooted across the bench seat, and looked up at him. They were almost to her apartment, so he settled for draping an arm over her shoulder and letting her lean on him until he pulled to the curb near her building. He killed the engine and unbuckled both of them, then pulled her into his lap and kissed her until their lips were numb.

"You wanna come in?" she asked, her words slightly slurred.

He was hard as nails in his jeans. "You know I want to. But I'm going to say goodnight. Thanks for coming out with me."

"Thanks for dinner." She gave him one more kiss, and it didn't feel like a goodbye kiss. It felt like a *see you later* kiss. It felt like a *we're together, so this kiss is just to tide you over until tomorrow* kiss.

"Tomorrow," she said, echoing his thoughts. "Trivia."

"I'll study up."

She laughed and climbed off his lap, then got out of the truck. "You better."

Chapter Seventeen

Trivia didn't draw the same crowd as live music, but the bar at The Cove was still two-deep by the time Mimi arrived after work. Nash was already there—at a table with Jay and Cami, and she could only wonder how many surreptitious photos had been taken of the three of them. It wasn't a secret this was Jay's place, and he'd been a fixture for long enough for the locals to know if you wanted a picture, all you had to do was ask.

But it was still a novelty to see stars as big as Camille Corsair or Nash Speedwell in town.

It was almost Labor Day weekend, and the vibe was tinged with a desperation to wring the last from summer before the return to routine in fall. Mimi stopped by the bar to grab an iced tea, waved to some folks she knew from around town, and chatted with the bartender. Most of the patrons she didn't recognize, which meant they were probably tourists, which was great for Misty Harbor's overall well-being. Summer and fall tourists made the math work for businesses the rest of the year.

She leaned back against the bar to watch Nash interact with Jay and Cami for a moment. He looked good—of course, when did he not?—in a white linen button-down and khaki shorts. He looked like he fit right in. How did he transition from burly fighter to suave cowboy to preppy New Englander to red carpet-ready star? And how had he transitioned into her life so easily?

Then again, his lifestyle had never made anything like dating possible before. He'd even said he was going out of town this weekend, only a week after arriving. Did either of them think there was a chance of this lasting longer than the few months he'd be there for *Sawyer's Cove*? Was this an exercise in heartbreak?

He'd dictated the terms of this so-called relationship from the beginning, and when he left Misty Harbor, she'd be the one left alone.

But that was how it was supposed to be, wasn't it?

She'd always counted on being alone. This didn't change anything.

And she had to admit, she'd had fun getting to know Nash better. He had a way of looking at her that made her feel special. Just like that little frisson she got listening to his music, the way it felt like he was singing only to her, she felt like that when he had his attention on her, and she liked it—even if it was an illusion. It was his actual job to stare into people's eyes and make them think he was looking into their souls.

She shook off her contradictory mood and made her way to the table. Nash smiled when he saw her, scooted his chair closer to Cami so she'd have room to sit in the fourth spot. She gave Cami a cheerful wave and nodded at her brother. He glanced between her and Nash but said nothing.

"When is trivia going to start? Should I even be here? I have so much work to do," Cami said regretfully. She did look unusually ragged, her blonde hair pulled back haphazardly, no makeup, and a sheaf of papers spilling out of the top of the bag slung over the back of her chair.

"Cams, you promised you'd take a break for one hour. Just one. You can go back to work after this if you want to," Jay said soothingly but firmly.

"It's just that Selena's flying in Friday, and I need to be able to hit the ground running once she's here."

"Are you talking producing stuff or acting stuff?" Mimi asked. Cami was wearing two hats—producer and star—for the revival of *Sawyer's Cove*.

"Both! I haven't even looked at my lines," Cami

wailed. "I'm going to be terrible. Do I even remember how to be Amy Green anymore?"

"You're going to be amazing," Jay said reassuringly. "And if you want, you can run lines with me and Nash tomorrow."

"Ugh, you guys are going to be prepared for the table read, and I'm going to be tripping over my words like amateur hour." Cami truly looked concerned, and Mimi was worried about her normally collected friend.

"First of all, you could play Amy Green in your sleep," Nash said calmly. "Second of all, you're killing it as a producer. This shoot is already so organized, it's going to be like a vacation after my last shoot. Cold, rainy night shoots and tons of greenscreen? Give me dialogue-heavy scenes in a cozy bar any day of the week."

Cami gave Nash a grateful smile. "You're right. We're very organized. I just have this feeling something's going to go wrong, and we don't have much wiggle room in the schedule."

"Stuff always goes wrong in productions, but you and Selena will take care of it. You make a great team," Jay said. "And speaking of teams, let's crush the competition, shall we?" He nodded to the stage, where Rhonda Henderson, who ran the *Sawyer's Cove* walking tour group and worked at the crystal shop on Spring Street, was adjusting the mic stand.

"We're doing a different theme tonight, since we have a few special guests in the audience," Rhonda announced.

Mimi looked around in interest for the special guests, until she realized every other eyeball in the place was on her table because the special guests were the three *Sawyer's Cove* actors. She blushed under the scrutiny by proxy and tuned back in to hear Rhonda explain there would be four rounds of trivia. The first three would be general Hollywood-themed questions, and the fourth would be *Sawyer's Cove*-specific.

Jay groaned. "I'm the worst person to ask about *Sawyer's Cove* stuff."

Nash commiserated. "Yeah. People are always quoting lines of the show to me I don't even remember saying."

Cami straightened her shoulders, suddenly focused. "Shelve the attitude. We can do this. What's the prize again?"

"A fifty-dollar gift card to The Cove," Jay said. "You already drink for free."

"Yeah, but it's the principle of the thing," Cami said, rubbing her competitive little hands together. "What do you think, Mimi?"

"I think we got this," she said. She rarely made trivia night, but she usually did okay, except when it came to sports.

Rhonda went over the rules—no eavesdropping on other tables' discussions, no phones, and exact answers only.

After the first round, Mimi wasn't sure about their chances against the other eight foursomes in competition. She'd contributed one right answer about the first

Best Picture Oscar winner, and Cami had been right about a question involving Katharine Hepburn, but they'd missed the other three questions.

The second round went better, where they got every answer correct, thanks to Jay getting lucky with a guess about how many Terminator movies had been made.

Mimi had trouble focusing on the questions at all once Nash slotted his leg next to hers. She felt his body heat bleeding through her thin cotton skirt. His thigh was firm and muscular, and she was remembering with Pavlovian predictability the times they'd snuck away from late night drinks in this very spot to mess around. It was good Jay was present as an unwitting chaperone, occasionally throwing them curious glances, because otherwise she would have been tempted to drag Nash out the back, trivia be damned.

She got it together to help them finish the third round strong, and they went into the fourth and final round tied for first with three other teams.

"Come on, guys. We lived this," Cami said.

Mimi was delighted the competition had gotten Cami's mind off her stress, if only temporarily. Jay seemed pleased, too, and he had a hard time looking anywhere but at Cami's face.

She glanced over at Nash, wondered if he'd ever been with anyone who made him happy the way Cami made Jay happy. Her heart clenched confusingly when she imagined him at a table like this, playing trivia with another girl at his side. She'd be conventionally pretty and thin and have some glamorous job, like lifestyle influencer or personal stylist. She'd go with him on shoots and work from her phone. Mimi would never be able to do that and keep her job at the library. And she loved her job.

She was starting to worry she was going to get hurt by the end of this experiment in dating a star.

"You okay?" Nash asked, nudging her knee with his under the table.

"Sure," she said automatically. "Why?"

"You looked a little sad."

She was surprised he'd noticed, or that she'd let her emotions surface far enough for him to read them. She forced a smile. "I just really want to win." Winning trivia would be nice, but this game she and Nash were playing had higher stakes than she was certain she was prepared for.

"Then let's win," he said, as if it were effortless.

Rhonda announced the first question in the final round. "What is Parker Wild's middle name?"

Half the room groaned, and someone threw a balled-up napkin in mock disgust at Jay. He just shook his head. "Parker has a middle name?" he said, surprised. "I sure as hell don't know it."

Cami bit her lip. "Wait, I think I know this. Remember the graduation episode?"

Mimi remembered it was the second to last episode of the show. "Yeah?"

"It was on the diploma. They had an insert shot of it, and I remember..." She closed her eyes. The table held its breath. Her blue eyes shot open. "Yes!"

She grabbed the answer sheet in front of Jay and scribbled something on it. Mimi bent over to see the answer. Cami had written "Eugene."

Eugene?

Mimi exchanged a laughing glance with Nash.

The next question was kid stuff—most of the tables seemed to be able to come up with the name of Cloudy Cove High's principal. Rhonda let loose the third question, with a wink at Nash. "Who was Will O'Connell's first kiss?"

Mimi was embarrassed at how fast the answer popped out of her mouth. "Zack Murphy."

Nash whistled in admiration. "Nice."

The last two questions had them stumped. Not one of them could remember the name of the dog Lily Fine adopted for a couple of episodes in the second season, but they put down "Rufus" just to have an answer. And the last question seemed to have everyone in the bar scratching their heads—how many times did Sawyer North use his signature catchphrase on the show?

"Just put forty-two," Jay said under his breath. "The answer is always forty-two."

They handed in their answer sheet and waited.

Rhonda read the correct answers after she'd tallied the winners. The dog's name had been "Shrimpy," and the entire room grumbled, except for one table that let out shouts of glee.

"Well, that's it, we're toast," Cami said stoically.

And as for Sawyer's catchphrase, the magic number was a mere fourteen.

"It's okay, baby, you can still drink for free," Jay said, kissing the side of Cami's head. "Besides, wouldn't it be cringe if we won a trivia contest about us in my bar?"

"Fine," Cami said, with a mock pout. She drained her beer and stood up. "That was fun, if frustrating, and now I'm going to knock my head against some budget numbers. We're trying to find the money for a Ferris wheel."

With that cryptic remark, she was off, Jay staring after her with heart eyes Mimi would have found disgusting a week ago and now kind of understood, because when she turned to Nash, he was looking at her with, if not heart eyes, squinty ones that made him look hot. Why were smile lines so attractive?

"I better do some work, too. This place doesn't run itself, you know," Jay said, standing and stretching ostentatiously.

Mimi gave Nash a sly smile. "Looks like we're the last two standing—er, sitting."

"So it seems." He leaned back in his chair. "You aren't drinking tonight?"

"I wanted to keep a clear head."

"Smart."

"Speaking of—you need a ride home?" She nodded in allusion to his beer.

"I'm okay, only had two. You got your car back?"

"Better than new," she said. "Four new tires, and new wheels, too. Turns out I was due. Probably why I didn't have enough traction to get up the hill in the first place."

He frowned at that. "You should have gotten those

done earlier. Tires are important, and your car is a tin can."

"Hey, she's been with me a long time," Mimi said defensively. "I know how to take care of my car." She decided not to tell him Jay had suggested she get new tires months ago and she'd let it sift to the bottom of her to-do list.

"You don't need a ride home either, sounds like," he said thoughtfully.

"Nope." They looked at each other for a long moment. "Well, okay, then. I guess I'll see you around?"

He chuckled and grabbed her hand, stroking the back with his thumb. She shivered. "Hey, remember when we used to sneak into the back and go at it like rabbits?"

"Vaguely," she teased.

"Bummer that Jay's around," Nash said. "I kind of liked the sneaking around thing."

"Really?"

Mimi was surprised. He'd been so hands-off all week, barring their make-out session the previous night that had been so hot, her lips still felt tingly. Then again, she had to agree—sneaking around had been part of the fun. She glanced around. No one in the place seemed to be paying them much attention now. The novelty of Nash Speedwell had apparently worn off.

"So, you want to hang out tomorrow?" she asked, since they weren't heading to the back room anytime soon. He was still holding her hand, though, which felt unexpectedly nice.

"I'm flying to North Carolina tomorrow night. Should be back Monday or Tuesday."

"Oh." He'd be gone for at least four days, and Mimi's weekend was suddenly bereft of plans. He'd been her social life every day for a week.

"What about lunch?"

"I have a meeting," Mimi said regretfully.

"Okay, then wanna go make out in my truck?" he drawled.

Her pulse leapt, and she lowered her voice. "Abso-fucking-lutely."

Chapter Eighteen

JULES: Plowing our way through season three here—and we're covering one of my favorite episodes.

ERIKA: Oh, mine, too! Parker and Will's storyline in this episode is just, like, give me these two cuties being supportive of each other. Why didn't they explore this dynamic more?

JULES: Well, as you remember, the show starts with Parker and Sawyer as unlikely BFFs, and Will is the somewhat awkward third guy friend, but by this point, with Parker and Sawyer being on the outs, it really gives these two room to breathe, and they are fire. Like, if I didn't know Parker's soulmate and true love was Amy, I'd be shipping these two hard.

ERIKA: They do have great chemistry.

JULES: We can only hope they're going to have a lot of scenes together in the new series.

ERIKA: I'm still not over it. In, like, four months we're

going to have brand-new *Sawyer's Cove* content. How is this our life?

From *The Sawyer's Cove Rewatch Project Podcast: The Magic Show*

Jay's living room had been transformed since the last time Nash had been there. It had been a large, depressingly empty room waiting for something to happen to it, and something—or rather someone—had. Cami had swept back into Jay's life and kick-started him into turning his house into a home. Now there was an over-sized sofa, art on every wall that wasn't taken up by a window, a new ornate light fixture hanging over a heavy wooden coffee table that held a stack of books, a laptop, two coffee mugs, and the detritus of that morning's breakfast.

"Sorry about the mess," Jay said offhandedly as he cleared a spot for their highly classified *Sawyer's Cove* scripts. They were stamped with their name on every page so leaks could be traced. Both were printed on green paper, which signified the version of the script they were on was the latest one, though there would probably be changes before they settled on a final shooting script.

"It's cool, man. This place looks so much better."

"Thanks." Jay grinned. "I needed a reason to finally unpack."

"You know you've got the dream, don't you?" he asked his friend.

"What do you mean?"

"You've got this sweet house, sweet gig, sweet girl. How'd you end up being the one who figured it all out?"

"You're not doing too badly yourself." Jay flipped through his script until he came to the page he wanted. "Or does being up for Astronaut Man or whatever not count?"

Nash had explained to Jay the reason he was flying out of town that weekend. He had a day of meetings with the powers that be about Moonshot, then a day of chemistry reads. He'd booked a third day at a recording studio in the city to lay down his track for the charity album. Then back to Misty Harbor for the table read, where he'd see some of his co-stars for the first time in years, plus meet the new cast members. Yeah, it was going to be a big week.

And on top of everything was Mimi—she was both a distraction and the person who was grounding his feet to the floor. She'd become an effortless part of his life after a week, and he didn't like the thought of being away from her for four whole days. Which was silly, because they'd spent long chunks of time, months, a year, even, without a single encounter. And they hadn't even had sex since he'd gotten back to town.

He shook his head. "It's Moonshot, and that's not a done deal, and I don't know if it's the right move for me." He was looking forward to the pitch from the producers, but he was keeping his hopes reined in.

"Seriously?" Jay's eyes went round. "It seems like the perfect project after *Hawk and Bone.*"

"I know, but I'd be playing this one character for a decade. Probably wouldn't be able to take many side gigs, if any. There's not a lot of flexibility. Plus, they shoot in North Carolina."

"So? That's a hell of a lot closer to home than Eastern Europe."

"Yeah." Nash sighed. It was hard to put how he was feeling into words. To anyone on the outside, taking this gig—if he even got it—made perfect sense. It leveled up his career, and the contract would be more money than he'd ever seen, even in his most successful years. He'd forever be associated with one of the most popular franchises of all time. And he wouldn't have to worry about where his next paycheck was coming from for quite a while. Then again, by the time he fulfilled the contract, he'd be almost a decade older.

It was hard to imagine how he'd be able to keep Mimi in his life on a regular basis if he was constantly in another state.

"We should get started," he said instead of confiding his fears in her brother.

"Sure. Thanks for doing this." Jay picked up his script again, his grip so tight, he was wrinkling the pages.

"Of course, I need it, too." He opened his script. "Scene seven?"

"Yeah."

Nash scanned the page. It was Parker and Will's first scene together. The first episode was a combination of reintroducing all the original characters, filling in the audience on what they'd been up to in the last twelve years, and introducing the new generation that would bring the youthful energy.

His character, Will, had been living in New York City after getting his law degree and going to work as a public defender. He'd been mentoring a young gay kid named Danny, who'd gotten into trouble with the law. To send him down a different path, Will decides to bring him up to Cloudy Cove to live with his parents.

Meanwhile, Parker has been living in Cloudy Cove all this time, or at least since he and Amy finally broke up for good. The question that had plagued every *Sawyer's Cove* fan since the series ended was, did Parker follow his true love Amy to Stanford, where she'd been accepted to college, or did he stay in Cloudy Cove?

The show was now revealing he did go, and they stayed together for six months, until the strain of his being a non-college student and her being so busy with school became too much for them and they broke up. She moved to San Francisco after graduation but has come back to Cloudy Cove to care for her sick mother. Parker works nights at a bar and has scraped together all his resources to help take care of a young cousin who needed to get away from a bad family situation. Badass beauty Lily Fine now teaches the next generation at Cloudy Cove High.

Nash thought the writers had done an incredible job of weaving in the new characters and giving the original five Cove kids convincing stories to tell. He knew the fans would be initially critical of anything the show attempted, but hopefully enough of them would take the new season on its own merits, rather than rate how the storylines stacked up to what they personally thought should have happened to the characters. He supposed they'd find out for sure when the show aired that winter.

It took him and Jay a few minutes to get into the rhythm of the dialogue. Their characters were seeing each other after years of no contact, and it was stilted at first, but that was okay. Will had gotten a bit more uptight, and Parker had become a bit more jaded. But they both had good hearts, and as Nash sank into the scene, he could feel Will's regret at not having kept in better touch with his friend, at not having been able to help him when he needed him in the past. He remembered how Will always put other people first, that he had a bit of a savior streak, and he was impressed Selena and the other writers had picked up on that thread of his character and run with it.

They looked up at the end of the scene and smiled at each other. Jay had stumbled a bit over the first half of the scene, but he'd seemed to loosen up. He sounded like Parker, and he knew what it was like to have people leave you behind. Jay had always been able to connect with his character on a level Nash had envied. It wasn't that he didn't have anything in common with Will, though the guy was way brainier and had a much more advanced vocabulary than Nash ever would, but he didn't embody Will the way Jay embodied Parker. Will was a suit he put on, and while he liked the suit and was comfortable in it, he was always relieved to take it off at the end of the day.

Besides, being a straight actor playing a gay character had always come with its share of complications. He'd seen the role as a challenge when it had been offered to him fifteen years ago, but now he wondered if he'd known the pressure he was in for if he'd have made a different choice about taking the part.

In theory, an actor should be judged on his ability to play the role, not on his identity. But that didn't mean identity wasn't relevant. Jay had used his experience as the child of a single mom to inform his role as Parker, whose dad had abandoned him as a kid. Nash had used his skills playing guitar to give Will a storyline about playing a song for his boyfriend.

But the writers had given Will amazing stories and memorable dialogue people had found inspiring, not Nash. He'd just said the lines they wrote for him the best way he knew how. Yet he got the credit for being this important gay character on screen. He'd never felt he'd earned the accolades. It was daunting to face all that again.

"So, you think we can pull this off?" Jay asked anxiously. He fiddled with the pages of the script, folding corners down and pulling them back up again compulsively.

Nash conjured up his most sincere expression. "Hell yes, we can pull this off. You're golden. Keep doing what you're doing. Besides, it's eighty percent how you look, right? And you look like Parker Wild. Selena's scripts will do the rest."

"You're saying I should just show up and look pretty?" Jay said dryly.

"But not as pretty as me. Or Crosby—he might have it in his contract that we're not allowed to be hotter than him."

Jay laughed. "Poor Crosby. It'll be good to see him, though. What's he been up to lately?"

"Theater, mostly, I think." Nash thought about the last time he'd heard from the eponymous star of *Sawyer's Cove*. "But from what I understand, it was pretty painless to convince him to do the show."

"Cami told me he said yes almost right away."

"Should be fun, getting the crew back together."

"I don't know why I'm so nervous," Jay said. "Oh wait, it's because I haven't been on a set in twelve years."

"You're a natural. And we can rehearse more. You want to do the next scene?"

"Sure." Jay turned the page. "And thanks. You're a good friend." He scanned the script and added blandly, "Even if you are screwing around with my sister."

"Hey, now," Nash said, his hackles up instantly. "You were cool last night—don't give me a hard time about this now."

"Sorry, sorry." Jay looked at him speculatively. "It's just weird. You two get along really well. Okay, Mimi gets along with almost everyone. But you don't exactly seem that couple-y. And I guess I'm grateful, because my eyes don't need to be exposed to that, thanks, but are you sure this is a good idea? Mimi doesn't do relationships, man. And you're not exactly known for your long-term monogamy."

"Are you calling me a slut?"

"Far be it from me to call either of you sluts. But let's acknowledge you both have a reputation for brief affairs. Very brief, in Mimi's case. Which I'm sure is not news to you."

"It's not." Nash tried to decipher how he felt about discussing this with Jay. He supposed the guy had skin in the game since he cared about both of them. But Nash was under no illusion if things did turn sour, Jay wouldn't back Mimi up 150%. Which did give him pause. Was he prepared to lose Jay's friendship if he and Mimi managed to blow this thing up?

"Look…" He didn't quite know how to explain to her brother how being with her made him feel that wouldn't be wildly inappropriate. "She's awesome. You don't need me to tell you that. And we get along. And we're compat-ible in…other ways."

He laughed lightly when Jay made a fake gagging sound.

"All I can tell you is, we have something I'd like to think would remain, even if the physical side of things stopped for whatever reason. So don't worry, dude. I'm not expecting her to pull up stakes and be my international gal pal. I know her life is here. And she's, like, the least likely person to put pressure on me for anything I'm not ready to give. She's cool."

"Yeah." Jay looked like he wanted to say something else. "Okay. I guess I'll trust you two can figure it out."

"That's very mature of you."

"But I also want to say…Mimi is the coolest. But she's also not used to people going out of their way for her. She's the type who always makes things happen for herself. She put herself through college. She revolutionized the library. She's half the reason The Cove is doing so well, with the great bands she's brought in over the last few years. Don't take her for granted, okay?"

Nash stared at Jay. Take Mimi for granted? Had he been doing that? He supposed he'd been taking up a lot of her time since he'd arrived in town. But he had this impulse to be with her, and it was hard enough to wait for her to finish her workday so he could see her. Maybe that was a little selfish. And here he was, taking off for four days and expecting her to be available when he got back. Jay was right. Their situation was kind of complicated. The problem was, he didn't know how to fix it.

"Okay," he said after a pause. "And thanks."

"For what?"

"For trusting her with me, I guess. And I know that sounds paternalistic as shit, but what I mean is, it means a lot to me that you think I could be good for her."

"I get it. And yeah. You're pretty cool, too," Jay said, with a genuine smile. "So don't fuck it up."

"Understood."

Chapter Nineteen

Hungry for your peaches, hungry
for your pie.
Honey, for a taste of you I'd even
wear black tie.

> — "Peaches," The Nash
> Speedwell Experience

Landed.

Traffic out of Boston though.

Might have to take a rain check on
dinner.

How are you?

Mimi looked down at her phone. She was in her office, of course. She'd been in meetings most of the day, but had managed to drop in on the afternoon story hour in the children's section. Seeing the happy faces had given her a serotonin boost she'd need to get through the last chunk of her day. She'd also been looking forward to dinner with Nash, who'd been out of town since Thursday night. Today was Tuesday. He hadn't been able to get out of North Carolina yesterday and had told her he'd meet her for a meal to catch up, but now it looked like she'd have to wait another day to see him.

Which was totally, utterly, completely fine.

They'd often gone months without seeing each other. What was five days?

But Mimi had been restless and unfocused all weekend. She'd gone to the show at The Cove as usual Saturday night, then she, Jay, Cami, and Deb all had lunch on Sunday on Jay and Cami's back deck. They were taking a deep breath before the actors started arriving in town.

Deb had a hectic week ahead of her as well, as they were putting most of the guest actors up at the inn during the shoot. Much of the crew was already in town and at work; they'd been building sets in the old barn-turned-studio on the edge of the woods, where they'd built the original show's sets.

Mimi was curious about the production, but she'd been so busy with the library fundraiser approaching at a clip, she hadn't had a chance to check it out personally. Jay and Cami guaranteed she'd be able to stop by once production was underway.

Even though nothing about her routine had

changed, it didn't feel the same without Nash. She'd gotten used to him, to teasing him and flirting and having long, meandering conversations about anything and everything. Texting wasn't a substitute.

He'd been vague about his reasons for going out of town, but she understood it was for work—meeting with some producers or something—and he did say he spent a day recording the song he'd sung for her, and it had gone well. She'd smiled when he reported that. A new Nash Speedwell song was something to look forward to.

She typed out a brief text, telling him she'd take that rain check, then finished up her workday mechanically. Three weeks out from the fundraiser, they were close to being sold out of tickets, which was exciting. She only hoped the attendees would bring their credit cards and be willing to bid extravagantly on the silent auction items. Some of the auction proceeds would go toward the scholarship fund, and some would go toward the library's general operating fund. There was no end to the ways she could spend money to enrich and expand the library's programming.

It had been a couple of hours since Nash had texted, and even if there was no traffic, he wouldn't have made it back yet. She thought about the evening ahead, going home to her tiny apartment, eating leftovers, and watching TV. She usually looked forward to her quiet, solitary evenings, but not tonight. She wanted to hear about Nash's weekend and tell him about the progress she'd made on the fundraiser. They'd made out hot and heavily in the cab of his truck like teenagers the night before he left. She was feeling pretty good about her chances of getting to the next base with him.

Wait. She reviewed her feelings and realized something. She missed him. She missed Nash. Like, actively missed him with a fierceness she felt like a bone-deep ache. She missed him, and she wanted to see him, if only to make the pain go away.

She shouldn't text him while he was driving, but maybe he'd pull over to get gas at some point.

How's the traffic?

She'd just walked in the door of her apartment when her phone chimed.

We're moving.

Home in thirty.

She smiled.

I'll get some takeout and meet you at your place?

She sent it before she could think better of it. Maybe he'd think she was needy or clingy or some other word that made her squirm with mortification.

Or maybe he'd just think she wanted to share some takeout with him.

In any case, his answer came right away.

Sounds amazing.

See you soon.

She stared at the screen of her phone for a second, frozen. Heart emoji? WTF? She took a deep breath and felt her own, real, live heart racing in her chest.

"Okay," she said to her empty apartment. That was a puzzle for another day. Right now, she was starving and had some takeout to order.

Chapter Twenty

Take me or leave me, I'm all I
need, but together we're better,
we can make harmonies.

— "Untitled" for Rainbow
Canyon, The Nash Speedwell
Experience

Mimi's car was parked in his driveway, and she was leaning against the driver's door, clutching a paper bag, eyes on her phone. She looked up when she heard his truck, and she smiled.

A grin spread across Nash's face, stretching out his cheeks and probably making him look ridiculous, but he couldn't help it. He was so damn glad to see her. He'd been in stop-and-go traffic for three hours, on a bumpy, crowded flight for hours before that, and had been heartily sick of his too-firm hotel bed before that. He wanted his comfortable bed with its gorgeous view, a cold beer, a hot meal, and his girl. Not in that order.

And there she was, sexy in a sleeveless blouse and cut-off jean shorts and a pleased with herself expression as he climbed out of the truck, grabbing his bag and guitar from the back. He stopped in front of her, gave her a quick peck on the lips.

"Let me wash the airplane off me, and then I'll give you a proper greeting."

"Counting on it," she said. "I'll plate up dinner."

She followed him into the house and went straight for the kitchen. He liked that she felt at home in his place, as temporary as it was. He dropped the Gibson off in the living room and went upstairs to shower and change in record time. He avoided thinking about Mimi and her perfect, generous mouth while he was soaping up in the shower, lest he get sidetracked. Instead, he turned the tap to cool and rinsed as quickly as possible. He was back downstairs to hear her crack open a can of beer. She had pulled pork, mashed potatoes, pickles, and macaroni and cheese on two plates and was taking a chug from her can.

"Got one of those for me?" he said, pointing to the can.

"Yeah, I got a six-pack."

He grabbed one from the fridge himself, then sidled up to her, boxing her in against the island counter, slotting his hips against hers. She grinned up at him, set aside her beer, and responded to his vibe by settling her hands firmly on his ass.

He nuzzled the side of her neck, nipping kisses against the warm, woman-smelling flesh. He licked her pulse, and she let out a breathy gasp. He captured the tail end of the gasp with his mouth, sucking the air out of her, sticking his tongue right inside. She opened to him immediately, and they kissed hard and deep, hips grinding together, her small, perky tits pressed against his chest.

Her entire body molded to his, and he swore he could feel her heart beating against his ribs. He pressed in harder, wanting less space between them, wanting to feel her warm and wet all around him. He wanted to be inside her, like, yesterday, and when he realized his hands were going for the snap of her shorts, he stopped and pulled back with a mild curse.

"What?" Her lips looked as if they'd been stained by crushed pomegranate juice, and her cheekbones were highlighted by stripes of pink.

"Damn, I—" *Oh, what the hell.* "—I missed you, Mimi."

She looked at him, her hazel eyes liquid with warmth. "I missed you, too."

"You did?" He could see the truth in her eyes, but he hadn't expected her to admit it so readily.

"So, are we going to fuck or—?" She lifted a querying eyebrow, and he laughed.

"Dinner first?"

"And then?"

"And then we'll see." Saying he'd die if he didn't get inside her tonight was a bit dramatic, even if it felt like the truth. But he didn't want to pressure her into anything. After all, it had been his idea to wait.

"And then you're going down on me at the very least," she said. Her directness didn't surprise him, but it did make his cock leap in his jeans. She shifted her hips and smiled knowingly. She could clearly tell exactly how on board he was with that idea. But she let him move away, open his own can of beer. The first taste was refreshing and helped quench his thirst for her, in the short-term anyway.

"Dinner," he repeated.

"It might be a little cold," she said, with a frown.

"My fault," he said. "Microwave?"

"No. Let's just eat." They carried their plates to the patio, where an evening breeze had kicked up off the water, blowing away the damp heat of the day.

"Tell me about North Carolina," she said between bites. "Unless if by telling me, you'd have to kill me, because I don't want to know that bad."

He laughed and again felt like he'd struck gold by finding her. "I'll give you the non-classified version. I met with some producers and a director and a couple of studio executives. They were cool. Then I did some test readings on camera."

"Like a screen test? Don't they know you by now?"

"Yeah, but this was with some other actors. A chemistry test, to see if we can work together."

"And can you?"

He thought back to the half-dozen actors he'd read against. A couple of them he knew slightly—they were

TV actors, like him—but the rest were big, big stars. Bigger than Camille Corsair. Bigger than almost anyone. He'd been intimidated until he realized everyone was relatively chill, and he reminded himself he didn't even know if he wanted this gig. Once he'd been able to relax, he'd been pleased with his performance.

"I think so. They were cool." He knew if he told her the names of the folks he'd spent the most time reading with, she would have choked on her pulled pork.

"Congratulations," she said. "And how did the recording go?"

"That went well," he said hesitantly. By sheer luck, the producer he'd worked with on The Nash Speedwell Experience album had been nearby and agreed to come in to assist. It had been great to connect with Rachelle again, and she'd told him the song was good, but she'd asked him to try a couple of different endings, and together they'd picked one they were both happy with.

"You don't sound so sure."

"I think I'm the worst judge of my own music," he confessed. In truth, he did like the song, but he had no idea if anyone else would. "Could you—would you listen to it?"

Mimi perked up. "I'd love to."

He pulled out his phone. The sound quality wouldn't be amazing, but good enough. He found the file and pressed play.

Mimi put down her fork and cocked her head toward the phone as the first notes of the guitar came through.

He watched her listen. It was entertaining to try to

decode her small changes in expression, and the exercise kept his mind off the pounding feeling of fear he had in knowing she was forming an opinion and judging his creative work.

They'd chosen a repeat and fade outro rather than an abrupt ending. As the last strains finally waned, Nash closed the app and looked at Mimi.

She had tears in her eyes. He'd only ever seen her cry once before, and that was the last time she'd heard this song. "I love it," she said, smearing wetness on her cheeks with a swipe of her hand.

He shot her a look. "Are you sure?"

"It's poignant, you know? The melody is lovely. I love the change you made to the ending. But it's not just that—it's the message, Nash. About authenticity. About acceptance. Do you believe that? 'I'm all I need, but together we're better, we can make harmonies.'"

"I think people are strong, and if we let everyone be themselves, the world would be a better place. People who live life on their own terms are my heroes."

She gave him a considering look. "Me, too."

"Don't you live life on your own terms?" he asked, curious. She seemed to be fearlessly herself, always.

"I try," she said. "But aren't we all works in progress?"

"I suppose so." He certainly felt like he'd been grappling with himself, with the next phase of his life. What did he want it to be? Who did he want to share it with?

They finished their meal. The breeze turned cooler, driving them back indoors. He rinsed their dishes in the sink and stuck them in the dishwasher to run later.

"I didn't get dessert," Mimi said.

"You can be my dessert," Nash said, glancing at the vee of her legs. She'd brought up the idea of him getting his mouth on her, hadn't she?

"Finally," she said, but lightly.

He grinned at her, feeling like a kid about to unwrap a birthday present he knew was exactly what he wanted. They raced each other up the stairs and to his bedroom.

Mimi had her shirt off and her shorts halfway down her thighs by the time he caught up, his own shirt off in seconds. He watched her strip, familiar with her body, but fascinated by how different this felt from previous times. In the past, it had been about fun, about expedience, about getting off with someone he liked and found attractive and who was game for anything.

But now he had feelings for her—he'd never lied to himself about that—and if she didn't know, it was because she didn't want to see what was there. He didn't know exactly how she felt about him, but she'd said she'd missed him. Missing someone meant you felt something for them, didn't it?

He didn't need reassurance they were exactly in the same place—they didn't need to be in love with each other to have sex. But he found himself wanting to slow everything down so he could savor each moment. There was no race to the finish line this time. They'd put in the work to get here, to feel comfortable and trust each other, and he didn't want to waste that on a quick fuck. She wanted him to go down on her; he could do that.

But giving her head was simply a sex act. He wanted to give her an experience.

He started by drawing the curtains across the windows. He loved the view, but she was the only thing he wanted to look at right now. Then he crossed to the portable speaker he'd brought and pulled up an acoustic playlist on his old-fashioned iPod.

Mimi scooted up his bed, naked except for her thin scrap of a bra. Its vibrant blue color matched the dyed streak in her hair. She looked like a shock of electricity on the gray blanket and pillows, a tropical fish in a murky cove.

The only light came from the hallway, so he lit the lamp on the desk and closed the door. He had condoms in the bathroom, but he could always grab them later.

"Happy now?" she asked when he finally shucked his jeans and got on the bed next to her wearing nothing but gray boxer briefs that already felt tight.

He made sure she was looking into his eyes with her luminous hazel ones when he replied, "Yes." He was happy, and he wanted her to know why. He had no intention of taking her for granted again.

"I'm happy, too," she whispered.

His heart leaped, and he realized he'd been waiting for a sign from her that he wasn't in this feelings thing all by himself. She was there with him, and he was unreasonably relieved. Those words were the signal he needed to take off the brakes. He kissed her. She tasted familiar— he'd kissed her plenty in recent days. He hadn't made out so much since high school. But it hadn't gotten old yet, tongues tangling, breath hot, sipping her like potent wine.

But tonight she'd offered him dessert, and he was still hungry.

He moved down her body, pausing to suck her nipples through the thin fabric of her bra, leaving obscene wet spots behind. She trembled and arched into his mouth, as if trying to get inside it. By the time he nipped over the swell of her belly, down the junction of her thigh and pelvis, he could smell her, ripe and heady, and he could see her, glistening folds sparsely covered by light brown hair she obviously kept natural. He liked that she didn't meticulously remove every piece of body hair. He nuzzled her gently, glanced up to find her watching him with her lips parted, her sexy little overbite giving her an eager look.

"You good?"

"I'll be better after an orgasm," she said breathlessly.

He grinned. "Coming right up," he said, rolling the first word with exaggerated emphasis.

She laughed. "Nice pun."

Her hands were clutching the blanket, and he tapped one gently. "You can touch me, if you want." He wasn't going to *demand* she pull his hair, but maybe she'd get the picture.

She followed his suggestion and threaded her fingers through his hair, getting a firm grip as he went back to work, licking a long stripe over her folds before stopping to concentrate on the apex of her sex. He could feel her clit getting harder as he sucked, and she tightened her hold, which meant he was on the right track. He grasped her hips and pulled out every trick he knew, licking, kissing, and finally spearing his tongue into her dripping pussy. The musky taste made his cock so hard, he had to rut against the bed to get some minor relief.

When he went back to her clit, her grip intensified again. He relished the sting as she pulled gently on his hair, and he was grateful for its current length. He'd often kept his hair so short there was nothing to grab onto, but the sensation of being held against Mimi's luscious wetness was intoxicating.

"Harder, please. Nash," she sobbed.

He renewed his efforts until she was suddenly stiffening beneath him, and he felt an extra spurt of fluid coat his chin just as she relaxed her hold. God, she was insanely hot, and he could have spent all night eating her out, except for the fact that he might actually die if he didn't feel her surrounding his cock with her tight, wet heat.

He licked his lips and raised his head. She was breathing hard, eyes closed, body flushed pink from forehead to thighs. He must look a mess, felt her coating his entire face. Even his eyebrows felt damp. He managed to reach a box of tissues on the nightstand and do a quick clean-up job before palming his erection through his boxer briefs.

"That was intense," she said, opening her eyes blearily. "Wow."

"I like 'wow,'" he said. "And yeah." They'd always sparked in the sex department, but that was like a runaway forest fire. And he was still burning with need for her.

She looked so unbelievably sexy laid out on his bed, all glowing and well-serviced. He peeled down his boxers and stroked himself roughly.

Mimi pushed up on an elbow, nodded at his crotch. "Hey, you want some help with that?"

"Yeah, but this is good, too." Honestly, jerking off to her seemed almost as good a plan as getting inside her at this point.

"Come here." She motioned him toward her, helped him get the boxers all the way off, then spread her legs. "I'm so wet, you'll just sink right in."

He groaned. "Wait. I need to get a condom."

She bit her lip and opened her mouth, hesitating. She then seemed to think better of whatever she was going to say. "Okay."

He threw himself off the bed and cursed his earlier cavalier attitude about the condom. Unless things had changed since the last time they'd talked about this, she was on birth control, and they were both healthy, but he made a point of never going without the extra protection of a condom. He didn't want to be hit with a surprise just because he was lazy about gloving up, and he'd never been with anybody he'd even considered skipping it with. But with Mimi, everything was different. If she'd said she didn't mind him going without, he would have done it in a heartbeat.

Jesus. She'd really gotten into his head.

Not to mention his heart.

Chapter Twenty-One

He was a cowboy lover, galloping
in hard and riding away wet.

— "Stetson," The Nash
Speedwell Experience

Despite the toe-curling orgasm Nash had dramatically delivered, Mimi wasn't done with him yet. She snuggled into the super-soft sheets and waited, flashing back to the image of his mouth working her clit like a pro, her hands bunched in his thick brown hair.

She'd almost told him she didn't need him to wear the condom but chickened out at the last minute. He seemed to take forever in the bathroom but finally came back with an entire pack.

Mimi approved. "I like your ambition, cowboy."

"Gotta have goals," he answered with a wink that made her pussy clench.

He was surreally attractive, a real-life screen star with the bone structure to prove it. But he was still just Nash, a little goofy, a little insecure, gentlemanly yet dirty when it counted. He was kind of perfect, if she was honest with herself.

And he seemed to think she was great, which was as it should be—Mimi knew her worth, thank you very much—but it was still a little random. How had this man decided she was the one he wanted to be with? In her experience, the universe didn't align itself in her favor like that.

But somehow it had. She was having sex with a man she cared about deeply. She didn't do that. Even though she and Nash had slept together before, this was the first time it was more than a hookup. She'd be seeing him tomorrow. And the day after. And maybe the day after that. And she realized suddenly she was on board with that plan. Even though it was new, and scary, and she didn't know what she was doing half the time, it didn't matter. Because he was right there with her. She wasn't alone in this. They were fumbling through together. And that seemed to make it okay.

She took a deep breath and smiled at him. He'd donned the condom and was stroking himself through it. He'd done an amazing job taking care of her so far tonight, and she wanted to make him feel just as good.

She rearranged them so he was lying back on the bed and she was on top, then she leaned forward and took him in her mouth. She'd blown him before, but it had been a while. She'd forgotten just how heavy his fully erect cock was, and it took her a second to adjust to the weight of him in her mouth. But she liked the way he filled her up. He let out a soft stream of curses as she took him deep, backed off, then repeated. She brought one hand up to cup his balls, and he froze.

"Shit, shit, shit. Stop, honey, or I'm going to—"

She pulled off, licking the latex taste off her lips. "You're so hard."

"Yeah, eating out your pussy makes me fucking hard as nails."

She groped around behind her until she found another condom. She removed the one he was wearing, put on a fresh one. His eyes never left her hands.

He grunted. "You're going to kill me."

"You'll survive," Mimi declared. She then straddled his waist and sank down on him, pausing to adjust until her opening was flush with his thighs. She'd been aching to have him right there since he'd come back to town, maybe longer than that, and it felt as fabulous as she remembered.

"God, you feel good," he said, bucking up until she was sure she could feel his tip spearing her as deep as anyone had ever been.

They quickly found a rhythm, and just as Mimi was getting frustrated because she wasn't getting exactly where she wanted, he flipped them and pushed her legs onto his shoulders. She loved that this wasn't their first time, or even their tenth. They'd been together enough that he knew she liked it deep, that she didn't mind him manhandling her a little, that she in fact preferred it when he put his Hollywood muscles to use. He snapped his hips into her, making her see stars. Her hands scrambled for purchase on those gloriously overdeveloped shoulders, slippery now with sweat.

First-time hookups were fun, and new was usually exciting, but sometimes it was just weird or not good or awkward if both people weren't exactly compatible. With Nash, it was different in so many ways. She knew his body better than any other she'd had her hands on besides her own.

Every moment they spent together, the formerly uncharted territory of Nash was being replaced by shared memories, by mutual understanding. She was getting to know him better than she ever thought she would, and she was surprised by how satisfying it was.

Almost as satisfying as the explosive orgasm that rocked through her and took her unawares. One second he was thrusting into her, the next she was shocked with pleasure, pleasure that kept building, until her mouth opened on a silent scream, the orgasm going on and on, showing no signs of giving up.

Nash didn't give up either. Despite being close to the edge earlier, he was holding out like a champ. He just kept giving it to her, and she kept taking it.

"I'm still coming," she gasped, and he smiled grimly, face red with exertion.

"Yeah, that's it, keep coming, Mimi."

She obeyed, the tightness building within the pleasure until she was shouting again. The closest thing she could compare it to was an orgasm within an orgasm, sharp and sweet and zinging through her nervous system like a pinball lighting up every post along the way.

He was right there with her, yet again, muscles bunched and chest heaving as he emptied himself into her.

They were both hot to the touch, as if they'd caught a fever. Kissing him after he'd pulled out and disposed of the condom, he tasted like salt, briny like the sea outside the window.

"Hot," she said.

"I'll turn on the fan."

"That's not what I meant." She kissed him again, the adorable man. "But yeah."

"Want some water?"

"You spoil me," she teased. "Orgasms and water."

"Only the best for you," he murmured. But he didn't sound like he was kidding.

She felt something in the region of her heart move, as if a pebble holding a boulder in place had been dislodged and something titanic was shifting inside her. It felt scary and big and too much to keep inside.

"Nash?" she said suddenly.

"Yeah, honey?"

Her mouth went dry. She scrabbled for words—any words. "Thanks."

"Entirely my pleasure, Mimi."

As soon as he opened the door and disappeared

downstairs to get them water, she became aware of the thickness of the air in his room, of the smell of sex. She thought about getting up and using the shower, but that might imply she was staying over. He hadn't asked her to. That had never been part of the deal before. But that was then. Now, they were…involved. More than hooking up. Did that mean she was supposed to stay over?

She already had, the night they fell asleep on his couch. It wasn't as if a precedent was being set. Not really. Before she could decide or do more than slip her underwear back on, Nash was back with two glasses.

"Do you want to grab a shower?" he asked.

"Um…" She swallowed some water.

"Or are you a morning shower person?"

"Will I be here in the morning?"

"Do you want to be?"

She thought about it. She had to work. But she didn't want to go home. She hadn't gotten her fill of him yet. It would be fine if she got up early enough to stop by her apartment to change.

"Yeah, I do."

He smiled big, and for a second she experienced a moment of pure joy. She didn't have to leave this man, and he didn't have to leave her. Not right now. They could be together all night long. It felt right, until she thought about logistics. Toothbrushes and pajamas and the fact that she didn't do co-ed sleepovers. This was another first, no matter what she'd tried telling herself earlier.

But again, he made it easy for her. He had an extra

toothbrush, got her a clean towel, and offered her a T-shirt to sleep in.

"Wearing your clothes is becoming a habit," she observed as they got into bed, together, and turned out the lights, together. It felt so grown-up. So adult. Weird but good.

"I like seeing you wear my clothes," he admitted. "You look good in them."

"I look good in plain white T-shirts?"

"Very sexy."

He was right. She felt sexy and satisfied. And tired. But she still had trouble falling asleep. It was a strange bed, with a strange smell and strange noises. And Nash was right there. She could hear him sniffing and turning as he got comfortable, those intimate little noises that came with sharing a bed.

She marveled. She was sharing a bed with Nash Speedwell. Over the years, she'd been so careful to keep her distance, not to confuse her familiarity with every plane of his face from watching him on screen with real-life intimacy.

She was intimate with books, with music. She often poured a glass of wine, put on her favorite album, and read the afternoon away in a tepid bath.

That was the type of intimacy she was comfortable with—intimate with herself, with her own company. She didn't know how to allow someone else in, had thought maybe she wasn't capable of it. But she was beginning to see not only was she capable of it, she craved it. She craved him.

It wasn't working to pretend this was only casual, only an experiment.

Mimi still didn't know how to be in a grown-up relationship. She felt like she'd mostly failed at her meager attempts. But Nash was still here. Still waiting patiently for her to get a clue.

How much longer would he stick around and let this play out? Was he as invested in this as she was beginning to be? Or was this just an extended version of their former game?

She yawned and stretched and tried to find a comfortable spot on her pillow. She was overthinking things. She listened to Nash breathe and told herself tomorrow was another day.

Chapter Twenty-Two

ERIKA: Oh, you know what I also heard? They cast
Stephanie Mae!

JULES: Not to be mean, but am I supposed to know who
that is?

ERIKA: I actually only know her because my cousin is
obsessed with her show. She's been acting for years on
cable sitcoms and stuff, but this would probably be her
most mainstream project.

JULES: Okay, cool. According to the Internet, they cast a
complete unknown named Henry Yu to play a character
named Kai Wild. *Wild.* So how is he connected to
Parker?

ERIKA: OMG, do you think Parker has a son? With Amy?

JULES: Well, according to my intel, this Henry Yu guy is
22, so probably not.

ERIKA: Oh. Bummer. They would have the freaking
cutest babies.

"Surreal, isn't it?" Jay said.

They were standing in front of Smith's Soundstage, the home base of *Sawyer's Cove* production past, present, and future. The soundstage had been converted years ago from an enormous barn on a large farming operation. It had metal siding and heavy doors, but the entrance they'd been told to use was propped open by a rock.

Nash lifted his eyebrows at Jay. "Great security, man."

Before Jay could answer, a man the size of a truck stepped outside and asked them for their IDs, which he checked against a list before issuing them badges.

"I spoke too soon." Nash followed Jay inside and down a hallway.

"This is Cami's first production, but she knows what she's doing," Jay said mildly.

"Apologies for implying otherwise." He breathed in the slightly industrial scent of the hallway and could have sworn it smelled the same as it did when they were all clueless teenagers working their first big job.

"I can't believe the last time I was here, I was nineteen. It feels like yesterday, man."

"I don't know," Jay said slowly, "I feel like a different person now."

"What do you mean?" Jay had been out of the game for a long time, but he'd basically lived and breathed his character.

"We were just kids; everything was an adventure. It was different stakes. Now we're adults. Our decisions have consequences. I feel like this time it's all on us, you know? All these jobs, all this money. What if we screw it up?"

Nash knew what Jay meant was, what if *he* screwed it up. Nash was confident he could play Will O'Connell, and he thought the writing was solid enough that the episodes would be good. Whether anyone watched or not—well, that was a function of marketing and luck. Would they hit the culture at the perfect time for a rediscovery of a nostalgic favorite? Or would they be watched by the die-hard fans and ignored by everyone else? They didn't have control over that.

"Listen, right now all we have to do is go in and read lines with our friends. It's supposed to be fun, remember? It's play. You know Parker Wild like the back of your hand. Be him for a few hours. I know you can do that."

Jay rubbed his neck and then cracked it, rolling his shoulders to loosen up. "Yeah. I can do that," he said with more certainty.

"Let's go have some fun, brother," Nash said.

They found the right room, a medium-sized conference room with a big table and a dozen or so chairs. A stack of goldenrod-colored scripts sat on the table, along with a water dispenser and some platters of food. A cluster of people stood around, talking animatedly as if this was a cocktail party, not a workday.

"Oh, my God!" An auburn-haired woman rushed up and threw her arms around both of them at once, somehow gathering them to her in one gigantic hug. "What happened to the sweet boys you used to be? Who are these giant men?"

"Hi, Ariel," Nash said, laughing.

She let him go first and clung to Jay a little longer. "I missed you," she said, a whisper of tears lacing her voice. Ariel had never been one to hide her emotions.

"Missed you, too, Ariel." Jay gave her a crooked smile. Nash hadn't given Jay the opportunity to drop him completely once the show was over, but he knew Jay hadn't kept in touch with anyone else. That included their other co-star, Spencer Crosby—Sawyer North himself—who was walking up behind Ariel.

"Jay. Nash," he said in that slightly formal, stand-offish way he had. "Good to see you."

"Hi, Crosby," Jay said, friendly, but not as warm as before. They shook hands. The two of them had always gotten along fine, but never had been close. Crosby was a tough nut to crack. He wasn't close with anyone, it seemed, though the peacemaking Ariel had done her best to include him.

"Hey, man," Nash said, ignoring Crosby's outstretched hand and hauling him in for a back-slapping hug. "It's been too long."

Crosby held himself stiffly through the hug, but he was faintly smiling when he stepped away. "Last time was at the Rainbow Canyon fundraiser in Malibu, I believe."

"Oh yeah, thanks for doing that." Nash remembered cautiously asking Crosby to help when he found out the recipient of Rainbow Canyon's annual service award was a huge fan. He'd asked Crosby to put in an appearance and take some pics with the guy, and Crosby not only had agreed and shown up, he'd actually smiled and been charming. One of the organizers of the event had even let it slip that Crosby donated a chunk of change that night, too.

He wasn't a bad guy, but it seriously took a crowbar to get him to loosen up.

"Hey, you made it." Cami joined the group and stood next to Jay.

Nash caught the subtle brush of her hand against Jay's arm. He loved seeing their casual intimacy, but he was jealous. They were going to get to spend the entire day together, while he had to wait until they wrapped to see Mimi.

They'd woken up early and gone for a walk on the beach as the sun rose, stopping to admire the view and make out a little before she'd gone home to start her day. He was still feeling the buzz of having her in his bed last night. They'd made plans to meet for dinner—maybe she'd be into a repeat of the after-dinner activities as well.

"We're not late, are we? Nash wanted to carpool." Jay's voice conveyed no anxiety, but Nash could still tell his friend was nervous.

"Carpooling is encouraged, and you're right on time. We're still waiting on Selena and a couple of others," Cami said.

"Wow, the five of you look so incredible together." A

girl walked over, cell phone in hand. "Can I take your picture? For, like, posterity?"

"And social media?" Ariel asked, but not unkindly.

"Good idea, Steph," Cami said. Somehow, she got them all lined up and facing the girl in under ten seconds.

While he dutifully smiled for the pic, Nash realized the picture taker was Stephanie Mae, one of the new cast members. She'd been cast as one of the fresh-faced Cloudy Cove teens. Nash had never met her in person, but he'd read up on the new cast members to get a feel for their resumes before they started work. She was young, eighteen, and had cut her teeth on a popular cable channel where she'd been one of the only Korean-American actors to headline her own show. She also had an artificial right leg, a silver prosthesis affixed to her thigh, which Nash could see ended in a sparkly blue sneaker.

She snapped the picture, then gave them a brilliant smile. "We're making history today, folks."

"Couldn't have said it better myself."

Selena Echeveria swept into the room, followed by Becca, her assistant. Selena was a round woman in her thirties, with a riot of black curly hair and crimson-painted lips. All eyes turned to her, the showrunner, the one with the overarching creative vision for the entire reboot.

Nash couldn't be prouder of the woman he'd first met when she was an assistant writer on the original show. She rocked and deserved this chance. They *were* making history, and he was grateful to be a part of it.

Everyone took their seats around the table. He found himself between Ariel and Jay, and across the table from Stephanie and Henry Yu, another one of the newbies. Selena quickly took her place at the head, while Becca passed out scripts.

Selena had them go around and introduce themselves and outlined the schedule for the rest of the day. She then put on round red reading glasses, turned to the first page in her script, looked at Crosby, and said, "All right. Act One, Scene One. Sawyer—you're up."

And they began to read.

Six hours later, Nash was exhausted in the best possible way. His friends had all stepped up to the plate, and they'd had a blast reading through the first two episodes. The new kids on the block had been good, too. They'd clearly been cast well, and they'd done their homework. They fit right in, as if they'd been part of the cast for years.

In fact, the entire thing had felt surprisingly natural. More like a theater troupe who played off each other than separate actors with their separate egos, trying to make their mark on the production. He supposed they'd built up trust with each other that hadn't fully gone away in the intervening years. And Selena was just as good as Ryan Saylor, the original creator and showrunner, at bringing out the best in each of them.

Even Crosby was smiling as they milled around after Selena called a wrap for the day.

"Nice work, Nash," he said as he grabbed his denim jacket from his chair.

Nash blinked. Crosby wasn't known for his liberal distribution of compliments.

"Thanks," he said after a beat. "You, too. This is going to be fun."

"Yeah, I guess it is." He looked at his phone and casually said, "You want to grab some dinner?"

Nash wanted to say yes. He'd love the chance to reconnect with Crosby. But he had plans with Mimi. Crosby's smile dimmed at Nash's hesitation, and he hurried to explain. "That sounds great. I'm just supposed to meet my—" he waited only a beat before finishing the sentence with "—girlfriend for dinner."

"Oh. You brought someone with you to the shoot?" Crosby asked with uncharacteristic curiosity.

"No, she's a local. Mimi. Um. Orlando." He kept the smile on his face, even though he had no idea how Mimi would react to him calling her his girlfriend or outing them to Spencer Crosby. They hadn't talked about any of this, and he felt like he was impinging on her privacy. But he was also being honest.

"Mimi? Jay's sister?" Crosby's lips twitched. The little shit was amused.

"Yes." He glanced around the room. Jay was gone. They'd arranged earlier that he'd catch a ride out with

Cami so Nash would have the truck to himself. "That's right. Jay's sister."

Crosby whistled and shook his head. "I thought this time there'd be less drama. Of course I was wrong."

"Hey, there's no drama. We're adults."

"And Jay knows you're fucking his sister?" Crosby said.

"Jesus Christ, Crosby. Mind your own business."

"Sorry," he said. His mouth turned serious. "I only met her once or twice. Nice girl?"

Nash smiled with teeth at the characterization of Mimi as "nice." "She's fucking spectacular," he said, hearing the edge of a warning in his voice. "Smartest person you'll ever meet. You'd like her."

"Well, I wouldn't want to impose on couple time," Crosby said acerbically.

"It's not like that." Oh hell, they'd been talking for two minutes and were already devolving into sarcasm. "Why don't you join us for dinner? You can get to know her yourself."

Crosby's eyes widened, as if his bluff had been called. "Nah. It's okay."

Nash suddenly realized while he had Mimi, and Jay, and Cami, and even Pauline and Deb, Crosby had no one. At least not in Misty Harbor.

"No, seriously. Come with me. Mimi was just going to order pizza because I didn't know how late this was going to go. I'm sure she'd love to have you, too. We can hear about what you've been up to. Your latest Broadway show and all that."

"You sure?" Crosby seemed hesitant but hopeful, and Nash felt bad for the guy who was usually pegged as an asshole because people couldn't see past the aloofness to understand he was shy. "I don't want to crash your party."

"No, it's cool. Follow me there, okay?"

"Okay," Crosby said. "Thanks."

Chapter Twenty-Three

JULES: From what I understand, pre-production has been going on for a while, and they're going into production any day now.

ERIKA: Which means, theoretically, if you went to Misty Harbor, you could probably catch a glimpse of them actually filming.

JULES: We could be extras! Why aren't we there?

ERIKA: Because if we ever met anyone from the show in real life we'd probably turn to stone?

JULES: Speak for yourself. I'm great with famous people. Remember that time I waited on Diego Luna?

ERIKA: Didn't you spill cream on his shoes?

JULES: Yes, but he was super nice about it.

FROM *THE SAWYER'S COVE REWATCH PROJECT PODCAST: REBOOT ROUNDUP*

"Your phone's buzzing. Want me to get it?" Trevor called from the living room while Mimi was opening a bottle of wine in her closet-sized kitchen.

"Uh, who is it?"

Trevor had come by the library just as she was leaving to bring her some leftover apple turnovers, because he knew they were her favorite, and she'd impulsively asked him if he wanted to come home for dinner. She'd been trying to find a time for him to meet Nash, and even though she knew she shouldn't ambush him after a workday, she'd also found herself wanting to have the focus pulled from their relationship for a minute.

Last night had been so intense, and she was still sorting out how she felt about it. Trevor was a buffer. Maybe they didn't need one, but it couldn't hurt to split the pizza three ways until she got her footing. Besides, Trevor was a sweetheart. He deserved a nice surprise.

"Oh, it's a text from Mr. Actor Guy. Who's that?" Trevor walked in, holding out her phone, which she grabbed from his hands. "Mr. Actor Guy" was how she'd entered Nash's number all those years ago, as a joke, and a way to remind herself that what they had was part of a fantasy. It wasn't real.

Only somehow, in the last couple weeks it had become the most real thing in her life.

"There's someone else joining us for dinner. And I need you to be cool about it."

"I'm always cool," Trevor said, pushing his straight shoulder-length hair behind his ears.

She raised her eyebrows at him.

"Okay, well. Sometimes." He pursed his glossy pink lips. "Who is it? Someone from the show?"

"Nash Speedwell." She glanced at her phone and read Nash's texts.

Bringing Crosby for pizza.

Hope that's ok.

If it's not ok I'll make it up to you later.

;)

"And Spencer Crosby, apparently." She'd only met the guy once, that she could remember. Oh well, the more, the merrier. She pushed away the uncomfortable thought that maybe Nash wanted his own buffer.

She sent back a quick thumbs up and looked in her fridge to see if she had some bagged salad she could use to make more of a meal. When she turned back from the fridge triumphantly holding a package of baby spinach, she caught sight of Trevor's face. It was completely blank. He didn't so much as twitch a blue eye-shadowed eye.

"Hello? Are you okay?" She snapped her fingers in front of his face, and he swayed.

"Did you just say Nash Speedwell and Spencer Crosby are coming here? To this house? To eat pizza with us? Is that what you said?" Trevor's voice was eerily monotone.

Mimi laughed. "Yes, that's what I said. And you said you'd be cool."

"I'm cool. I'm so cool. This is me being cool. Uh huh."

The doorbell rang. Trevor screamed.

Mimi set down the bag of spinach and shook her friend by the shoulders. "Snap out of it."

"Don't *Moonstruck* me. This is incredible!" Trevor's pale face was blotchy red with excitement.

"Seriously, I will send you home if you can't handle this," Mimi warned.

"Okay, I'll be good. I swear."

Mimi took a second to push a hand through her own hair to make sure she didn't have any curls sticking straight up, then answered the door.

Her breath caught at the sight of Nash in a light blue button-down shirt and navy slacks. He looked so... professional. And hot.

"Hey," he said.

She swore her panties dampened a little.

Fuck, she'd miscalculated this. She'd thought they might want some distance, to normalize things, slow them down even. Instead, she wanted to drag him to her bedroom and do wicked things with him.

But they had guests. "Hey." She opened the door wider, and he walked through with an easy familiarity. A slightly shorter man followed him in, instantly halving the space in her tiny living room.

Spencer Crosby was a Raphael painting brought to life, with his curly light blond hair, viridian green eyes, and almost translucently pale skin. His sculpted cheekbones and prominent chin cleft were gilding the lily. He was stockier than Nash, filling out his light green longsleeved Henley with lean muscle. He wore a smile, but it looked forced.

Mimi gave him a genuine one. It was easy to smile at Sawyer North, one of her favorite characters from the original show. And she remembered what her brother always said about Crosby, that he acted tough but was just shy.

"Hi there," she said, injecting friendliness into her voice.

"Hi, Mimi." He looked around, managing to seem politely dismissive of her tiny, cluttered apartment. "It's good to see you again. I'm sorry for the last-minute addition to dinner."

"It's all right. Good to see you, too," she said, trying to sound like she meant it. "And I have a friend visiting me, so we're a little party."

"A friend?" Nash said.

"Trevor. He's in the kitchen. Nash, can you listen for the pizza? I'll get the wine. Spencer, is red okay?"

"Sure, but call me Crosby," he said. "Need any help?"

He had good manners; she'd give him that. "Just make yourself comfortable."

Trevor was standing next to the fridge where she'd left him. She grabbed the bottle of wine and two glasses. "Can you get the other glasses?"

"I don't think I can do this," Trevor whispered.

"You are going out there, and you are going to be

chill. Just pretend they're customers at the Bakeshop. Two regular people."

He took a deep breath. "Totally. I can do that. I was super chill when I waited on Ryan Phillippe one time."

"Exactly, you can do this. Now get the glasses."

She returned to the living room that also functioned as her dining room. The small round table where she ate most of her meals was piled with books she hadn't gotten around to clearing. Maybe they should eat on the couch around the coffee table. It was just pizza. With that in mind, she set up the glasses on the coffee table, and Trevor shadowed her.

"Crosby, Nash, this is a good friend of mine, Trevor Kendrick."

Trevor's hands shook as he set down the glasses, but he gave the guys a smile and waved. "Hi. What can I get you? I mean, can I get you some wine? Oh, I guess Mimi's pouring the wine. I could get you something else, though."

When she'd told him to act like he would at the Bakeshop, that wasn't what she had in mind.

Nash stepped in. "Wine sounds great. How do you and Mimi know each other?"

"Well, everyone in town knows Mimi." Trevor looked over at her. "But she pretty much just saved my life, that's all."

"He's being dramatic," she said quickly, handing Nash some wine. He caught her eye and gave her a look she couldn't interpret. She bent down to get a glass for Crosby.

"Yes, I am a known drama queen," Trevor said. "But that doesn't make it untrue. I was a miserable teenager when my parents moved us to Misty Harbor. I had no friends. We came from the city, and there I could just blend in. Here I kind of stood out, no matter how invisible I wanted to be."

Mimi handed Crosby the wine, who took it absently. He seemed to be riveted by Trevor's story.

"I started going to the library after school, because I knew if I was home alone all afternoon I'd start heading into a dark direction and Mimi noticed me and gave me a volunteer job and I got to be friends with some of the other volunteers and then all of a sudden I was still a miserable teenager, but a miserable teenager with friends. And this tiny town grew on me." He smiled at her, toothily, and Mimi smiled back, touched by his account of their meeting.

She'd been doing her job, but that's why she loved it. She could change people's lives, usually in small ways, but once in a while in a big one.

"Misty Harbor is very charming," Nash said, "and Mimi is a lifesaver. That's a great story, Trevor."

"Remarkable," Crosby murmured.

"How did the table read go?" Mimi asked to change the subject. She didn't like the spotlight being on her for very long.

"Better than expected," Nash said, while Crosby answered, "Decent."

"That sounds good," Mimi said. "Was Jay all right?"

"Your brother is knocking it out of the park. He's

twice as prepared as anyone else. Practically off book." Nash sounded proud.

"Going to make us all look bad," Crosby said mildly.

High praise, indeed. "Well, the pizza should be here any second. I thought we could just eat here." She gestured to the couch as the doorbell rang. She thanked the delivery guy and took the box to the kitchen.

Nash said, "I'll help," and crowded into the room behind her.

Before she could start serving, he had his hands on her waist and was spinning her around to give her a smacking kiss on the lips. "Missed you today," he said on a low growl.

She let herself enjoy the rush of being kissed by a handsome man in her own kitchen. "Missed you, too," she said honestly. "Sorry about Trevor."

"He seems like a good kid."

"He's twenty-two, but yes. He's been wanting to meet you. Apparently, you're a bisexual icon or something."

"Oh." Nash's smile dimmed. "Okay. Thanks for the warning." He stepped away from her.

"What?"

"Nothing. I'll just tone down the PDA."

"Why?" Mimi didn't point out that so far there had been no PDA, as they were currently out of sight of the other two.

"Nothing, I just don't want to—I don't know. People have this idea about me in their heads, and I don't—"

"Hey, there's no pressure. Trevor knows you're a real person. You don't have to be this perfect avatar."

"Yeah. No. Right." Nash sighed. "Sorry. Do you want help with the pizza?"

"I want you to kiss me again," she said. "And then I want help with the pizza."

He obliged her, with a chaste kiss that was somehow still deeply arousing. They threw some pizza and the baby spinach on four plates and went out to the living room, where Crosby was sitting on the couch while Trevor sat on the floor on the other side of the coffee table.

"I like your—" Crosby motioned to his cheeks. "What's it called?"

"Nars Orgasm," Trevor said flirtatiously. "It's the only blush I wear."

Crosby's cheeks were slightly pink as well by this point. Maybe it was the wine. Mimi internally shrugged. At least they were getting along. "Okay, dig in, everyone. Oh, I'll grab some salad dressing."

When she came back out, Nash was sitting next to Crosby, leaving the ell of the couch for her. "This pizza is great."

"Told you Antonio's is better than Harbor Pizza."

Crosby elbowed Nash in the side. "Your girlfriend *is* wicked smart. You always used to rave about Harbor Pizza, but I always said Antonio's was better. Thinner crust."

"Girlfriend?" Trevor said, eyes popping like an anime character. "What's he talking about?" He turned to Mimi, who froze mid-bite. She looked at Nash.

"Uh," Nash said. "Um."

"What?" Crosby said, sounding honestly confused. "Nash said you were his girlfriend. Did I get it wrong?"

What the hell? Nash told Crosby she was his *girlfriend*?

Trevor looked between the two of them, a smile growing wide on his face. "OMG, you guys are together? How did I not know this? Mimi, you're too fucking discreet. I wouldn't have told anyone. I mean, I won't tell anyone, if you don't want me to."

"It's not a secret," Nash said tightly. "Is it?" This last to Mimi.

She swallowed with difficulty. Why was *he* being weird when he'd called her his girlfriend without checking with her first? Now she was the jerk for being caught off guard by the G-word.

"Nash and I are...dating," she said, drawing out the last word, as if she wasn't sure that was the term she wanted to use.

"Wow. You really are straight, aren't you?" Trevor said, his earlier enthusiasm dulled.

Crosby coughed on his sip of wine.

Nash nodded gravely. "Yeah, afraid so."

"It's okay. You can't help it," Trevor said philosophically. "So, what's with all the fundraising for Rainbow Canyon and signal boosting queer PSAs and stuff? Mimi said you were a good ally, but that's a lot."

Nash shifted in his seat. She felt a little bit bad he was on the spot, but she was still reeling from being called his girlfriend against her will.

Before she could jump in and change the subject,

Nash set his plate down on the coffee table and said, "I got a lot of kudos for playing Will O'Connell, gay teen role model extraordinaire. People looked up to him."

Trevor nodded enthusiastically. "He's the best. The opposite of a disaster gay, but still believably queer." He smirked. "And hot."

Crosby rolled his eyes. He might have been shy, but he clearly still had an ego. Nash just grimaced. Mimi's pizza was forgotten as she soaked up the fascinating exchange.

"I've always felt uncomfortable taking any credit for Will. Ryan Saylor invented him, wrote his lines, and I just played him the best I could." He scrubbed a hand over his face. "But then I'd get letters, and messages, and in interviews people would tell me how much Will meant to them, how it pushed them to do things in their own lives they were scared to do. And they wanted to thank *me*. I really didn't know what to do with that early on. It made me uncomfortable, feeling like some kid somewhere was depending on me for something I had no personal experience with."

He sighed. "Once the show was over, I felt like I'd gotten away with something. Some people were like 'you were so brave to play a gay character'—it didn't seem all that brave to me, since I didn't have any pushback in my own life. I didn't experience any backlash. I've always felt any praise sent my way was undeserved."

"That's why you donate so much—you're assuaging your heterosexual guilt?" Crosby's voice wasn't judgmental, but there was a thread of something in it Mimi couldn't read.

"Yeah. Doesn't money solve everything?" He smiled wryly.

Mimi felt her heart melt like the cheese on Antonio's pizza. The charity album, the endless fundraisers. He funneled all that money toward people who needed it a hell of a lot more than he did. Nash's privilege enabled him to help people, yet he only saw himself as a burden to the community that had embraced him.

"It helps," she answered, even though she knew his question was rhetorical.

Crosby just shook his head, as if Nash was a mystery he wasn't going to attempt to solve.

Trevor had been watching Nash avidly, his bright eyes trained on the actor's face. "I think you've helped a lot of people, unintentionally or not, and it doesn't matter who you like to fuck, Nash, you still get credit for being a good person."

Mimi had never heard Trevor sound that serious before. She'd always thought of him as young; he was a lot younger than her, after all. But she realized he'd grown up into an adult with passions and convictions, and she felt good knowing she'd been a small part of helping him on his journey, just like Mr. Russell had helped her. Just like Nash was helping kids and young adults by funding programs they needed. Trevor was right, Nash was a good person.

She smiled at her friend, then turned to Nash. He looked gobsmacked.

"Thanks, Trevor," he said gruffly.

"You know how sometimes you meet your idols and wish you hadn't?" Trevor said suddenly. He didn't wait for anyone to answer before he added, "You guys are super cool. And I'm proud Misty Harbor is the home of *Sawyer's Cove*."

"Me, too," Mimi said. It was arguably a frivolous teen show, but it meant a lot to a lot of people, and that mattered.

Crosby cleared his throat and looked at Trevor. "The fans are who really kept it going all these years. So, thanks."

Trevor beamed.

Mimi let out a breath. "Well, that was surprisingly emotional for pizza night."

"How about dessert?" Nash said. He lifted his eyebrows at Mimi. She immediately flashed back to last night, when she'd been dessert, and her cheeks grew warm.

Trevor glanced between them. "Okay, let's leave the hets alone. Crosby, you want to go grab some ice cream?"

Mimi was about to protest on Crosby's behalf, but he surprised her by getting up from the couch. "Sure. Is the ice cream place on Spring still there?"

"Nope. But Zelda makes her own, including a watermelon chocolate chip that'll change your life, and I've got keys to the Bakeshop."

"I have a lot of questions, but I'm game," Crosby said. "Thanks for dinner, Mimi. Hope we can hang out again sometime."

Mystified by why Crosby would volunteer to hang out with Trevor, she just nodded. "Sounds great."

Trevor hopped up and gave her a peck on the cheek as he left. "Have fun," he sing-songed. "Nash, I'm sure I'll be seeing a lot more of you. By the way, if you ever hurt Mimi here, I'm officially revoking your friend-to-gays card."

"Understood," Nash said, cringe-smiling.

Suddenly, they were down to two, the remains of dinner scattered around. She started clearing up the plates. "I'm not sure what was going on there, but I guess they're good?" she asked Nash.

"Don't think about it too hard, honey," he said.

She walked past him toward the kitchen, but he caught her arm as she passed. "Do we need to talk about this?"

"Talk about what?"

"About how hearing the word 'girlfriend' made you look like you wanted to throw up?"

Chapter Twenty-Four

Pick up the phone, don't wanna
    text.
Your voice in my ear makes me
    forget all the rest.
It's no damn use. Our signals are
    crossed.
You hung up on me, but I'm still
    hung up on us.

— "Hung Up," The Nash
Speedwell Experience

Mimi's face blanched, and Nash's heart sank. He had the feeling he'd messed up somewhere along the way, and even though Mimi had confirmed they were dating, her lack of enthusiasm for the label he'd accidentally brought to the conversation still made him uneasy. What if he'd read her wrong and this was still just a glorified fling for her? What if she wasn't falling for him the way he'd been falling for her for the last eight years?

"Let me put the pizza away," she said quietly. "Then we'll talk."

He followed her to the kitchen, helping her put the leftovers into containers and her fridge. It was small, like everything about this place. He always felt a little like an ogre stomping around in a fairy's cottage when he came over. Mimi claimed to like the efficiency—less to clean, perfect size for one. Which was part of the issue, wasn't it? She'd built her life single-sized, and here he was, knocking into everything, disrupting her carefully constructed world.

But he wasn't sorry. His life was a series of temporary camps. Hers had been set in stone for years. They both needed to break out of their comfort zones.

She wiped off the countertop, straightened the dish towel hanging from the oven door handle. Apparently finished stalling, she said, "So, I'm your girlfriend?" in a carefully neutral tone.

Of course she'd get right to the point.

"That's how this feels to me," he said. "You admitted we're dating. And we already talked about being exclusive."

He paused, and she filled in the silence.

"You make it sound like I'm ashamed of us."

"Are you?" He needed to make sure.

"Of course not," she answered quickly. "Though I kind of wish we'd talked about the labels thing first."

"We're talking about it now."

She turned away and opened her freezer. "All that talk about ice cream," she said, bringing out a pint of rocky road and opening the lid. "You want some?"

He let out a sigh of frustration. Talking about relationship stuff with her wasn't easy. "Mimi, come on. Crosby asked if I wanted to have dinner with him, but you and I already had plans, so when I explained, it just came out."

"So you didn't mean it?"

"I did mean it. Are you pissed?"

She pulled a spoon out of a drawer. "I'm not mad… it's just that I've never been someone's girlfriend before. It feels weird."

"Weird how?"

"I built my identity around being single. And to suddenly be in a couple—I feel like a fraud. Like I'm not myself anymore."

He considered that. "I had the great fortune of getting to know the single and proud Mimi. And even though I know you even better now, I know you're the same person. I don't want you to change just because I want us to sleep in the same bed."

She took a bowl out and spooned some ice cream into it. "I know you don't want to change me. I don't want to change you. But don't you think we're different people just by being together?"

"I like who I am with you," Nash said. He held his breath. Did she feel the same way?

She put away the ice cream. Was it him, or did she slam the freezer door a little hard?

Mimi wasn't looking at him, and he experienced a moment of unsteadiness, like everything they'd built was about to come crashing down.

This was it. She was going to end things, and he knew with complete certainty he didn't want that.

She then went back to her silverware drawer, pulled out a second spoon, and put it in the dish next to the other one. She took a bite with the first spoon, nudged the second toward him.

He let out a slow breath, then picked up the spoon. The ice cream was cold and rich and tasted like hope.

"You know, we don't have to use 'girlfriend' and 'boyfriend' if that's squicky for you."

"How do you know the word 'squicky?'" she asked around a mouthful of ice cream.

"That's not important. We can define things for ourselves. And all that matters to me is that we're a couple now. You're the person I'm dating, and the person I'm fucking, and the person I'm starting to make plans with. The person I have a lot of feelings for." He forced himself to stop. Was that already saying too much?

"So I'm your person?" she asked tentatively.

"Exactly. And I'm yours." He set down his spoon and took her hand. "If you want me."

She dropped her spoon with a clatter in the now-empty dish and took his other hand with hers so they formed a circle of two.

"Wanting you isn't the problem, Nash. I'm scared to need you. I'm scared to lose myself."

"I won't let you get lost, Mimi. Being with you makes me feel more 'me' than when I'm with anyone else."

She kissed him, her lips cold, her tongue sweet.

He kissed her back so hard, they bumped into her kitchen counter. They'd already had sex on this kitchen floor once; it had been hot. And cramped.

He didn't want cramped. He wanted to spread her out, to unfurl her limbs and screw himself inside her so far, she'd feel him for days. He wanted to leave a piece of himself behind, so she knew even when she was alone, he always wanted to be with her.

"Want you, Nash."

"I want you in a bed."

"You going to sleep over?"

"Yeah." He grinned. "I want to sleep over in my person's bed."

She wrinkled her nose. "It's not very romantic," she said. "'My person.' Maybe we can think of something else."

He picked up her hand, and they went back through the living room to the tiny hallway that led to the only bedroom. "I could be your gentleman friend."

"Too fancy."

"Companion?"

"Too bloodless."

Her room was small, too, but it had a big enough bed. It was covered neatly in the same patchwork quilt it had been made with since he'd first started coming over years ago. The same photo of her and Deb and Jay at Jay's high school graduation sat on the dresser, the ubiquitous stack of books covering the nightstand. One new thing caught his eye—a cobalt blue gown in some wispy material hung on a hanger over her closet door.

He was too distracted by her immediately pulling her shirt up and over her head to ask what the dress was for.

"Lover?" she suggested as she removed her bra and tossed it onto a chair.

It was his turn to make a face. "Too hip."

She slid out of her pants, crawled onto the bed on all fours, facing away from him. Her firm, round ass was on display in a pair of practical black panties. His cock swelled, and he got started on getting naked.

"Well, we'll keep workshopping it," she said, glancing at him over her shoulder. "Now why don't you get back there and fuck me so hard, I can't remember the Dewey Decimal System."

"God, librarians are so hot," he groaned, peeling off the rest of his clothes in a hurry. His dick hung thick and heavy between his legs. He draped himself over her body and rubbed, the skin-on-skin contact bringing him to full hardness.

Dropping kisses on the creamy skin of her back, he found his favorite mole on her right shoulder blade and felt it with his tongue. He rutted against her clothed ass, the barely-there fabric silky on his cock, a tantalizing barrier to him getting what he really wanted. He could smell her pussy, and when he reached around to finger her clit, the fabric was soaked.

She bucked into his hand, arched her back, and he strummed her clit hard and fast, like a guitar string. He ground his cock against her, and she was trapped there, between his dick and hand, pressure from both sides. She let out a sharp cry.

"Nash." She was breathing fast, and he knew he'd made her come.

Without waiting for her to come down, he pushed the fabric of her panties aside far enough to slide right into her. Fuck, she was wet, and she pushed herself back on him, taking him all the way. He waited a beat to let her adjust, then pulled almost entirely out and slammed back in to the hilt.

She screamed. "Yes, please, do that again."

He complied in a smooth slide of pure pleasure, his hand gripping her waist tight, pulling her back on him as he thrust forward, the sound of skin slapping on skin loud in the quiet room.

He vaguely registered his own grunts of exertion, her increasingly high-pitched moans. He wondered if her neighbors could hear them, then he figured they could have the vicarious thrill. She felt unbelievably good. He wanted to pump her full of come and then lick it out of her.

Fuck. He stilled mid-stroke when he realized what he'd done. He'd mindlessly mounted her without putting on a condom. It had seemed the most natural thing in the world to do, but he hadn't asked.

"Don't stop," she panted. "Come on, cowboy."

He pulled out all the way. "Shit. Mimi. I'm sorry. I—I wasn't thinking."

She twisted around, looking at him with concern. Her face was red, and her hair stuck up in every direction. She was so beautiful. And he'd majorly fucked up.

"What?" Her gaze dropped to his still-hard dick. His bare, still-hard dick. "Oh. Fuck."

"Yeah. I'm so sorry."

She pressed her lips together, and he made a move to climb off the bed, to give her some space, but she grabbed his arm.

"Wait. It's okay." She bit her lip. "I didn't remind you, and I didn't even—it's okay. You know I'm on birth control."

"Yeah, but…I don't do that. Ever."

"You can put one on now. Or—"

"Or?"

"Or it felt really fucking good. I don't mind if you don't."

He realized he trusted her, but even more, if the unexpected happened, he could see himself happy about the prospect of having a baby with his person.

With Mimi.

She turned all the way onto her back and guided him on top of her.

He caught her mouth in a kiss, hoping she could feel some of what was going on in his head. She wrapped her legs around him, and his cock found her entrance easily. Being inside her uncovered was like nothing he'd ever experienced. It felt like freedom—the freedom to be himself with the one person he wanted to know him the best.

He started slow, until they found their rhythm again. He came, deep and hard and unexpected while they kissed, and he swore he could feel himself empty out and then fill back up again with a deep well of euphoria. She felt incredible. He felt incredible. They were incredible together.

"God, Nash," she said, low and a bit bewildered.

He raised his head from where it had fallen onto her shoulder and looked at her, bleary-eyed. "Yeah. That was—"

"Incredible," she said.

"My thoughts exactly."

She kissed him, and he slowly pulled out of her. She sat up and reached for a box of tissues on the nightstand. "Sex without a condom is a lot messier."

They cleaned up haphazardly, brushed their teeth, then Nash crawled under the covers with her. He stroked her shoulder until she fell asleep. He did his best to ignore the sneaking suspicion that as good as things seemed to be, they might not be able to last.

Chapter Twenty-Five

Please join the Misty Harbor Library Board
For the Misty Harbor Library Annual Fundraiser
Dinner and Silent Auction
Honoring the Legacy of Arthur Russell
Saturday, September 24
6PM
Silent Auction
Live Music
Semi-formal Dress
Tickets Required

The Tuesday before the night of the fundraiser, Mimi was going over the guest list when she made a curious discovery. They'd sold out of tickets for the event a week earlier, and as she scrolled through the spreadsheet of the guests' names, she clocked nearly a dozen people who were directly involved with *Sawyer's Cove.*

Jay and Cami had bought tickets, naturally. But Ariel Tulip and Spencer Crosby were also listed. Not to mention showrunner Selena Echeveria, and several of the new cast members whose names she remembered from Nash talking about them. There was even a director's name on the list, and she thought a couple of the names she recognized were in the prop and costume departments. She was happy their temporary guests were supporting the library, but it was still a bit strange to see those two distinct worlds colliding.

Once filming had started, and Nash's schedule had gone from nine-to-five to sometimes early morning calls and days that stretched late into the night, she used her extra time to put in more hours on fundraiser prep. They still made a point of coming together as many nights as they could, sometimes at Mimi's apartment, more often at Nash's more spacious house. They'd spent nearly every night together for the past two weeks. It wasn't even a question at this point. They each had changes of clothes and toothbrushes at the other's place.

Mimi had somehow acquired a boyfriend, no matter how hard she tried to think of a term she liked better, and she had to admit, she'd never been happier. There was something comforting about going off to work in the morning to do her normal kick-ass librarian thing, knowing she was going to come home to a friendly, improbably handsome face, and a supportive ear. Someone who wanted to hold her and kiss her, someone who made her feel cherished.

But as she scanned the guest list again, and a third

time, looking for a name she didn't see, she had a sickening realization. She'd never specifically asked Nash to be her date to the fundraiser, and his name was a glaring omission.

She'd never brought a date to one of these evenings before. They were work functions, but they were also opportunities for the library staff to bring their partners and show off all their hard work. The board members were bringing their spouses. Fiona, the research librarian, would bring her husband, Mac. She hadn't met Olive, the children's librarian Delia's wife, but she'd been told they'd get along because they both loved British procedural crime shows.

The night was about raising money and schmoozing with the donors, but it was also about celebrating the library. She realized with a pang she wanted Nash by her side, helping her enjoy the fruits of all her hard work.

And she'd gone and messed it up. She hadn't asked him to be there—she'd just assumed. She knew how well assumptions worked in relationships—she'd berated her brother once or twice over the same bad idea.

Letting out a little yelp, she checked the time. She was supposed to meet Jay for lunch at the Bakeshop in five minutes. Before filming started, they saw each other almost every day, between The Cove, the library, and just randomly bumping into each other around town. But with his schedule changing due to the show and all the time they were both spending with their significant others, she'd barely seen him in the last two weeks. She missed her brother.

She closed her laptop and ran down the street to Misty Harbor Bakeshop. She hadn't seen much of Trevor, either, since the weird night they all had pizza at her place, and she was disappointed to see he wasn't behind the counter today.

Jay was already in line, looking at his phone, but put it away when he spotted her. She gave him a breathless hug, and they ordered quickly. They usually sat inside near the window, but Mimi pulled Jay out back to the more private patio, choosing an empty table near the back fence.

"I have a problem," she said nervously.

"I can see that. You have the groove of despair." He reached out to smooth the dented skin between her eyebrows. "What's wrong, Mimi?"

"I forgot to ask Nash to be my date to the fundraiser. Everyone else bought a ticket except him, and I think I was probably supposed to ask, but I never claimed to be good at this relationship stuff, and I'm weirdly freaking out about it."

Jay's laugh was admirably restrained. He tried turning it into a cough, but she just rolled her eyes.

"Look, I know this is hilarious to you. Your big sister felled by—" She stopped short. She'd been about to say love. But that was another thing they hadn't talked about. She had a feeling the giant wave of positive-skewing emotions she experienced whenever she was around Nash, or thinking about him, belonged some-where in the vicinity of love, but again, everything was new to her. How did she know for sure? "The point is, what should I do?"

Jay schooled his face into something resembling brotherly concern. "I'm honored you'd ask."

"Well, you are, apparently, in a committed long-term relationship," Mimi grumbled. "You may recall I helped you pull your head out of your ass and get Cami back after you dumped her for some absolutely made-up reason."

It was a testament to how revoltingly happy Jay was to be with Cami that he didn't even snark at her. "And I'll always be grateful. Though I probably would have figured it out on my own eventually."

"So, help *me!*" she wailed.

"You're being too hard on yourself, Mimi. Nash doesn't expect perfection. He likes you the way you are."

"True."

"And if you want him to be your date, then yeah, I think you should ask him."

"You make it sound so simple," she said, looking up at the server who'd appeared with her beet salad and Jay's BLT. Jay swirled some ketchup into the tiny cup of mayo on his plate, then stuck a French fry in the resulting pink goop.

Mimi shuddered and picked up her fork.

"Relationships aren't rocket science," Jay said. "But I feel like there's something else bothering you."

Mimi had been thinking about this on and off for weeks since she and Nash had first talked about it. She hadn't wanted to bring up bad memories for Deb by asking her, but she honestly wanted Jay's take. He was the only other person in the world who could possibly understand what she was ruminating about.

"Do you think the reason I've never had a long-term relationship before is because of the way my dad's family rejected me?"

"What?" Jay looked astonished.

"They didn't even want to meet me, so I suppose I shouldn't take it personally. They'd probably really like me if they met me. Or not. They're assholes. Nash said that. He's really kind of smart." She looked unhappily down at her plate, wishing she had an appetite.

"I never knew you felt that way," Jay said softly. "You're always so forward-looking, you never get bogged down by the past. I didn't know it was bothering you."

"It doesn't bother me, most of the time. But I guess when you don't have a dad, daddy issues are hard to avoid." She looked at her brother. "How did you do it?"

He wrinkled his nose. "Who says I don't have daddy issues?"

"You don't seem to be bothered by it either," Mimi persisted.

"I'm not, most of the time." He smiled slightly.

She poked at her salad. "You know, I always wondered why you weren't more curious about your dad. I mean, you never thought about doing a DNA test or something to see if you could track him down?"

"It's complicated," Jay said. He caught her gaze with his, his brown eyes set in a face so different from hers. They didn't look related, but Mimi felt absurdly close to her brother in that moment.

He gave her a nod, as if he felt the same way, and went on. "I never felt like I was missing out. Some of my friends' dads growing up were so shitty, I could see I had it better than them. And Mom's awesome. You're pretty awesome, too."

She accepted the faint praise for what it was.

"And I guess when I was old enough for Mom to tell us what happened with your dad, I thought, you knew who your dad was, but you'd never get to know him. And I didn't think it was fair of me to find out about my dad when I knew you'd never be able to."

Mimi's breath caught, and she involuntarily let out an embarrassingly sob-like noise. "Oh, Jay...really?" That was the sweetest thing her brother, a known softie, had ever said to her.

"Yeah. It's their loss. You're the coolest, smartest, kindest, most badass librarian and person Misty Harbor has ever had the honor of claiming as one of its own. I feel sorry for them that they'll never get to know how incredible their granddaughter is."

She was undeniably crying now, that humiliating combination of sniffles and hiccups usually reserved for movies about animals finding their way home against inconceivable odds and books where the heroine dies at the end.

"Thanks, bro," she said, trying to toughen up through her tears.

He scooted his chair around their small metal table, pulled her in, and tucked her head to his shoulder. He kissed the top of her curly head.

"Nash is pretty smart. Because he knew he'd never find anyone else like you, and he made a move—despite your status as sister to his best friend. Guy's got some steel balls."

She laughed and hiccupped and used her brown paper napkin for a tissue. "You don't think this is going to end horribly, then?"

He thought for a minute, then sighed. "I can't see into the future, Mimi. But I can picture the two of you happy together down the road if both of you can be flexible about how you get what you need."

"What do you mean?"

"Look, you've probably had your fill of relationship advice from me, but I think I've learned a couple things. One being that compromise only works if you understand why you're making the compromise. Cami and I are happy in Misty Harbor right now, but we can't assume that's the way it's always going to be. But we know if we make a change, we're going to decide on it together."

Mimi's heart twisted thinking about Jay possibly moving away. She was selfish—she liked having her family nearby. But he was right. They had to be okay with change.

"You and Nash have different lives. So when you make compromises, you need to be realistic. You can't do your librarian thing from Bulgaria. He can't shoot all his projects in Misty Harbor. You'll both have to adjust if you don't want to be a victim of Hollywood-relationship-disease."

"That sounds like a lot of work," Mimi said doubtfully.

"Good thing you aren't afraid of hard work," Jay said, elbowing her lightly in the side.

She lifted her head and looked at her brother, her handsome, kind little brother who'd always been there for her. She may not have had a dad, but Jay had never let her face something hard alone if she asked for his help, and that knowledge gave her strength.

She might feel strong, but now she knew her problems were much bigger than not knowing basic relationship stuff. When the *Sawyer's Cove* shoot ended, Nash would be off to the next project, and it might be months before he found his way back to Misty Harbor. How was she supposed to be his girlfriend from across the globe?

Still, he was here now. And she wanted him by her side at the fundraiser, and for as long as she could have him. She'd try to take Jay's advice to heart and not stress about what would happen after the music stopped.

Jay sneaked a hand over and snagged a beet from her plate.

"Hey!" She sat all the way up and put a protective hand over her food.

"What? You weren't eating it," Jay said, brazenly sticking the beet in his mouth.

"I wasn't hungry. But I am now." She took a huge bite of her salad to prove it. God, little brothers were so annoying sometimes.

Jay grinned with beet-stained teeth. "Happy to help."

Chapter Twenty-Six

I'm hung up on you, but you hung
   up on me.
Maybe I'll find a better connection
   with the next girl I see.
It's no damn use. Our signals are
   crossed.
You hung up on me, but I'm still
   hung up on us.

— "Hung Up," The Nash
Speedwell Experience

It was after dark when she drove up to Nash's rental house by the beach. Nearly October now, the days were getting shorter and shorter. His truck was in the driveway, and the downstairs lights were on. She parked behind him, took her time getting to the door. She'd rehearsed what she wanted to say, and the preparation made her self-conscious. She'd never really enjoyed public speaking and gladly left all the acting in the family to Jay. But she wanted to get this right.

She let herself in with the key he'd given her a couple of weeks ago, kicked off her shoes just inside the door, then called out a hello.

Nash appeared at the entrance to the kitchen, wearing an unbuttoned blue overshirt with a white T-shirt underneath, and dark blue jeans. He was barefoot, too. The man looked like a walking cologne ad, his carefully curated stubble making her want to nibble his strong chin. The producers had decided a few weeks ago that Will would have lawyer-appropriate, neatly trimmed hair for the season, but with too-busy-to-shave stubble to soften the look. Whatever the reason, he looked amazing.

It was kind of unreal the person she came home to at night was on thousands of people's screens on a daily basis. But she was the only one who got to greet him with a kiss on the mouth.

"Hey."

"Hey," he said, voice warm with pleasure.

"Long day?"

"Not too bad. You want a drink?"

"Beer?"

"Sure. You ate?"

"Had a burrito. You?"

"Ate on set."

He got her a beer, and they settled onto the couch, Nash reaching over to swing her legs up onto his lap. He liked stroking her legs while they talked, and Mimi wasn't about to complain. Still, the entire scene was so domestic, it made her nerves kick up again.

"There's something I need to talk to you about," she said.

"Shoot."

"The fundraiser is finally being held this Saturday."

He raised his own beer toward her, as if in a toast. "Congratulations."

"And I probably should have asked you before, and maybe you have other plans already, but I was wondering if you'd go with me. As my date."

He reached over her to set his bottle on the coffee table. She couldn't read his expression.

"Are you sure? I know it's a big work night for you. You might not need me to distract you."

"I know I don't need you there." She took a deep breath. "But I want you there."

His grin broke slowly but brilliantly, like the sun through dense storm clouds. "That's all I need to hear, honey. I'll be there."

"Thanks."

"Of course."

They sat in silence for a moment. She'd gotten what she wanted, and painlessly, too. She debated keeping her mouth shut about it, then figured it would bug her if she didn't bring it up.

"And I want to apologize for not asking you earlier. It wasn't an intentional oversight."

"It's okay," he said, laid-back as anything. "I figured if you wanted me there, you'd ask. It's your call."

"Okay, thanks." She let out a relieved sigh and snuggled back against the couch cushions, her legs warm where they crossed his lap. Now all she had to do was make it until the weekend, make sure her Ts were crossed and Is dotted and everyone who came to the fundraiser had the time of their lives. Easy peasy.

"There's something I want to talk about with you, too."

"Go for it," she said, feeling lethargic in the comedown from her emotional freak-out that had ended so anticlimactically. Nash was touching her gently, and the couch was comfortable, and the beer was making her sleepy. Her eyes half-closed.

"I got a call from Mary-Anne today." His thumbs kneaded her ankles.

She opened her eyes. "Your agent?"

"Yep. I got offered a part."

"A new show?"

"No, a movie. Six of them, actually. They want me to be Moonshot in a brand new series based on the comic books."

"Oh, my God. That's huge." She wasn't the biggest comics fan, but even she knew movies based on those were bigger than almost anything else out there. "Congratulations!"

"Yeah. Uh. Thanks." He swung her legs down and turned to her more fully. His expression was tentative, a look she hadn't seen on him very often. "I'm not sure I want to do it, honestly."

"What? Why?"

"Well, for one thing, it's a huge time commitment. Six movies in six to eight years, and that's just an estimate. I'd basically be playing the same character for the better part of a decade. And with pickups and ADR and press, I probably wouldn't have time to do anything else."

"What about *Sawyer's Cove*?" She had heard from Jay the studio was happy with the dailies they'd seen from the first few weeks of shooting. They'd already completed principal photography on three of the ten episodes; those three were being cut together in Los Angeles, where all the post-production was happening.

"Probably couldn't do another season of it. They want to start pre-production on the next movie in the new year. I'll have press when the final season of *Hawk and Bone* comes out, so they said they could work around that, but that's about it for time off."

"Wow. That is a big commitment." Six to eight years of his life, spoken for in the blink of an eye. "Where do they shoot?"

"There would be some location work, but mostly at their facility in North Carolina. I'd probably have to get a place down there. But there would be chunks of down time."

"Hmmm." North Carolina didn't sound very far away, but Misty Harbor wasn't exactly next door to an airport.

"So, what do you think?" Nash asked hesitantly.

"What do I think? I think it sounds like they found the perfect Moonshot." She was happy for him. She really was. The hot feeling behind her eyes was just because she was tired, not because she felt like crying at having the end of their relationship thrust into her face.

"You think I should do it?" He sounded...disappointed?

"I don't think I get a vote," she said quickly. "This is something you need to work out with your agent and management or whatever. If it's a role you want, I think you'd be amazing at it."

"Thanks for the vote of confidence, Mimi, but I'm not asking if you think I'd be good. I'm asking if you think it's the right thing to do."

She blinked rapidly, took a sip of her beer to buy time. "What do *you* want?"

He opened his mouth as if to say something, then sighed and stood up, leaving her alone on the couch. "I don't know, honestly. The people seem good. I know I could play the role. The money is unreal. I could retire when it was over and be more than comfortable for the rest of my life, even after making sure Rainbow Canyon gets its share. It would be crazy to turn it down."

"Then it sounds like your mind is made up," she said, willing her voice to stay even.

"If it was purely a business decision, I would have already said yes," he returned. "But you know that's not what I'm asking."

"I don't know what you want me to say." She stood up so he didn't have as much of a height advantage. "It's your career. Your life."

He just stared at her. She sensed she was failing at whatever test he'd set out for her, but she refused to be the woman who asked her boyfriend to give up a huge opportunity just to stay with her in Misty Harbor. Jay hadn't been able to bring himself to do that with Cami, and for the first time she truly understood where he'd been coming from. How could their relationship survive that kind of burden, that kind of pressure?

She tried to remember what Jay had said about compromise and flexibility, but all she could think was, if Nash left Misty Harbor—left her—because of this, it would be because he couldn't say no to this opportunity, and not because he got tired of her or she sucked too hard at relationships, or that he simply didn't want to be in her life anymore. She'd survived perfectly well before with her mom, brother, friends, and one-night stands. She could do it again. She would do it again.

"I guess I thought maybe you'd have more of an opinion," he said slowly.

"You said it yourself, it would be crazy to turn it down." She forced herself to hold eye contact with him while she said the words.

"Okay. Thanks. I guess." He frowned.

She bristled. What was she supposed to do? Ask him to give up a multi-million-dollar opportunity? Beg him to give up his career and stay in this tiny town? She supposed they could do long distance, but that seemed like simply another way for their relationship to do a slow slide into oblivion.

"Look, I'm tired. I think I better just head home." She didn't know what he wanted from her, and, sadly, it didn't feel like sex would solve this problem.

"If you're tired, you shouldn't be driving. Just stay here."

"Yeah, I don't think so." She went to the kitchen and dumped the rest of her beer down the drain, then set the bottle in the recycling bin.

"Then let me drive you," he said.

"Why?"

"Because I worry about you on the road at night."

"You don't need to worry about me. I've been driving at night for longer than you have," she said, with a touch of acid in her voice. "I'm going to go home and sleep in my own bed. By myself," she added, as if that part wasn't obvious enough. She really was tired, and cranky, and she wanted to start this conversation all over again, but somehow as a different person who knew how to navigate choppy relationship waters.

"I get it. You need space." Nash put his hands up and stepped back, as if literally giving her breathing room. Somehow, the gesture only inflamed her more.

"I don't need space. I want space," she spit out, aware she sounded childish, and maybe a little unreasonable. "Thanks for the beer." She grabbed her bag and headed for the front door.

"Will I see you tomorrow?" Nash asked.

"I don't know. I have a lot of last-minute stuff to do for the fundraiser," she said, though she knew her evening would probably be free.

"I work nights Thursday and Friday."

"So then...I guess I'll see you Saturday," she said.

"At the fundraiser," he confirmed. "Should I pick you up?"

"I'll have to be there early," she said. "Better that we meet there."

"All right."

She hesitated, her grouchiness draining away in the face of their rational conversation. But she was still tired and confused, and it wasn't fair Nash was just cool with everything while she had a mini-meltdown about this stuff every week.

"Goodnight," she said awkwardly, steps away from the front door. She wondered if he'd come and give her a goodnight kiss. She wanted it, wanted the reassurance that no matter how crummy she was at this, he'd be there to catch her, to make it all better.

But he just said, "Goodnight, Mimi," with none of his usual swagger.

Her heart felt heavy as she walked to her car, and her feet dragged, as if her body wanted to overrule her brain and force her to turn around, run back to him, and throw herself in his arms.

She sat in her car for a moment as the engine warmed up unnecessarily. A few days apart would be good for them. They each needed perspective. He needed to decide what to do about the part, and she needed to remind herself that she'd be able to learn to live alone again once he left to take it.

Without further hesitation, she pulled out of his driveway and headed for her own apartment, and her life built for one.

Chapter Twenty-Seven

Misty Harbor Library Fundraiser
Silent Auction Lot #42
Spend a day on the set of *Sawyer's Cove*
Be an extra in the upcoming revival of the cult
favorite television show being filmed right here in
Misty Harbor!
Bidding starts at $500

Saturday afternoon, Mimi walked into the room off the main ballroom in the inn where the silent auction was being held. Delia and a volunteer were walking around, finalizing the auction items. She was shocked at the sheer number of lots, many of them one-of-a-kind memorabilia.

Not only had Jay and Cami come through with what they'd promised, they'd also gotten other members of the production to put in signed photos, scripts, and other collectibles. Nash had dropped off a box set of the first three seasons of *Hawk and Bone*, signed by the major cast members. Since Mimi knew they were all international actors who probably had super busy lives, she had no idea how he'd gotten all of them to sign the same thing. It must have cost him a fortune in postage.

"Shouldn't you be at home getting ready?" Delia asked, tsking her. "This party needs its hostess." The petite children's librarian looked chic in an amethyst cocktail dress.

"I'm about to go home and get dolled up," Mimi promised. She pulled out her phone to check the time and saw she had a voicemail. How had she missed a call? She'd been glued to her phone all day as she coordinated the caterers, the rentals, the PA system. Speaking of which, her band was already supposed to be here to do a sound check.

Her mom strode into the conference room just as she hit the button to listen to her voicemail. Deb marched over, lovely in a silvery blue sheath. "Don't you need to get ready?" she asked, tapping her wrist in a mom gesture for *get a move on.*

Mimi held up a finger as she listened to the message. "Oh, no."

"What?"

"This is not happening right now." She groaned and shut her eyes, trying to figure out what to do.

"What's going on?" Deb asked again. "Bad news?"

"The band isn't coming. They ate some bad shrimp and are puking their guts out."

"Gross." Deb put her hand on her stomach. "Well, what about a local band?"

"It's such short notice. I don't even know where to start." Dammit, everything had been going smoothly, the party timeline unfolding just as she'd planned for weeks. Being an over-organized person had its drawbacks sometimes, but today all her hard work had been paying off. She'd been relatively unstressed, knowing every element of the evening had been planned and checked and double-checked. But she hadn't planned for this.

Deb pulled out her phone. "Let me help. I'll call your brother."

"What could he do?"

"He's got the contact info for the acts that have played The Cove, right? He can start contacting people while you get ready." Her mother dialed before Mimi could even react. "You can't show up in jeans and clogs," she said.

Mimi experienced the lurching feeling of having something important snatched away from her, but she did feel better knowing her mom was on top of this. And while Jay was probably busy getting ready for the event himself, if he could help, he would.

"All right," she said, reluctantly ceding control. "I'll go home and change. Let me know if you guys come up with anything. Worst case scenario, we can hook up someone's phone and stream a playlist. The band is mostly for entertainment between dinner and dessert."

"It's going to be fine," Deb said. "Now go."

Nash stood in front of his closet in trousers and an untucked dress shirt, considering the rest of his outfit for the fundraiser. Wanting to look good for Mimi's big night, he'd had his L.A.-based stylist send him a couple of options. He wished Chloe was there now to give him advice. Tie or no tie?

Even though they hadn't seen each other since Tuesday, he and Mimi had texted a few times. He wanted to chalk up her distance to the distraction of the fundraiser, but he'd been unsettled. Somewhere, they'd gotten their wires crossed, but he thought if they could talk, they'd straighten them out again.

He'd realized after Mimi left it hadn't been fair to ask her what she thought about the movie deal without giving her time to think about it. Of course her initial reaction would be supportive—she'd want what was best for him. Problem was, he didn't know what was best for him.

He knew what Mary-Anne and his management team would say: he was finally hitting the big time; if he took this role, he'd forever be associated with one of the most successful franchises in history. He'd be a household name.

He wasn't exactly longing to being more famous. He was already recognized nearly everywhere he went. Misty Harbor was a strange pocket of the world where everyone knew who he was, but it was an unspoken town pact not to draw attention to the very recognizable people they had in their midst. It was nice to have a chance to be himself and live a semi-normal life.

But it still hurt that Mimi hadn't once seemed to care that if he took this role, it would affect them, a lot. He understood intellectually she wouldn't tell him not to do it just for her. She'd never stand in his way if there was something he really wanted to do. But he still wanted her to care. He wanted her to *want* him to make a different decision.

Which was totally passive aggressive and unfair. But he still wanted it.

Fuck it. He grabbed a tie—he could start with it on and take it off later if it was that kind of party. He heard a car outside and frowned. It was too early for Jay to pick him up. He started down the stairs, picking up his pace when he heard urgent bangs on the door, accompanied by Jay yelling.

"Open up, Nash!"

The bellow had him thinking the worst. Was Mimi hurt? What was going on? He yanked open the door, heart racing. "What?"

"It's Mimi," Jay said, looking grim.

A hundred horrible possibilities flashed through his brain as his stomach suddenly acquired a painful knot. "What is it? Is she okay?"

"Oh, yeah, she's fine," Jay said, suddenly so relaxed, Nash wanted to murder him. He was on an emotional tightrope, and Jay was bouncing up and down on it.

"What the hell? Then what's wrong?"

"She needs help. The band canceled, and she has

three hundred people arriving at the inn in an hour to be wined and dined and entertained."

"Shit." Nash knew how important the live music was to Mimi. Even if none of the guests would complain if there was no entertainment, she'd promised them a show, and she'd feel terrible if she couldn't deliver. "What can we do?"

"I called a few local bands that have played at The Cove, but they're all booked for weddings and stuff. A couple haven't gotten back to me yet. It's such short notice." Jay's voice slowed. "I was thinking, and I know this is a big ask, but I was wondering if you'd consider doing something. Even a short acoustic set would be better than nothing."

"Me?" The idea was completely out of left field. "I'm not a professional musician."

"You're a damn good guitarist, and you know it. I could maybe track down an electric guitar, or I was thinking Jeff could help us set up a decent mic to pick up your acoustic guitar." Jeff was the sound guy on the show, and Nash was aware he'd be attending the fundraiser as a guest.

Nash hunched his shoulders as he thought it over. He'd vowed to himself he'd never be in this situation, but this wasn't him trading on his name to try to sell tickets. It was almost like a private show—he knew a lot of the people who were going to be at the event. They were his friends. They wouldn't boo or hiss. And Mimi needed this. She needed *him*, even if she didn't know it.

He pointed a shaky finger at his best friend. "You're going to talk me through the stage fright, okay?"

"Anything you need, buddy," Jay said.

"I'll do it."

"I thought you would."

"You did?"

"Men in love do whatever they have to."

Nash's stomach twisted into another, more complicated knot. He'd basically figured out he was in love with Mimi the first time they'd fucked and it hadn't felt like just sex. It had been making love, and it had felt incredible. But it still felt weird to have her brother toss the word out there.

"Is that okay with you?" he asked cautiously.

"I'm rooting for you two," Jay said with a shrug of his shoulders, as if it was nothing. But Nash saw through his nonchalance. He was giving them his blessing, which all three of them knew wasn't required but was very much appreciated.

"Thanks, man."

"You know, I never really cared that much about not having a dad, and Mimi's the best sister in the world, but I always wanted a brother," Jay said, looking down at his dress shoes.

"Really?" Nash had never been particularly close to his own brother, who was a stockbroker with two Weimaraners and golfed every Sunday. He wondered if he didn't invest more in their relationship because he'd had Jay since he was sixteen—someone who got him, who teased him, who supported him and challenged him and always had his back. "You've always been like my brother, Jay, since the first week of the show, when we got in trouble for eating the set decorations."

"How were we supposed to know those bananas were a prop?" Jay grinned.

"Love you, Jay."

Jay's eyes widened for a split second but then crinkled up again as his smile returned. "Love you, too, brother. Now go get your guitar."

Chapter Twenty-Eight

He was a cowboy poet, composing
on his pony, rhyming couplets
as he rode

> — "Stetson," The Nash
> Speedwell Experience

Found a musical act. Will take care of
everything. See you at the inn.

Mimi stared at her phone in disbelief. She wanted to feel relief that her brother had apparently fixed the problem, but the Mimi who'd been planning this event for months couldn't accept what he'd said at face value.

Who??

She waited for a reply, but she didn't even see any dots. Argh. She turned her attention back to the mirror. She was almost done with her makeup, which she rarely wore but knew how to apply, thanks to Deb's patient tutoring back in the day.

Her eyelashes were thickly black and accentuated by the tasteful blue shadow that matched the wide streak in her hair, which had morphed a few days ago from electric to cobalt blue to match her dress. Her hair had gotten long this summer, and her hair stylist had put a relaxer into it, so it was more wavy than curly tonight. Her high cheekbones were accented in blush. All she needed was the finishing touch of lipstick.

She carefully applied a classic carmine red and kissed a tissue before declaring herself finished. She picked up her purse, swore when she saw Jay still hadn't replied to her text, and headed for her car, careful not to damage her beautiful gown by slamming it in the door or catching it under her low-heeled shoes.

When she got to the inn's ballroom half an hour before the official start time, everything looked ready. The dozen-odd round tables were set, waiting for guests to arrive. Inn employees were filling water glasses and attending to last-minute details. There were security guards at every entrance to the ballroom to make sure only ticketed guests were admitted, and as another layer of protection for their more high-profile attendees.

In a few minutes, the place would be buzzing with people and activity, and she'd be too busy to eat any of the delicious food she'd ordered. She didn't have an appetite anyway.

Jay was on the stage, talking to someone she thought worked on *Sawyer's Cove*—Joe, or Jeff, maybe? He was setting up some mic stands in front of a chair on the stage.

Her heart sank. It didn't look like a band was getting set up. She'd promised everyone a *band*.

She was about to interrogate Jay when Nash walked onto the stage from the rear door, carrying his guitar. She was momentarily flummoxed by where he'd come from—he'd have had to been let into the back staging area by a hotel employee, or Jay, she supposed, who knew this place better than a lot of people who worked here.

What was he doing here so early? And why was he carrying his guitar? Was he lending it to someone to play?

He looked so handsome, she wanted to cry. Three days without seeing him had been stupidly hard. He was wearing a gray suit, white shirt, and, with a start, she realized his tie was the same shade as her dress. Coincidence? Somehow, she knew it wasn't. He wore shiny black cowboy boots, and he looked healthy and hale, his Will O'Connell stubble tidily groomed. He looked like one of those improbable thirty-year-old billionaire heroes on the covers of the romance novels she loved.

She was too far away to hear what he was saying when he leaned over to talk to the guy fiddling with the mics. He then sat down in the chair, plugged his guitar into an amp she noticed for the first time. He strummed a few chords and bent his head over the guitar. He mumbled something unintelligible into the mic, then cleared his throat and touched his ear. She edged farther into the ballroom until she was almost at the dance floor they'd set up in front of the stage when Mimi had expected folks to be eager to dance. Finally, he caught sight of her.

"Mimi." Nash's voice, loud over the speakers, echoed around the room. He managed to sound surprised, chagrined, and apologetic all at once with her two-syllable name.

"What's going on?" she asked, though she had a sneaking suspicion she knew what was going on. Only it didn't make sense. Nash never performed live. He just didn't do it, and it never would have occurred to her to ask him.

He shook his head at her—he couldn't hear her, so she crossed the dance floor and stopped next to Jay, who looked great, too, in a black suit and crisp white shirt. He whistled flamboyantly.

"You look amazing, sis." He opened his arms, and she gave him an obligatory hug.

"What's going on?" she said again.

"Your entertainment for the evening," Jay answered. "The Nash Speedwell Experience."

"Seriously?" She looked up at Nash, who gave her an awkwardly toothy smile.

"If you're okay with it," Nash said. The mic picked up the words, and they boomed across the ballroom.

Mimi winced. "Are you sure?"

"Your brother is very persuasive," Nash said, averting his mouth from the mic this time.

Mimi looked at said brother. She wondered what Jay had said, or what he'd blackmailed him with, to make this happen. "Oh, really?"

"Nash wanted to help," Jay said.

She could get the whole story later. For now, she needed to know Nash could pull this off. "What songs are you going to do?"

"Um…" Nash looked downright scared for a second. "Songs from the album?"

"Maybe you could write down a quick set list, Mimi," Jay suggested. "You know his album by heart, don't you?"

How did he know that? She shot him a look. "I guess I could do that."

"Thanks. We'll take care of the rest. Jeff's helping with sound. It's going to be great."

She wasn't completely convinced this wouldn't be a disaster, but Nash looked more worried than she felt, so she'd keep her qualms to herself. "Thanks for doing this, Nash. You're saving the day."

"Just like a superhero," Jay said casually.

Nash glared at Jay. Was that supposed to be a reference to the role he'd been offered? Had he decided to take it? Was this just the beginning of the end for them?

Mimi turned away before she could get too much in her head. She sat down at the nearest table and began typing out a set list on her phone. She thought about the album, about the songs she and Nash had talked about, listened to, the few he'd sung her. He went on with the sound check, played half of his song "Cranberry Girl," sounding pretty good, if a little high and nervous. She tried to ignore him, focus on the list. When she'd put together half a dozen songs she thought would both work acoustically and keep the crowd's energy up, she texted them to him.

People started to stream into the ballroom in groups of two and three. Nash set down his guitar in a stand that had materialized from somewhere, Jay plugged his phone into another cord, and soon a lively mix of pop classics was on rotation over the sound system.

Nash climbed down from the stage and gave her a kiss on the cheek. "You look wonderful," he murmured. He smelled like his expensive body wash. She wanted to wrap her arms around him, to take comfort in him, to wipe away the last few days of worry and loneliness and stress. But she had a job to do now, and she didn't know if they were in a place where she was allowed to take relief from him. If he was taking the job and leaving in a matter of weeks, wouldn't it be more painful to prolong the goodbye?

She kept her hands by her sides. "Thanks for being here," she said instead. "And thanks for stepping in."

"Thank me after," he said. "I might be flat and out of rhythm."

"You'll be great." He was an entertainer. And she'd heard him play. His fingers were magic, his voice was sex, and he knew how to perform a song so you felt like he was singing right to you. Everyone in the room was going to have a huge crush on him by the end of the night—if they didn't already.

"So, you want to mingle?" he said.

She saw a few members of the board of directors she needed to talk to. "Yeah. Wish me luck."

"Good luck," he said. But when she went to say hello, he stayed with her, walking next to her, patiently being introduced to the board members and their spouses, shaking hands and smiling politely and making small talk like a pro. He helped her segue out of one conversation to greet an important donor, who blushed and tittered at Nash. He took the attention in stride.

When they extricated themselves by telling the donor not to miss her chance to bid on the silent auction items, Mimi let out a sigh. "How are you so good at this?"

"After Hollywood schmoozing, this is a piece of cake," Nash said.

"Well, you're making me look good. Thanks."

"You don't need any help looking good, honey." There was no time to search his face to see if the heat she'd thought she'd heard in his words was reflected in his body language, because suddenly Spencer Crosby was right in front of them, flashy in a shiny suit with a metallic silver shirt.

"Crosby, thanks for coming," she said warmly.

"Wouldn't have missed it. And Nash wouldn't have let me," Crosby said in his mannered way.

Trevor came up right behind Crosby and tackled her with a giant hug. He was dressed to the nines in a slim black suit, black shirt, black tie, his hair pulled back into a neat queue, sheer lipstick, dramatic purple eyeshadow. He looked sophisticated, but he was still Trevor, quivering with enthusiasm.

"Mimi, you look gorgeous. The room is gorgeous. Your date is gorgeous. This is like prom for library nerds," Trevor said.

She laughed. "Thanks. You look gorgeous, too."

"Pauline!" Trevor waved madly to the world's foremost expert on Captain Zachariah Bragg. Pauline wore a satiny canary yellow A-line dress with matching heels. On her arm was Colin, in a baggy suit and sneakers, smiling from ear to ear. Pauline looked pretty happy herself, and everyone traded greetings, then Nash, Colin, and Crosby left to fetch beverages.

"Are we at Almack's, waiting for the proverbial lemonade?" Pauline wondered.

"I don't understand that reference, but my advice is to enjoy being waited on," Trevor said.

Mimi counted heads again. "Wait, you didn't come *with* Crosby, did you?"

"We're here together. As friends," Trevor said.

"Since when are you friends with Spencer Crosby?" Mimi asked.

"Since that night at your house. He's a sweet guy."

"Sweet?" Mimi had always thought Crosby was the best actor of the bunch, because he seemed nothing like the passionately clueless character he played on *Sawyer's Cove*. But she'd been wrong before.

"Well, awesome," she said brightly.

"And what about you? How are things going with Mr. Actor Guy?" Trevor said slyly.

"You two are clearly speaking again," Pauline noted.

Trevor's jaw dropped. "What? You were fighting? What about?"

"We weren't fighting. Exactly. And none of your business." She'd filled Pauline in on the bare bones of their disagreement. "We're okay. I don't want you guys to worry about me. This night is about celebrating all our hard work over the past year."

"And raising a lot of money," Pauline reminded her.

"True." In all the drama, Mimi had almost forgotten she was supposed to make some remarks to the crowd. Jay had volunteered a while back to emcee the event, and he was climbing onto the stage right on schedule to announce the opening of the dinner buffet.

As people made their way to the buffet lines, the noise level rose. Nash came back with a glass of bubbly for Mimi, which she drank without tasting. Colin handed Pauline a beer, and Crosby handed Trevor something dark in a lowball glass. Mimi and Pauline had earlier planned to split up so they could keep their eyes on everyone and make sure there were library employees scattered around if people had questions, so they broke up their small party and went their separate ways. Trevor and Crosby floated over to a group of *Sawyer's Cove*-affiliated people, including the showrunner herself.

"Hey."

Mimi dragged her eyes to Nash.

"Everything's going great. You can relax."

"I'll relax when it's over," Mimi responded.

But his words helped. She managed to eat some of the really yummy dips, and she got through her thank you speech without bungling it. She reminded everyone to get their bids in by the end of the musical performance, as they needed time to close the auction before the end of the event.

"And I want to announce a change to our program," Mimi said. "Alabaster Poppy, unfortunately, couldn't make it tonight, but a good friend of mine, and a good friend to not only the library, but to Misty Harbor itself, has graciously agreed to perform some songs from his album. Nash Speedwell will be performing for us in a few minutes."

A huge swell of applause and some cheering from the *Sawyer's Cove* tables overpowered her as she turned off the mic and sat down. Nash was smiling calmly, as if he did this every day, but when she brushed her hand over his, he grabbed on tightly.

"It's going to be great," she said under her breath. "We're an easy crowd. And your songs are beautiful."

"They are?" He sounded as if he genuinely didn't believe her.

"Of course, Nash. You write some of the most beautiful poetry I've ever heard."

"Poetry?"

"I'm a librarian. I've read a lot of words. I know what I'm talking about. You are a poet."

He laughed, rich and full, and even if he thought she

was making fun of him, he seemed slightly more relaxed than he did a moment before.

Then he sobered up. "What if I forget the words halfway through?"

"Then look at me, and I'll mouth them to you." She knew at that moment her pride was secondary to making him believe he could do this. "I know your entire album back to front and upside down."

"You do?"

"I do."

"You did pick all my favorites," he said, pulling out his phone and looking at the set list. "How did you know?"

"Those are my favorites, too." She brought his hand up to her mouth, kissed the back of it briefly. "You're going to be awesome."

Jay had been sitting at a different table. He came over now, clapped Nash reassuringly on the shoulder. "Ready to go, Champ?"

"Ready as I'll ever be," Nash said.

"Break a leg," Mimi said. "Does that expression work for music?"

"I hope so." He squeezed her hand hard, just once, then let it go. He climbed the stairs, and Jay and Jerry worked the sound system, helping Nash get set up. The buzz of conversation quieted as he tapped the microphone, and a hint of feedback screeched before subsiding.

Mimi held her breath as Nash started to sing.

Chapter Twenty-Nine

Pick up my glass, buy a stranger a
    drink.
Gonna drown my sorrows; damn
    jukebox on the blink.

> — "Stranger," The Nash
> Speedwell Experience

The only way he could get through the first shaky chords of "Stranger" was to keep his eyes half-closed so he could pretend he was sitting in his living room, totally alone. But once he started feeling the song and could tell his voice sounded all right over the speakers, he loosened up enough to lift his eyelids a tad. Mimi had suggested starting with an up-tempo song, one that immediately got people's feet tapping.

He saw them respond almost right away—they might not know the song, but they could appreciate the beat and semi-humorous lyrics about a lonely Hollywood star drowning his sorrows in a glass of whiskey in a Sunset Strip bar.

His eyes were completely open by the time he finished the song, and he took in the room in its entirety, the round tables filled with faces tilted toward him, some of them friends, some of them strangers. All of them seemed to be having a decent time.

He relaxed a fraction more when he spotted Jay at the edge of the stage, swaying along to the music and standing by to make sure all the tech stuff stayed in place. Jay had his back.

He wrapped up the first song, and the sound of the applause and whistles was overwhelming. The blood had been roaring too loud in his ears earlier when Mimi had announced him, but now he could fully appreciate the audience's reaction. He thought he heard someone yell, "Go, Nash!" When the clapping died down, he spoke into the mic.

"Thanks for having me here tonight." More applause. He grinned. This was kind of fun. He let a little more drawl slip through his voice. He loved the old country performers, how they told stories through their songs, and how they portrayed a world-weary effortlessness. He relaxed his posture, wished he had his cowboy hat. Maybe next time.

Wait.

"You sure are a beautiful crowd," he told the audience, trying to stay in the moment. "We're here tonight to raise money for a place close to all our hearts."

He found Mimi's face in the crowd. She was smiling so hard, it looked like it might hurt. He realized with a rush he was making her proud, and it felt better than cutting an enormous check to Rainbow Canyon, or writing the perfect rhyming couplet, or nailing an emotional acting scene. It felt better than anything.

"The Misty Harbor Library is more than a place to check out books. It's a place to belong. So make sure you do your part, so its mission can continue."

He took a deep breath, waited for the audience to settle, and launched into his next song.

Nash was sweating through his shirt, had long since loosened his tie, much to the delight of certain audience members, who'd felt free to catcall him. He'd winked back, and the calls had gotten louder. He didn't know if this was helping the library raise money, but at least everyone was having a good time. Shockingly, including him.

Mimi had suggested he close with "Puzzle Piece," which was the first song on the album, and she'd chosen well. But he also wanted to play his new song, the one he'd written for the charity album. As the chords died away on "Puzzle Piece," he spoke.

"One more, then I'll let you all get to your dessert. I wrote this song for an upcoming charity album to benefit a great organization called Rainbow Canyon, but I think the message is universal. And I want to dedicate this one to Mimi Orlando. Y'all are incredibly lucky to have her guiding this place and working on your team. She made this song better; she makes this town better. She makes me better, to tell you the truth."

He looked straight at her. Her cheeks were flaming pink, but she didn't look away when he tipped an imaginary hat toward her. Someone hooted—it might have been Jay—and then Nash began to play. By the end of the song, folks were up on their feet, swaying and clapping along with the chorus. It was hard to get super intense with acoustic, but Nash played as hard as he could. He finished the song, wiping sweat from his forehead with the back of his hand.

He sort of didn't know what to do after that, but Jay, perhaps sensing his discomfort, jumped onto the stage and grabbed the mic. "Nash Speedwell, everybody!"

Nash stood and Jay pulled him into a hug.

"You did it, man," Jay said into his ear.

"Huh." Nash wasn't ready to declare his stage fright completely conquered, but he had to admit, he could see the appeal of singing to a bunch of adoring fans once in a while.

"Thanks, Nash. Now, grab dessert courtesy of Misty Harbor Bakeshop, and then you have exactly fifteen minutes to finish bidding on the silent auction items before we announce the winners."

There was a mad scramble. Everyone knew how delicious Bakeshop desserts were, and Nash liked to think he'd riled up the crowd's energy to encourage bidding up the auction items.

Now that the attention was off him, Nash sagged a

little. He was hot and sweaty, and he needed a gallon of water. He hadn't sung like that since he'd recorded the album, and his voice was out of shape. Still, the rasp he'd acquired by the end of the set sounded okay, complemented the music even.

"Let's get you cleaned up," Jay said.

"Sure." He was dazed and felt the adrenaline coursing through him like a drug. "That was awesome."

Jay laughed and patted his shoulder. "It sure was."

He looked around, trying to see Mimi amongst the crowds of people at the dessert bar or heading to the silent auction room, but she seemed nowhere to be found.

"Come on," Jay said, leading him to the door behind the stage he'd gone through earlier that evening. There was a little changing room back there, and Jay had presciently suggested he bring an extra shirt to change into. He knew he should take a breather, make himself presentable, but he was so high from the performance, he just wanted to see Mimi and kiss the daylights out of her.

But he followed Jay obediently. There'd be time for kissing later.

"Hey, could you grab me a water?" Nash asked once he and Jay were backstage. He took off his jacket and hung it up.

"Here you go," a familiar voice said.

He whipped his head around. Mimi was there, holding out a water bottle. He drank her in first, from her elegant eyebrows to her painted red smile. He took the bottle gratefully, without losing eye contact.

"Thank you."

"Well, I'm gonna scoot," Jay said quickly as Nash just stared at Mimi and Mimi stared back.

"Bye, Jay," Mimi said distantly.

"Yeah. Bye," Nash echoed. There was fire in Mimi's hazel eyes, and he couldn't look away.

"Oh, my God. Okay. See you later."

Jay slammed the door on his way out, but Nash barely registered anything but the beautiful woman standing in front of him.

"I can't believe you did that," Mimi said finally. "It was amazing. You're amazing."

"I wasn't sure I was capable of it, to be honest. But I'm glad I did."

"Me, too," Mimi said. "And I hope this won't be the last time The Nash Speedwell Experience performs live."

"I'm not making any promises, but I hope not."

"But why did you do it? Did Jay blackmail you or something?" Mimi asked.

The answer came out of his mouth before he could shove the words down. "I did it because I'm in love with you."

"Oh." Mimi's eyes closed.

No, no. Nash needed them open. He needed to know what she was feeling. He needed that window to her emotions just in case she started shutting herself off from him.

"Mimi, that doesn't have to change anything. I love you, but I'm not asking for anything other than what we have," he said hurriedly.

Her eyes opened. A sheen of tears covered the multi-colored irises. Happy tears? Sad tears? Angry tears? Nash didn't know how to interpret them.

"Well, maybe you should." She spoke slowly, deliberately.

"What do you mean?"

"I mean, you've been giving me so much space, you've been so careful not to ask me to change, but I think I'm starting to want to change. I was right when I said being in this relationship is changing me, changing us, and I finally realized that's not a bad thing. I've made this comfortable life for myself, but I accidentally made a wall around it, limiting myself to Misty Harbor and what I could have here because I was scared to ask for more. Scared if I really made myself vulnerable to someone, they'd reject me, just like my father's family. I'm happy here. But you've opened my world and made me see even if my life works, it could be so much bigger, richer. You brought that to me. And I'm so grateful."

"You've made a great life for yourself, Mimi. I love it here, with you. I don't need us to go traipsing across the globe to feel fulfilled."

"But your life is so much bigger than mine. It's not exactly easy to be a superhero from Misty Harbor."

"You do it every day," Nash said. "You're a hero to every kid who walks into the library looking for a place to belong, to every adult looking to make their life better, to every grandparent who wants to share a moment with their grandchild. You are a hero."

"That's sweet. But we're talking about you. About that role. And I think if you want to do it, we could figure something out. Long distance. You wouldn't have to be there all the time, I could come visit on the weekends, stuff like that?"

The uncertainty in Mimi's voice made him hopeful. "But tell me, is that what you'd choose? What if I turned them down? What if I spent more time on music and less on acting?"

Mimi's eyes grew wide. "Is that an option?"

"I just want to know your honest, unvarnished feelings. Not what you think. Not what practical solutions you can come up with. I want to know what you *feel*."

"I don't know—"

"Please. Tell me."

"I want to be with you. I want you to stay in Misty Harbor, with me. I—I love you, too."

Nash's breath caught in his throat, and he felt suspiciously like tears were welling up. He schooled himself, managing a full breath before he gathered her close, heedless of her beautiful dress and his sweaty shirt.

"Hearing that makes me so happy."

She pulled back to look at him sternly. "But that's not a good enough reason to turn down an opportunity like the one you've been offered."

"Maybe it is," he said. He didn't care about the superhero franchise—he already felt like he could fly. Mimi loved him back. Everything else was a distant second. "We'll figure it out later."

"Okay." She sounded slightly doubtful, but she met him halfway in a scorching kiss that left them both breathless.

"I should get back. I have to announce the silent auction totals," she said a minute later. She touched the tip of her finger to his bottom lip. "You have a little lipstick here."

He grinned. "I'm a mess. I'll clean up and meet you in a minute, okay?"

"Okay." She smiled at him. "You were really great out there, Nash."

He'd almost forgotten about his performer's high, in the rush of hearing Mimi say she loved him.

"Thanks."

After she'd gone, he quickly changed shirts, not bothering to redo his tie or don his jacket. He did take a minute to wipe the lipstick off his mouth and fix his hair. His heart felt like it was full of helium.

Mimi loved him.

Chapter Thirty

We don't have to touch, we don't
have to tease.
We don't have to kiss, we just have
to breathe.

— "Sleep With Me," The
Nash Speedwell Experience

Mimi looked at the number the silent auction coordinator had given her. That couldn't be right. She looked up, and Delia nodded at her.

"Seriously? We made this much on the silent auction *alone*?"

"There was a bidding war on that *Sawyer's Cove* set day experience, so I asked Camille if she'd donate two packages to the two highest bidders, and she said she'd do three, if all three matched the top price."

"Wow." Mimi had high expectations for the

fundraiser, but the number she'd envisioned as a successful haul was a fraction of the number that would encompass the silent auction, the ticket sales, and direct donations. Not only would they make their goal, they might have enough to endow a second complete scholarship in Mr. Russell's name.

"This is incredible," Mimi said.

"You did it," Delia said. "You should be so proud of yourself."

Mimi didn't want to take all the credit, but she allowed herself a moment to take pride in a hard job well-done. "Thank you. I better go make the final announcement before everyone takes off."

"Oh, I think you're going to have a hard time getting rid of everyone," Pauline said, materializing from somewhere. "Jay put on an eighties mix, and there's some serious boogying down going on."

"Oh, cool." She smoothed her dress. "Okay."

Pauline wasn't wrong. It looked like every single one of the nearly three hundred guests was on the dance floor, hopping around to the B52s. A glance at the depleted dessert bar led her to conclude they were all high on sugar. She waited until "Love Shack" was over to pause the music and grab the mic.

"Sorry for the interruption," she said, "but I have a quick announcement. Thanks to the incredible generosity of you all, and those who donated to the auction, I am pleased to announce we have raised over one hundred thousand dollars for the Misty Harbor Library and the Arthur Russell Memorial Scholarship.

We're going to ensure Arthur Russell's legacy lives on for years to come. Thank you all so much."

A cheer rose from the crowd. Mimi suddenly caught sight of Nash on the periphery. He raised his hands to his lips and yelled, "Take a bow, Mimi!"

She grinned at him and did exactly that.

Hours later, Mimi was dead on her feet. The fundraiser had devolved into an impromptu eighties dance party. Nash had pulled her onto the dance floor, and they'd joined in the fun.

Eventually, people started saying their goodbyes. Deb gave both her and Nash hugs and promised to call tomorrow. The playlist finally spit out a slow song. Mimi allowed Nash to pull her close, and she rested her cheek on his shoulder as they swayed to the strains of "In Your Eyes."

As they moved slowly around the floor, she saw Jay and Cami dancing in a similar position, though Cami only came up to about Jay's lapel. They looked good together, comfortable and as if their twelve-year separation had never happened. Her heart felt full knowing her brother was truly happy. She could finally understand why it sometimes seemed like Jay's feelings for Cami were lighting him up from the inside.

Mimi felt like her love for Nash was pouring out of her, seeping through her pores, staining her with emotion for everyone to see. It was scary to think Ariel, over there dancing with Jeff the sound guy, or Crosby, who was chatting with Trevor, could simply look at her and know the contents of her heart. Could they know she was in love with one of the most famous men in the country and if—when? —this ever came to an end, it would be plain to all her love wasn't enough to make it last.

But that was her insecurity talking. And it was hard to feel insecure when Nash's strong arms surrounded her, the reassuring pulse of his heart matching the beat of her own.

The song ended, and Nash checked his watch. "It's late. You must be so tired."

Mimi was exhausted. She let her yawn be her answer. "I think the hotel staff would probably appreciate us officially ending this shindig."

The clean-up had already started, but she would come back in the morning to make sure everything had been taken care of.

"Can I come to your place tonight?" she asked.

"Of course. Can I ride with you? Jay drove me before."

"Sure." She said her final farewells while Nash picked up his guitar and other shirt. Jay disconnected his phone, and silence filled the ballroom.

She gave her brother and Cami goodbye hugs, thanked them again for all they'd done. She was waiting in the lobby when Nash found her, his guitar case strapped to his back. He smiled and took her hand. "Shall we?"

They drove to his place in silence. Nash seemed content to hold her hand while she drove, rubbing circles on her palm with his thumb.

They stumbled into the house, and he deposited the guitar in the living room.

"You hungry?" he asked.

"I'm too tired to eat," she said.

"We'll have a big breakfast tomorrow."

"Sounds great." They climbed the stairs, undressed by the bed. Mimi couldn't imagine where she might wear the dress again, but she still carefully laid it over the back of a chair to take to the cleaners eventually.

Nash went into the bathroom and started the shower, unselfconscious in his nakedness. He called from the bathroom, "Wanna share?"

"Sure, you can prop me up and make sure I don't fall asleep," she said, joining him under the warm spray. Nash lathered up his expensive gel and rubbed her arms with it, followed by her chest, her belly, her thighs. His hands were sure and strong, not sexual, just taking care of her, cleaning her so she could tumble into his bed and sleep away the stress and exhaustion of the last week.

"I love...the smell of this body wash," she said.

He smiled at her. "I thought you were going to say you loved something else."

"Oh." Right. She'd told him she loved him. And she did. She didn't know what else to call the overwhelming feelings of happiness, joy, pain, sorrow, and worry being with him and being without him caused her. "That, too."

"Please tell me tonight isn't the only time I'll get to hear it," he said lightly.

"It's not," she protested. "I can say it. I can say it whenever I want to."

"Sure you can." He smiled, but not in a mean way. "No rush."

"What about you?" she said. "I don't remember hearing it out of your mouth recently."

He'd been scrubbing his hair, and he ducked under the water and rinsed. When he was suds-free, he held onto her shoulders lightly, looked into her eyes, and said, in his most devastating rasp, "I love you, Mimi."

He was an actor, so he could deliver a line. And that was a damn good line reading.

But he wasn't acting, and that wasn't a line from a script. It was real.

"Shit." She swallowed.

He lifted his eyebrows, as if silently challenging her to say it back.

With the noise of the shower running, and with the safety of his warm, familiar presence, she felt like she could say it, but—

"I'm scared," she confessed.

"Oh, honey. Is it weird it makes me happy to hear you say that?" Nash said.

"Why, because you're scared, too?"

"Of course I'm scared. I'm scared we're going to mess this up. I'm scared of making a wrong decision. I'm scared somehow I might do something that dims your vitality, and I'd never want to be responsible for that. But

I'm happy because you telling me you're scared means you trust me. I just want to know you're in this as deep as me, you know."

"How deep are we talking about here?"

He let out a shaky laugh. "Let's just say as nontraditional as our relationship has been from the start, someday I'm going to want a ring. Fair warning."

A ring? Mimi had never been the kind of person who thought about her wedding or played pretend marriage with schoolyard friends. She would have said Orlandos weren't the marrying kind, until Jay and Cami found each other again.

She sealed her lips together as she thought. Nash wasn't talking about getting married tomorrow, or even next year. But he wanted a commitment. And for the first time, giving him that didn't seem hard. Because she wanted it, too.

"I think I'm okay with that," she said.

His face lit up. He was absurdly easy to please. She wanted to do better than his minimal expectations. "I want to be with you. And I don't want to break up over something stupid. Or even something big. I'd like to think we're smart enough to figure out how to deal with things life throws our way."

"You are the smartest person I know," Nash said.

"I still don't know how to do any of this," Mimi warned.

"We'll figure it out together."

"Okay." She turned off the water, and she shivered now that the heat of the shower was gone. Nash went to reach for a towel on the bar outside, but she stopped him. "I love you."

He simply said, "Thank you." And that was that.

Mimi had somehow gone from confirmed singleton to pre-pre-engaged in a matter of weeks. But she supposed that's what happened when you fell in love with the person who made you happiest, who turned you on the most, who understood you the best. You held onto them, and you didn't let them go.

Chapter Thirty-One

I've been waiting a lifetime to get
    in this bed
With you, honey, so let's go to
    sleep.
Maybe we'll wake up wed.

— "Sleep With Me," The
Nash Speedwell Experience

Nash knew it was partly coming down off the high of performing and sheer exhaustion from the long day they'd had, but he felt like he was in a dream as they slowly toweled dry and made their way to the bed. He was too tired to bother putting on any sleep clothes, just slid under the soft sheets. Mimi followed his lead, getting in next to him naked, clean and pink and smelling like his body wash.

The sheets felt cool on his skin. Mimi burrowed

close, warm and soft, and he thought that was everything he'd ever need, right here in his arms. He had the love of the most amazing woman on the planet. Even though she was plastered to his side, he felt the overwhelming urge to be even closer to her. In the protective bubble of blankets, he shifted until their legs were tangled together, his arms completely encircling her. Her breasts pressed into his chest, and his cock nestled against the soft swell of her sex.

They were too tired to fuck. He loved the energetic way they usually went at it, athletic and without inhibition. They'd do that again, after about twelve hours of sleep. But he wasn't too tired to rock against her, to kiss her shoulder, to murmur in her ear, "I love you, Mimi."

She fluttered out a sigh, like she was on the verge of sleep. "Mmm." She kissed his neck where her mouth was conveniently positioned. "Nash."

He thought maybe she'd settle back down, go fully to sleep, but she kissed him again, open-mouthed and hot, sucking a little. He knew she wouldn't give him a hickey, not when he had scenes to film first thing Monday, but she still worked his neck with her tongue and teeth, and he hardened in response.

They moved in slow motion, limbs heavy with exhaustion, shifting so they were facing each other on their sides. Mimi's leg curved possessively over his hip, rocking back and forth until the friction was almost too much. He stilled them, positioned himself so he could slide into her welcoming pussy.

There. That's what he'd been craving. Now they were

just about as close as they could be. He didn't even want to move; he just wanted to be, joined to her, sweaty and hot under the sheets, in their dark, safe space, where all that mattered was their love.

He wasn't surprised when Mimi lost patience with him and started moving against him, trying to rebuild the friction. He reached down and rubbed her nipple hard. She let out a small cry and arched toward him. Then he went lower, slipping between their bodies to circle her clit with his finger, while she slowly ground herself on his cock, minute rocking driving them both closer to the edge.

Suddenly, Mimi yanked him even closer, trapping his hand between them, going stiff and shuddering with pleasure. She relaxed and sighed, and she found his mouth with hers, brushing her lips languidly against his.

Her pussy was furnace-hot when he carefully turned her on her back and drove into her, with deep, firm thrusts that had his orgasm building quickly. She let her legs splay open lazily, so open and fragrant, like a flower dripping with nectar. Her sweet honey was all he needed to live. He bent his head, clumsily kissing her as the flood of his orgasm overtook him, pumping his come into her, so together they were one sopping wet mess.

He didn't care how sticky they were when they'd been shower-clean minutes before. He'd sleep in a wet spot every night for the rest of his life if it meant he got to sleep next to Mimi.

Mimi, as ever, was more practical. She extricated herself from his hold long enough to locate some tissues and used them to mop them up halfheartedly. She shuffled back to his side, using his shoulder for a pillow.

"I could have sworn I was too tired for sex," she said sleepily, moving around, getting comfortable.

"But not too tired to make love," he couldn't resist saying. She could make fun of him all she wanted, but that's what they'd done.

She was silent for a beat, then said, "Guess not."

He fell asleep smiling.

Though it was officially fall, Sunday morning dawned warm and bright, as if summer had made a resurgence. Mimi was wearing borrowed clothes again, this time a pair of his boxers and an oversized tank top he wore to work out sometimes, which was slipping off her shoulder. He spied the raspberry pink of her nipples when she leaned over to take a bowl out of the dishwasher. They scavenged his mostly bare cupboards for breakfast —oatmeal for her, half a leftover chef's salad for him— and brought it outside on the patio. The sun had baked the concrete pad, and they turned their chairs to face the beach. The ocean air felt good on Nash's face. He'd slept hard and deep, but they'd both awakened early.

"This is nice," Mimi said, her long legs stretched out in front of her.

He squinted at her, wishing he'd thought to bring out his sunglasses. "Yeah, it is."

"I'll go by the inn this morning to make sure the

clean-up went okay, but I'm free later. You want to hang out?"

"Sure. I need to work on my scenes for tomorrow, but maybe we could go for a walk."

"And dinner?"

"Definitely dinner."

Mimi licked her spoon. "So, have you decided what you're going to do about the offer?"

He wrenched his thoughts away from the things he wanted to do with her after dinner and set his empty plate on the ground. "I've been giving it a lot of thought. It's complicated. And I'm sorry I was weird the last time we talked about this. It wasn't fair of me to put so much pressure on you to have an opinion."

"No, I get it. I just...I guess if we're going to be together, we have to be able to talk about work stuff that affects both of us. Right?"

He let out a relieved breath. "Yes, exactly."

"So, let's talk. You know I think you'd be amazing as Moonshot. But the more I think about it, the more I wonder if you'd be taking it for the right reasons."

"What do you mean?"

"If I've learned one thing about you, Nash Speedwell, it's that you don't always put yourself first. You're always giving stuff away—your money, your time—and all that adds up to your life. I just want to make sure you wouldn't be taking it just so you could donate more to causes."

It had crossed his mind. "Think of all the people I

could help with superhero money," he said. "We're talking millions."

"Yeah, but what about you? What about your life? You can't trade your life away just because you feel bad about your white cis het privilege."

His laugh was loud. "Okay, way to tell it like it is, Mimi."

She smiled at him, a little shyly. "I mean, you have so much else to give the world. Your music, for one. Maybe you'd even want to do some live shows now that you've popped your concert cherry."

"That's not exactly how I would have described it, but okay." He frowned. He'd felt awesome after the show, but beforehand he'd felt like he was about to face a firing squad. Maybe it would get easier? "I'm not ruling it out."

"If you want to do this role because you think it would be a fun challenge or a solid gig, or it's your dream to play a superhero you read about in comics when you were a kid, then I'll be happy for you, and we'll figure out the schedule. We'll just rack up a lot of miles."

"You'd do that?"

"Of course. Jay told me a while ago compromise works both ways. I'd never expect you to give up your job to live here in Misty Harbor twenty-four-seven-three-sixty-five."

"But it wouldn't be fair for me to expect you to leave everything and come on the road with me."

"Exactly. We have to work something out in the middle."

"That's so mature and adult of us," he said.

"I know, right?" She stretched her long arms above her head. He tracked the tank top as it rode up over the swell of her belly. "So what do you think? Are you the next Moonshot?"

He'd spent plenty of time weighing the pros and cons over the past week. He knew what he wanted, but he was kind of scared to admit it.

"Honestly? I don't want to take the part."

"Then don't take it," she said, as if it was as easy as turning down Danica at the bar on another IPA.

"The thing is, taking the superhero role feels like the safe path. It ticks all the boxes—fame, money, security."

"In spades," Mimi agreed.

"But I think I want the adventure of not knowing how the next few years are going to play out. I want the freedom to say no."

"No is very powerful."

"I think I've gotten into the habit of saying yes. I spread myself too thin, and I forgot my life is actually mine. You reminded me that I want a life, a real one. Every time I'd come to Misty Harbor, it was like a fantasy land, where I could just be a guy in a small town, hanging with my best friend and his incredibly sexy sister."

Mimi laughed, and she didn't stop.

He turned to her, grinning uncertainly. "What?"

"It's just—" Mimi hiccupped as she tried to stop

laughing, "—when you'd show up, it was like *my* fantasy life come true, the super sweet, super-hot, super talented guy who came to town for scorching sex."

"We're each other's fantasy?"

"Apparently."

"How lucky are we that we're going to be living our fantasies every day?"

"Is it still a fantasy if it comes true?" Mimi asked, getting out of her chair to sit on his lap. His hands slid up her bare legs and settled on her hips.

"I think our fantasy became reality," he said, then kissed his fantasy woman on her warm, soft lips that felt as real as life.

Chapter Thirty-Two

Erika: We're not above idle gossip on this show, but this piece of news is actually confirmed.

Jules: By Nash Speedwell himself.

Erika: The other week we were talking about how cute it would be if Nash and Jay Orlando's sister were dating.

Jules: We're clearly visionaries because they are, in fact, dating. There was a picture of them canoodling on Camille Corsair's socials, and Nash liked and commented, and he sounds pretty smitten. How delightful is it that he's enamored with Jay Orlando's sister?

Erika: We should stop calling her Jay Orlando's sister. Her name is apparently Mimi.

Jules: Sexy.

Erika: And she's a librarian.

Jules: No way. I think I'm in love.

Erika: Exactly how many people are you crushing on right now?

Jules: Not enough.

From *The Sawyer's Cove Rewatch Project Podcast: Reboot Roundup Redux*

Six weeks later

Mimi was in her office, rocking out to her favorite album. The Nash Speedwell Experience was excellent cleaning music, and her office needed a thorough cleaning. She didn't technically need to be at work, but she was leaving early tomorrow to be Nash's date to the *Sawyer's Cove* wrap party, so she'd decided to put in an extra hour.

Pauline stuck her head around the door. "I'm taking off."

"Sounds good, dear. Fun plans?"

"Colin and I are going to try that new tapas place in Southville."

"Things still good with you two?"

"It's going surprisingly well." Pauline smiled.

They'd officially transitioned from dating to together for about a month, and Pauline had confided over beers at The Cove that he'd been very open about the parameters of their relationship. Colin wasn't asexual, but they'd figured out how to communicate what they were and weren't up for. Mimi was happy her friend was able to be with someone who cared about her so much and seemed to understand her sexuality.

"Well, say hi for me," she said.

"Going to The Cove this weekend?"

"Yeah, I think we'll be there Sunday night."

"Let's text," Pauline said. "Later."

"Later."

As she went through a pile of papers on her desk that were mostly sailing toward the recycling bin, her phone dinging was another interruption. She picked up her phone and saw a text from her brother.

> I'm trying to get your boyfriend to do a few songs at the wrap party. Could you work on him for me?

Mimi bit her lip. She was always in favor of hearing her top singer-songwriter play live, but aside from an impromptu living room concert he'd performed a few weeks ago for her, Jay, Cami, Trevor, Crosby, Pauline, and Colin, he hadn't picked his guitar up to play in front of other people since the night of the fundraiser.

> Baby steps. But I'll try.

Nash was a bit of a pushover when it came to asks from the Orlandos. If both she and Jay were encouraging him to do something, he'd probably do it.

Before she could set the phone down again, it rang in her hand.

"Hi, Mom."

"Hey, sweetie. I was wondering if you'd heard Caroline Russell put the family house on the market."

"No, I hadn't." Mr. Russell's house was one of the old

Victorians on the north side of town. She remembered going there as a kid to trick-or-treat, being intimidated by the imposing late 19th century architecture, but persevering because everyone knew the man gave out books instead of candy, and Mimi had always had a voracious reading appetite.

Later, she'd gone to visit Mr. Russell when he was retired and sick. He'd been set up in the front room in a hospital bed, frail and wan, but he'd given Mimi a smile, told her how happy it made him that she was working at the library. The visit had been short, but it was one of her most cherished memories. His daughter had been living in Newport and came to stay with him until the end. When he died, the house sat empty while she went back to her life in Rhode Island. Mimi drove by it sometimes, wondering what would happen to the place.

"How much are they asking?" she asked her mother as she tried to sort through the other items on the desk, not really seeing them.

The number her mother quoted wasn't a steal, but it was fair for the house and land that surrounded it, though Mimi wasn't sure what kind of shape the house was in. It probably needed a lot of work. Besides, it was much too big for one person.

"Anyway, I have to run. See you for brunch Sunday? We need to talk about the Thanksgiving menu."

"See you then." They were planning a family-and-friends meal at Jay's for the upcoming holiday.

Being part of a couple hadn't impacted her social life as much as she'd thought it would. She still went out on the weekends, still hung out with her family. Nash went to work in the morning, just like her, though sometimes he had random days off, and then they'd meet for lunch downtown. In the evenings, if he was done with his day, they usually went back to his place and had dinner. She was introducing him to her British procedurals, and he was getting her to listen to more country music.

Sometimes they stayed at her place, but it was becoming more and more of a place to store her clothes and books and less an actual living space.

Problem was, all of that was going to have to change. *Sawyer's Cove* was officially done with shooting as of today. The first episode was due to air on Christmas Day, and they were going to show a rough cut at the party tomorrow night. Which meant except for his press obligations, Nash was officially out of work.

The charity album had come out a few weeks ago and done well. He'd been noodling around with a few new songs, and they'd talked about him recording a second album in the new year. Mary-Anne had been surprisingly understanding about his turning down Moonshot, having been able to land a role for another of her clients in the franchise.

But another deadline was looming large—Nash's lease on Warner's rental house ran out next week. She'd slowly started thinking of the little beach house as theirs, but it had already been rented to someone else for the winter. She tried to imagine Nash moving into her small apartment. He might be up for it, but there was barely enough room for the two of them when he did stay over—where would they put his guitar and clothes? He didn't have a lot of stuff here now, but she knew he had a bunch of things in storage in Los Angeles. He had kept a place there for several years and packed everything into a storage unit when he went overseas to shoot the first season of *Hawk and Bone*.

But all of this brought up the issue of whether he was going to make Misty Harbor his permanent residence. And if he was, then were they going to live together? And if they lived together, where would they live?

Mimi sighed. She supposed these were things she should discuss with her boyfriend rather than ruminating pointlessly on them in her office when she was supposed to be working.

Though working was difficult when she kept getting interrupted. A knock at her door had her looking up in irritation. Her scowl gave way to a smile when she saw who it was.

"Well, if it's not my favorite singer."

Nash grinned. He looked a little manic—his hair was ruffled out of his careful Will O'Connell coif, and his jacket collar was half-up, half-down. His eyes were bright, and he practically bounced into her office and gave her a smacking kiss on the lips.

"What's going on?"

"How much longer until you can leave? I want to show you something."

"Well, since people keep interrupting me and I can't get any work done, I guess I can leave now."

"Perfect!" He watched her pack up, buzzing with impatience. "Am I really your favorite singer?"

"Totally," she said. "You and Nina Simone."

"Good company." He tugged her toward the door. "Let's go!"

"Where are we going?"

"Do you know Sonia the real estate agent?" he asked as she switched off the lights in her office and locked the door behind her.

"She helped Jay buy his house."

"Great, well, she has a house to show us."

Mimi's stomach flip-flopped. "Us?"

Nash's steps slowed in the library's lobby. "Yeah. Us." He swallowed nervously. "Is that okay?"

"You mean you don't want to live in my shoebox? I'm shocked."

He relaxed a fraction. "I just thought we could both use a little more room. And wait until you see this place. It's exactly what I've been looking for. It needs some work, but it has—" He started toward the door. "Well, you'll see."

"Have you seen it yet?"

"No, it just came on the market."

Mimi felt a prickling on the back of her neck. "Wait—is it a big Victorian up by the woods?"

"Yes. How did you know?"

"Misty Harbor grapevine. Faster than social media."

She followed Nash to his new truck—he'd replaced his rental a month ago with the same model, only this one was shiny black, with even more features. She'd been aghast at the gas mileage but had to admit, the sound system was kicking.

"I'll bring you back to get your car later," he said, then he tore out of the parking lot with an actual squeal of the tires.

"Calm down, I don't think the local real estate market is exactly on fire."

Nash took his foot off the gas slightly, but they still got to the north side of town in record time. It was dark outside, but the house was cheerfully lit. A car was parked in the driveway—Sonia's, Mimi assumed.

"You know whose house this was, don't you?" Mimi asked as they climbed out of the truck and walked up the gravel path to the front steps.

Nash sounded surprised. "No. Whose?"

She didn't get to answer before Sonia greeted them at the doorway and started singing the praises of the house. It had been years since Mimi had been inside. It was basically empty, and it felt bigger than she remembered. It was deeper than it looked from the front, and it had more bedrooms than she could ever imagine them needing, even if they ended up with triplets.

They'd talked about kids once or twice, both agreeing it was something they were interested in talking about more. Mimi never had been against the concept of having kids, but she'd also decided, given her lifestyle, they were a remote possibility. Now that she and Nash were in this for the long haul, that was just one more thing changing in her vision of the future.

"Can we see the basement next?" Nash said after they'd seen the large but antiquated kitchen.

Sonia led them downstairs through a door in the kitchen. The basement looked like it was recently finished, with a carpeted floor and bright white walls. "This was all redone in the last few years. The owner thought about turning this into a rental property before she decided to sell."

"This is one of the things that got me so excited," Nash said. "I could totally convert this into a music room, even put in some recording equipment. It's all soundproofed."

"Really? That's so cool." She loved the idea of Nash having a place to concentrate on his music.

Nash asked Sonia more questions, and they went back upstairs. "Okay, and now the other part I really wanted you to see," he said.

Mimi couldn't understand what could have him so excited. She shrugged at Sonia, who looked between the two of them and smiled. "Of course. Right this way."

To the side of the kitchen was a more modern extension of the house, a story-and-a-half room that had picture windows in the back that looked into the big back yard and woods beyond. All three of the walls were made of built-in bookshelves. There was space for what looked like thousands and thousands of books.

"Oh. My. God." Mimi stepped into the center of the room and looked around. "This is incredible."

Nash was smiling like a little kid. "You like it?"

"I had no clue this was here."

"Mr. Russell had this addition built and the bookshelves installed about twenty-five years ago," Sonia said, looking down at her notes.

"Mr. Russell?" Nash asked.

"This was Arthur Russell's house," Mimi said. "I used to trick-or-treat here growing up. His daughter inherited it but never did anything with it until now."

"I had no idea," Nash said. "I just saw the pictures of this library, and I—well, I wanted you to have it."

Mimi's heart swelled in her chest until it almost hurt. "You're *Beauty and the Beast*-ing me?"

He looked momentarily perplexed, then nodded. "I guess I am. Is it working?"

She walked over to him and put her arms around his shoulders. "Nash, do you want to buy this house and live here together and be surrounded by books and music and laughter and maybe even kids one day, and oh my God, I can't believe I'm saying all of this, but I can't help myself because I love you and being with you makes me so happy."

He looked into her eyes, and she felt her future was going to be so much bigger, so much brighter, and so much more full of love than she'd ever imagined. "Yes," he said. "Very much, Mimi."

She twisted her head over her shoulder to see Sonia quickly averting her eyes, with an amused smile on her face.

"We'll take it."

Epilogue

Ten weeks earlier

Selena checked the house number against the address in her phone for the third time. The sleek, mid-century modern house looked completely out of place on this stretch of beach road, but she supposed the views afforded by the giant floor-to-ceiling windows would be spectacular.

She'd left finding a place to stay for the duration of the *Sawyer's Cove* shoot until the last minute, and she'd had to beg Cami to help her find something—anything —that meant she wouldn't have to stay at the Misty Harbor Inn. She'd stayed at the inn earlier in the summer during a location scouting trip, and it had been lovely, but she needed her own space. She needed a kitchen and windows that opened and unrecycled air.

This place was completely extravagant, but it was only a ten-minute drive to the set in one direction and ten-minute drive to downtown Misty Harbor in the other. And she wasn't renting the entire house anyway, just the pool house. Or that was the way Cami had described it to her, anyway.

She left her rented hatchback in the driveway behind a minivan and hesitated. She'd been told to collect a key from the owner of the house, her landlord for the next few months, but the house looked dark. The driveway ended in a wooden gate. Presumably, her pool house would be found beyond the gate.

God, it was hot. The sky was overcast, but that just seemed to make her feel warmer, a natural greenhouse effect. She was sweating in her airplane outfit of stretchy jeans and sweatshirt. She paused to remove her top layer and tie the arms around her middle. That was better. She adjusted her glasses. They were practically fogging up in the humidity. She was Southern Californian, born and bred. She liked a dry heat.

Before she could decide about going up to the front door, the gate swung open. A man walked through—he didn't see her right away, but took in her rental car with a frown.

"Hello," she called, and his gaze swung immediately toward her.

The guy was about six feet, wearing jeans and dirty work boots and a mud-streaked T-shirt that might have been white when it first came out of the multi-pack at the chain store. His skin had been tinted a reddish bronze by the sun. She couldn't see his face well under the battered ball cap pulled over his eyes, but she'd peg him to be about her age, thirty-seven, or maybe a little older. She hadn't seen a workman's truck, but this guy was clearly in the middle of some manual labor.

"I'm looking for Warner," she said. Maybe the guy knew if the owner was home.

"You the renter?" he said shortly.

"That's me."

"I've got your keys. Just a second."

He passed in front of her and went to the door, opening it as if he owned the place.

The penny dropped, and she smiled to herself. Well, she guessed he did.

She felt only a little bit bad about assuming he was a maintenance man or landscaper. How many times had she walked into a room and been taken for the assistant, when she'd worked her ass off to become a staff writer by the age of twenty-five?

He came right back out, a key ring in hand, and walked past her to the gate. "I'll show you around. I haven't had a renter here before, so if there's something that's missing, let me know. I'll give you a number you can text."

"Okay. Thanks. I'm Selena. I appreciate this, by the way. Cami said she had to pull some strings."

He didn't reply, just kept walking. She followed him through the gate into the back, where there was indeed a pool, beautifully landscaped garden, and small building set about a hundred feet back from the house. It wasn't the same style, more of a generic wooden structure, but it was as nicely landscaped as the rest of the place, and it looked like the perfect spot to hole up while she got through the shoot.

"This is so beautiful," she gushed. "The roses are incredible." She paused to sniff at the deep velvet red blooms. She spotted a part of the flower bed that looked freshly turned, as well as a pair of gloves and some kind of digging implement. Selena was no gardener.

He didn't stop, and she had to hurry to catch up to him as he showed her the two locks on the door to the small house.

"How long have you lived here?" she asked, to find out if he answered direct questions.

"There's no security system on this building, but I do have a perimeter system and a camera system."

"Okay." She hadn't been particularly worried about security.

"Try not to park behind me. I'll move over so we can park side by side."

"Got it."

He showed her the fuse box and fire extinguisher and headed for her front door.

"Enjoy your stay," he said to the doorjamb, then walked through.

"Wait!"

He stopped and turned around before she'd had time to come up with a reason to keep him there besides her curiosity about a guy who lived in a modernist mansion who was borderline rude and liked digging in the dirt.

"You said you'd give me a phone number."

He nodded and waited for her to pull her phone from her back pocket. He recited a ten-digit number.

"Warner, right?"

The man nodded. He lifted the ball cap off his head in an impatient gesture. But there was something about his light eyes and messy, sweat-dampened hair. She narrowed her gaze on the man's face. He looked familiar.

"You got a last name?" If he wasn't going to be effusive, then neither was she.

He hesitated the barest moment before saying, "Mathis. Warner Mathis."

She hadn't really expected her idle speculation to be confirmed. But it couldn't be a coincidence, could it? Still, there was something forbidding in the way he looked at her as he told her his name. She'd read the term "piercing gaze" in more than one of her favorite historical novels, but she'd never encountered the human embodiment of one before. His stare felt like it was penetrating to the skull beneath her skin.

He must have seen an expression of understanding cross her face, but she responded, as if nothing weird had happened, "Selena Echeveria."

"Echeveria," Warner repeated, with a decent Spanish accent. "Like the plant."

"Yes. The succulent."

Maybe she'd finally started speaking his language. "Welcome to Misty Harbor, Selena Echeveria."

"Thanks, Warner Mathis."

When he turned to go this time, she didn't stop him.

Later, when she'd gotten her bags inside the small

house and locked the door behind her, she unzipped one of her suitcases and found what she was looking for. The well-worn paperback had a glossy black cover. The title—*Gunsmoke*—burst off the background in blood red letters in the style of an old pulp fiction novel, though it had been published less than a decade ago. She flipped to the back until she found what she was looking for—a somewhat low-res black and white photo of the author that was a younger version of her landlord, Warner Mathis, the very same name on the cover of the book she'd read a dozen times.

She looked out the window, across the pool and empty yard, and stared at the large house where her landlord was presumably taking refuge from the heat of the day.

What on Earth was Warner Mathis doing in Misty Harbor, of all places?

Selena found herself smiling. She always did like a mystery.

Thank you for reading! Mimi and Nash's story is one of my personal favorites. To find out how Selena solves the mystery of Warner, read *Take It All*. And scan the code to download the free prequel to the Sawyer's Cove: The Reboot series right now!

xoxo,

Libby

Acknowledgments

Thank you to every librarian and library employee who makes libraries such amazing community resources, especially those who work at my two local libraries, the Norwalk Public Library and The Westport Library. Special thanks to Cynde Bloom Lahey, who does so much to promote local indie authors in Norwalk, Connecticut, and beyond.

Thank you to all my author friends near and far—I couldn't do this job without you!

Thank you to Jen Colburn Design, Wicked Smart Designs, Jessica Snyder's HEA Club for support and encouragement, Word Slayers, and Sara Kettler for her always above-and-beyond work. All mistakes in this book are mine.

Finally, thank you for reading *Take a Bow*. In writing this series I've created a world that I truly love spending time in. I hope you've enjoyed your time in Misty Harbor, too!

About the Author

Libby Waterford is the author of the Sawyer's Cove: The Reboot and the Never a Bride series. She's obsessed with her pollinator garden, DIY fermentation, and writing swoony first kisses and hopeful happily ever afters. Her steamy contemporary romances mix witty banter and all the feels with a solid dollop of good old-fashioned sexual tension. Libby wrangles her two ever-growing sons and a husband in Fairfield County, Connecticut.

Get a free story at libbywaterford.com and email Libby at libby@libbywaterford.com.

facebook.com/LibbyWaterford

instagram.com/libbywritesromance

bookbub.com/authors/libby-waterford

goodreads.com/libbywaterford

amazon.com/author/libbywaterford